That Which Should Not Be

BY

BRETT J. TALLEY

JournalStone

San Francisco

JournalStone books may be ordered through booksellers or by contacting:

JournalStone
199 State Street
San Mateo, CA 94401
www.journalstone.com

ISBN: 978-1-936564-14-9   (sc)
ISBN: 978-1-936564-15-6   (dj)
ISBN: 978-1-936564-16-3   (ebook)

Library of Congress Control Number: 2011931054

Printed in the United States of America

JournalStone rev. date: October 7, 2011

Cover Design: Denise Daniel
Cover Art: Philip Renne
Author Photo: Ann M. Donaldson

Edited by: Elizabeth Reuter

Dedication

For all those without whom this book would not be.

Check out these titles from JournalStone:

Shaman's Blood
Anne C. Petty

The Traiteur's Ring
Jeffrey Wilson

Duncan's Diary, Birth of a Serial Killer
Christopher C. Payne

Ghosts of Coronado Bay
J.G. Faherty

Imperial Hostage, Book 1 of the Destruction Series
Phil Cantrill

The Pentacle Pendant
Stephen M. DeBock

Reign of the Nightmare Prince
Mike Phillips

Available through your local and online bookseller or at
www.journalstone.com

"We live on a placid island of ignorance in the black seas of infinity, and it was not meant that we should voyage far."

The Call of Cthulhu

Prologue

Mr. Charles,

Enclosed please find a document which I believe you will judge most intriguing. It was discovered among Mr. Weston's personal belongings sometime after his disappearance. In fact, it was the only document located in the wall safe in his office. The contents are most fascinating, and despite the order and coherence thereof, I fear they raise grave concerns regarding Mr. Weston's sanity in the last days of his life. In order to ensure that Mr. Weston's will is probated post haste, I would recommend destroying this document at once lest it fall into vicious hands. I recognize this course may seem rather dramatic, but I believe once you have reviewed what can only be described as the feverish imaginings of a broken mind, you will agree it is better for all involved, not the least Mr. Weston himself, that it never sees the light of day.

Always,

David Ashton
Lovecraft, Hartford & Shanks

Part I

Chapter

1

Carter Weston:

The day has come, that day I always knew would, and my time is short. But I must protect the Book. I will not surrender it, no matter what the cost. And if my life is to be forfeit, then I shall die as I have lived, standing against the black tide that would cover us all.

I suppose this could be called my final testament, for my family should know why I've spent the better part of my life in the dark corners of the world, why I have dedicated myself to the unspeakable horrors that lie beyond civilized man's imagining. I have hunted them from hell-blasted planes to yawning chasms that know no end, from the moonlit towers of fallen temples to demon-haunted ruins of unimaginable antiquity. But never defeating them. Nay, would that it were so. Merely holding them at bay, as best I could, postponing what may well be their inevitable conquest. No, one cannot kill what can forever lie in repose. Sleeping. Waiting. And I fear the time of their awakening is upon us.

I hope my family can forgive me. I hope they can understand why I have lived my life as I have. I hope this testament will give them that comfort. For it was not always to be so. I had never expected to live in the shadows. There was a time when my interests lay with quainter things. Those were younger, brighter days. My father was a Harvard man, and in his mind, so was I. It broke his heart, I suppose, when I chose Miskatonic University of Arkham, Massachusetts, instead of that ivy-gabled institution. I think back often now on that choice and I wonder what paths my life might have roamed had I listened to him instead. Ah, but regret is a broken road that is better not taken. Still, how things could have been different.

I arrived with no more extravagant dreams than that of the life of an academician. And so I embarked upon a degree in history with a focus on the folklore of New England, a rich but narrow subject in which I intended to establish myself as the foremost expert. It was in this pursuit that I made the acquaintance of Henry Armitage.

Henry was a brilliant mind, and even as a young man he was keenly interested in the occult and the role it played in the tales and myths of the common man. He came to Miskatonic to understand the dark shadow of man's desires. The myths, I believed, at that time at least, leapt fully formed from primordial man, conjured merely to explain those things he did not understand. I was surprised to learn that Henry did not share this view. He believed there was more than a grain of truth embedded in those superstitions and ancient fears.

Perhaps in another environment the learned men of the University would have shattered such a faith, crushed it with the hammer of science. But not at Miskatonic. I heard the whispers, the rumors of the shadow that hung over the town of Arkham. Miskatonic was witch-haunted ground, and there were those who spoke of nameless rites echoing through its darkened halls. I pushed such talk aside. I would brook no opposition to my chosen University. In honest moments, though, I could face the truth, or at least the image of it. I belonged at Miskatonic and not in a trivial, romantic way. It called to me, pulled me, and since before I knew its name, I longed to be there. In truth, I never felt at home until the day I arrived on its grounds.

But I digress now, and I must focus on the tale at hand. My time is short; I know that now. The stories I could tell would fill volumes, but the sands in the hourglass run thin, and I must ration my words.

It was Henry who suggested I study under Dr. Atley Thayerson. It surprised me at the time, but for reasons I couldn't quite describe. It was entirely appropriate I should take Dr. Thayerson's class on Folklore and the Occult. In fact, I suppose it would have been surprising to anyone familiar with my academic studies if I neglected to do so. Yet, there was something inside of me, buried deep, that recoiled at the thought. Not for any rational reason, none that I can articulate. I had steeled myself against the growing sense of inevitability involved. But somehow, Henry's simple suggestion of the thing defeated my apparently unimposing defenses.

Henry and I enrolled together, and it quickly became apparent to Thayerson that we were to be his star pupils. I devoured the class and, in doing so, felt the birth of an obsession — the occult was to become my passion. This will, of course, come as no surprise to those who know me; I have made the study of that subject my life's work. But at the time, it was a revelation.

In any event, I requested, and Dr. Thayerson eagerly granted, the opportunity to work more closely on the professor's many and varied studies. It was then that my eyes began to open to the dark forces that move in the uncultivated lands beyond the borders of the world we know. But this was just the beginning for me, and my studies were merely that — an academic exercise. I spent my weekends and every free moment traveling about the Massachusetts countryside, as far into the wild as the roads would take me. Sometimes farther. To ancient towns and villages peopled by simple folk to whom even Boston was a far away Xanadu of modern wonder. I listened to their stories, obscure tales of late night visitations, of strange creatures that walked beneath darkened moons, of sleeping evils that invade men's dreams. I dutifully recorded these tales, and I smiled inwardly at the horrified looks on the simple villager's faces as they relayed them. I believed myself wise, and in my skepticism my wisdom was confirmed. But I had no faith.

No, I found the occult fascinating in the way that folklore had always held my thoughts. The study of myth helped mankind to understand truth. It offered no such truth itself. And then came that day in late January of my second year at Miskatonic when everything changed.

Chapter 2

The air was as crisp that day as any other in January, but there was an unnatural chill in the wind that portended the coming of a storm. The iron gray clouds that crept across the sky hung low, as if full to bursting with winter snow. I was perusing Cotton Mather's *Wonders of the Invisible World* in front of the lighted hearth in my room quite contentedly when there was a sharp knock on my door. It was Henry.

"Sorry to bother you, Carter. I met Dr. Thayerson today, and he seemed rather anxious to see you."

I remember placing a marker on my page. I did not return to that book for many years. I was confused. I had seen Thayerson only a day before, and he had seemed as relaxed and convivial as always. I could not imagine what could have provoked his anxiety to speak with me, yet again, so soon.

"Did he say if something was wrong?" I asked Henry as I slipped on my boots and heavy coat.

"He did not, just that I should find you and send you straightaway. He would say no more, and I admit I was concerned. I certainly hope nothing has happened."

I could see the anxiety in Henry's face. He did not, on that day, possess the iron temperament that time and bitter experience has gifted him with.

"I'm sure it's nothing, Armitage," I said, putting my hand on his shoulder. "I fear Thayerson is getting a little senile in his old age. He probably just forgot I saw him only yesterday. Besides, what could have come about in a single day that is so important?"

I left Henry there. He did not seem convinced, but obviously there was no time to tend to his concerns. I made my way across Arkham Green to Putnam Hall. I found Dr. Thayerson pacing his office in what can only be described as a fevered state. Upon my arrival, though, his expression suddenly changed, as if he wished to present the impression to me that nothing of any terrible significance weighed on his mind.

"Ah, Mr. Weston. Do sit down."

As I took the seat opposite him, Thayerson stretched his arms out across his desk and clasped his hands. He took a deep breath and cleared his throat.

"Mr. Weston, I have a favor to ask of you, and in the interest of complete honesty, it is no minor one."

I listened intently as he spoke, and I had already decided that whatever he asked I would do.

"Are you familiar," he said sternly, "with a book known as the *Incendium Maleficarum*?"

"The *Witch's Fire*?" I responded with some surprise. "Well, yes, Professor, of course. It is a book of some legend, if I remember correctly. I never studied its history directly, but I was under the impression it was merely a legend. No such book ever really existed."

"Oh, it exists," he said in the way men do when they speak of what they are sure. "I would also take issue with your translation. It is better to say it is the *Inferno of the Witch* or the *Flame of the Witch*."

As Thayerson spoke, the only fire was the one in his eyes.

"It means passion, total subjugation of oneself to the dark arts, to turn over body and soul to their devices. It is the most ancient of all books of witchcraft, the grimoire of grimoires."

"But, sir," I said, drawing on my limited knowledge of the subject, "what of the *Necronomicon* then?"

I watched as the color drained from Thayerson's face at the mention of that dread tome, inked in blood and bound in human flesh. In my youth and foolishness, it meant nothing to me to speak of it, though now I would no doubt react in the same way.

"The *Necromonicon*," he whispered, though with great effort, "is altogether different. It is no common spell book, or even an uncommon one. Its purpose is . . . how to say it . . . otherworldly." Thayerson now paused. "The *Incendium Maleficarum*, on the other hand, deals squarely with the forces ruling this world. The two books are dualistic, you see, and it is impossible to understand the one without the other. And when the two are brought together, the properly initiated is said to wield untold power over this world and beyond."

I watched as Thayerson spoke, and as he wove his tale I noticed that his hands were shaking.

"Well sir," I said calmly, "then I suppose it's good this book, even if it did exist as you have said, has now been consigned to the pages of history."

Thayerson leaned back in his chair and sighed. He looked at me with his deeply hooded eyes and said, "It appears a copy has been found."

I sat forward quickly in my seat. Even though this was not my area of interest, a find such as this would be an invaluable artifact, a glimpse into an ancient religion both long dead in its real form and deeply distorted by error and myth in the form it exists today.

"Where?" I exclaimed more than asked.

"Very near here," Thayerson said solemnly, "in a port town called Anchorhead."

I was shocked at this revelation. I had heard of the place. Its central point was a hill overlooking the port. The village cemetery had been placed on that hill. Death was ever-present there. That the markers of death could be seen by everyone from every part of the town at all times only helped to reinforce the knowledge of how dangerous living by the fruit of the sea could be. Then, Thayerson provided yet another shock.

"Carter," he said in an unexpected breech of formality, "I need you to retrieve that book. I need you to go to Anchorhead, acquire it by whatever means necessary, and return it here, to Miskatonic."

For a moment we sat in silence as I remained dumbfounded by this request. It was the last thing I had expected.

"It cannot remain out in the open," Thayerson continued. "We must keep it here in our library, safe from those who would use it to do evil."

"But, sir," I said, leaning forward, "if I may ask, if this book is of such importance, shouldn't you be the one to retrieve it?"

Thayerson visibly shuddered.

"I fear," he began, "that word of the book's existence is known outside these four walls, and not all that seek it do so for noble purpose.

But I suspect, strongly, they do not yet know its location."

Now he paused, and I watched as certain calculations were conducted in his mind. Then, he made a decision.

"I believe, Mr. Weston, I'm being watched. It is expected by certain parties that I will make an effort to retrieve the book. It is, therefore, imperative that I not attempt it."

"I see," I said, though in truth I felt even more mystified than before.

"Do we know where the book is located in Anchorhead?"

Thayerson sighed, showing me the palms of his hands in a sign of helplessness.

"I do not. I know only it is said a copy of the book has come to that town. By what means, I'm unaware."

I glanced skeptically at Thayerson. He saw the doubt in my eyes.

"I assure you this intelligence comes from a most reliable source," he said. "I would not send you if I doubted it. I know this is a difficult charge, Mr. Weston. But in truth you are the only one I trust. Not even Armitage. His heart is too close to the dark arts. You, and you alone, must go to Anchorhead and seek out the book. I would ask you to be discreet, to use the natural charm with which you have been gifted to your advantage. Spare no expense, and stay as long as it takes. I will deal with your affairs here. Good luck, Carter," he said, rising and extending his hand. "I've already purchased you a ticket on a north-bound train. It leaves Arkham Station in a little over an hour."

I took his hand and shook it firmly. He handed me a ticket, and I turned hurriedly to leave. As I did, Dr. Thayerson issued a final warning.

"Carter," he said, "be careful. There is much in this world far beyond your present imagining. And not all of it is harmless."

I simply nodded my understanding from the doorway and turned to go.

Chapter

3

As I stepped out onto the Green, a fierce north wind met me. With it came a smattering of snow flurries, harbingers of more to come I had no doubt. I returned to my room to find Henry waiting. He rose quickly to meet me upon my entrance.

"Well, what did the old man say?"

I gave him a wary look as I unwound the scarf hanging tightly to my throat. I had never lied to Henry before, but it appeared now was the time for firsts.

"He needs me to collect something for him," I said vaguely. Henry was my closest companion, and I trusted him completely, no matter what Thayerson said. But on the off chance Thayerson's paranoia proved to possess a grain of truth, I thought the less Henry knew or suspected, the better for his sake, as well as mine.

I packed quickly and light. I could not know how long I would be away. I assumed it would take some time to locate those individuals most familiar with the object in question. But as I knew little of what I was about to begin, I thought it best to avoid burdening myself with too much baggage. As I walked to Arkham Station, I barely noticed the strengthening north wind or the snowflakes falling in greater and greater quantity.

I needed a story, a cover for my intentions. As I took my seat in the railway car, I realized the difficulty of my position. I was no detective, and nothing in my academic career had prepared me to imitate that profession. It struck me that the people of Anchorhead were perhaps, and even likely, unaware of the significance of what they possessed. In that event, it might be as simple as finding the local librarian and inquiring as to artifacts of interest.

Of course, that begged yet more questions. Was the book in the possession of an individual? Was it held by the town in some collective capacity? If Thayerson was aware of its existence, would there be others on the trail, seeking it out, as well? If so, was I in danger? The last question fell upon me with a particular violence; it was the first time I had considered the possibility this exercise could end badly for me. I didn't think on it long, however, as the sudden jerk of the train's hesitant first steps out of the station jolted me from my thoughts.

For the moment, I allowed myself to forget the challenges ahead as I gazed out of the car window. I could see very little. The snow was now falling in torrents, and I realized this was no ordinary storm. It had all the markings of a nor'easter. Now, I was traveling to a town with which I was practically unfamiliar, with night having already fallen, in the midst of a coming blizzard. It was as if dark forces were conspiring to defeat me already.

My mind drifted, and I found myself thinking back to the earliest days at Miskatonic to one of the nights that defined my relationship with Henry. Henry would occasionally host parties to which he would invite those fellow students with whom we were particularly close. He was always a charming fellow, and I often noted people were drawn to him like metal flakes to a magnet. But in him also was an eccentricity, a fire that burned for those un-nameable creatures from beyond. And I knew that many of our so-called friends appeared only in the hopes that Henry would broach his favorite topic. His eyes would sparkle with a peculiar flame. One never knew what tales he might conjure.

So it was that night. After much wine flowed and the conversation meandered from professors to classes to the young ladies of Hampstead that lies across the Miskatonic River, Henry spread his arms wide on the table, and I saw that particular light come into his eyes.

"Did anyone read the *Times* today?"

I glanced at the five men seated around the table. I saw in their faces the answer was no. I could not help but smile. I had read the *Times*, and I had no doubt of what Henry would speak.

"Then, I suppose," he continued, "that you did not see the story regarding Dr. Charles Ashcroft?"

"I did not read the story," said an unremarkable boy whose name has long since escaped me, "but all of New England knows he has gone mad."

"Yes, yes," Henry said, waving him off, "but let us not get ahead of ourselves. That Ashcroft is mad is beyond doubt, but does one not wonder how a man such as he could lose his mind?"

"Why don't you tell us, Henry," I said.

"Oh, I shall, my good Carter, if only you will stop interrupting me."

The other men at the table laughed, and Henry smiled wickedly at me. I could not help but grin.

"Four months ago," Henry began, "Dr. Ashcroft left Boston, as I am sure you no doubt saw in the papers, on a scientific expedition for the ages."

Henry removed a pipe from his jacket pocket and struck a match. We all watched as he lit the tobacco within, waiting patiently for him to continue.

"He arrived," he said, extinguishing the match with a flick of his wrist, "on the northern shore of the continent of Antarctica with forty men, as many dogs, and a month's worth of supplies and provisions."

He then glanced up, looking at each man, starting with the one nearest him and moving down the table, as if to make sure we understood. He knew we were all well aware of Dr. Ashcroft's fate.

"Three months later," he continued, "a British whaling ship came upon a man on the far western shore of the continent. The sailors on board described him as a wild savage. Alone. Starving. And no doubt completely mad. We were all horrified, of course, to learn this man was none other than Dr. Ashcroft himself."

Henry paused and sipped his wine. The others looked around the table. They were anxious to hear the rest. Word of Ashcroft's fate had reached Arkham, but not the details. Henry appeared to have them, and their curiosity was irrepressible.

"The British," he continued, "passed Ashcroft off to an American clipper ship rounding the Horn from San Francisco en route to Boston. The ship's doctor attempted, as best he could, to learn what had befallen Ashcroft and his men. To learn the fate of the thirty-nine who had set out across that ice-locked desert. But whatever ailed Ashcroft was beyond his feeble talents, and the words that streamed from his gibbering lips were as ineffable as the shroud of horror that hung like a mask upon his face."

"Tell me Henry," I said, interrupting, "how is it that you know of all this? I have followed the news of Ashcroft's disappearance and rescue and learned no more than the barest details. Yet, you seem to know it all."

"Yes, Henry," said one of the others, "is this just one of your stories? An imagined tale for our amusement?"

Henry looked up at me as he held his pipe between his teeth and smiled.

"My dear Carter," he said between puffs of smoke, "patience is indeed a virtue you lack. But if you will allow me a moment, I will explain. This is no idle talk, and if you open your mind you may yet learn much about the ageless and ancient worlds that predate our own."

I merely nodded, and he continued.

"I know of what I speak, my good friends, because Dr. Ashcroft was moved from Boston to the Arkham Asylum two weeks ago. He lies not three miles from where we now sit. The learned men of Boston could make nothing of his ravings, but those doctors of Arkham, bred and trained at fairest Miskatonic, their minds are not closed to the sprawling mysteries that engulf us. From Dr. Ashcroft's seemingly mad ramblings, they drew forth a story, one which I will now relay.

"Dr. Ashcroft and his men set forth across the wasteland of the Antarctic with more than sufficient supplies to reach their goal, the southern pole. They would attempt a more southerly route than the expeditions before them, bypassing the Dome Argus where so many men have lost their lives. It was in that uncharted, cold waste that Dr. Ashcroft met his destiny. He should have known, he said, to turn back when he and his men came upon a mountain range where no mountains should be. He should have seen that something had gone horribly wrong. That the expedition had stepped into a world that presented impossibilities that ours does not hold. But when he viewed those peaks whose crest would look down upon the mountains of the Kathmandu, he saw nothing but an obstacle to be conquered. So he began his ascent, and his men began to die."

Henry paused then, for his pipe had extinguished. He struck a match, and as it flared, the light illuminated the room which had gone dark, casting for a brief moment furtive shadows that seemed to be watching us before darting back into the darkness.

"Every day they would climb, and each night they would make camp on the slopes of those fearful mountains. And then the light of the pallid sun would peak over the Antarctic horizon to show a camp of fewer men than when it had left them the night before. Some would simply disappear, perhaps stumbling off to their death in the cold waste, driven mad by the chill that could be beaten back but never defeated. Strange, then, that they left no footprints to mark their passing. Unusual that their tents were in perfect order.

"But not all the tragedy that befell Ashcroft's men was unexplained. Any attempting such an ascent would face mortal dangers. And on an uncharted slope those dangers were compounded by the unknown. How many fell into a yawning abyss, crevices that would appear and then seal themselves in seconds, entombing the screaming man below in eternal silence? Only Ashcroft knows, I suppose. But what we know is this — within a week, Ashcroft was left alone with whatever infernal powers had sought and procured his men's undoing and left him behind. As if they wanted him to seek. As if they wanted him to find.

"There could be no turning back. Ashcroft was high upon the mountainside and far from the eastern sea. He pressed on, though he couldn't have done so with much hope. It was then that he came upon a cavern carved into the side of the mountain. He plunged into the Stygian blackness within, feeling his way as best he could. Stumbling often, he rose to his feet only because of the command he heard within his own mind to continue. So powerful it was that even though he wished death to come, he would not simply fall to the ground and let it take him. Then, a vision seemed to creep into his mind. One of light, just beyond his reach. He made his way towards it, sometimes on his feet, sometimes crawling on his hands and knees. It was no vision, but his salvation. An opening. He rushed towards it, but when he reached the precipice, he saw the thing that drove him mad."

At that moment Henry fell silent, placing his once again extinguished pipe upon the table. My fellows sat leaning forward in their chairs, anxious to hear what maddening vistas opened up before Ashcroft. Only I remained relaxed, grinning smugly at Henry as he weaved what I assumed was an entirely manufactured tale. But then he continued.

"Who can describe properly what Ashcroft saw in the gray half-light in that valley? He could not. Not truly. Nor could his brain properly process it, as the very sight shattered his mind forever. What did he see? A citadel, nay, a city of unimaginable proportions and expanse, stretching forth in that hellish valley between the mountains. Cyclopean stone blocks of a hew and craftsmanship he could not know, cut from the earth eons before the Great Pharaoh raised his eyes to the plain of Giza and found it worthy of grandeur. Ruined towers and walled fortresses, dwellings of such size and dimension one might wonder if the mountains themselves did not call them home. All locked beneath solid sheets of ice. But it was not that which broke his mind. No, it was the thing that lurked in the titanic abyss, the infernal pit that lay in the center of that most ancient city. The thing that called to him in a voice that was not of man. The thing that, as he stood frozen in place from terror and wonder combined, began to rise."

Once again Henry stopped. He sat quietly in his chair, as if he had relayed nothing more than a somewhat interesting anecdote from class.

"And?" I finally asked. Henry raised an open palm as if in apology.

"And, that is all," he said. "Ashcroft remembers nothing from that moment until his arrival in Arkham. Whatever followed was too horrible, too monstrous for the mind, even one as strong as his. What he saw there . . .well, I pray to God we never know."

I looked around at my compatriots, and I saw true fear in their ashen faces. I smiled and said, "Bravo, Henry, you have truly outdone yourself this time."

"I'm not surprised, Carter, that you would disbelieve Ashcroft's report. Disappointed perhaps, but not surprised."

"Henry, please. It makes for a fantastic story and, from the looks on our friends' faces here, one that no doubt has a great power to instill fear." I saw the other men look down and blush. Fear was not an emotion to be lightly shown. "But what is more likely? That Dr. Ashcroft stumbled upon some Atlantis of antiquity only to witness a scene that drove him mad? Or that the expedition ran into great difficulty and when he was found, Ashcroft, half-starved and probably fully frozen, imagined a vast host of impossible visions?"

"Ah, but if that were true," Henry said, gesturing to me with his pipe, "wouldn't we expect that some of his men would have survived, as well? His dogs? His supplies? But it was only him. A man of some, though not exceeding, age, who managed to survive while all else perished?"

"Well, if you expect to bring logic into the discussion, how would that same man have made the trek from southern Antarctica to its western shore and survived? Surely such a thing is impossible."

"And thus you have hit upon the most compelling evidence for

Ashcroft's story. It is impossible, whether his men fell by natural causes or were hunted down by some fell beast. Ashcroft should be dead. Yet, he is not. Something must have saved him."

"So, the very force you believe killed Ashcroft's men and stole his sanity delivered him safe and sound to be rescued? Why? For what purpose?"

"No purpose but its own, I assure you. Why did it bring him to that dead city? Why did it lead him to the steps of an ancient necropolis, only to deliver him from its clutches? I cannot say. All I know is that it did, and that is enough for me."

At that point I simply sat back in my chair. There was nothing more to be said. Soon our friends had departed, and I was left alone with Henry.

"That was quite a story you told tonight," I said. "Do you believe a word of it?"

Henry laughed as he poured two glasses of brandy.

"Some of it. Do I believe that Ashcroft saw something fantastic? Certainly. Is every word he spoke the truth? Unlikely. That is where we differ, Carter."

"Where? That I do not give credence to insanity?"

"No," he said, "that you do not recognize that in all things there is at least a grain of truth. And that makes Ashcroft's story truly remarkable."

"You are from another age, Henry. Another age altogether."

"Yes, that may be true," he said, handing me my glass. "But the ancients knew certain things, Carter. Yes, I see what you are thinking. They were superstitious. Fearful. Hateful and destructive at times. But they knew man is not meant to understand all things. They knew man is not capable of understanding all things. And there is wisdom there, wisdom that we would do well to heed."

In truth, I did see much wisdom in his words. But I simply could not believe. I was, and remain, a man of faith. But that faith was the limit of my belief in the supernatural. I was, as Thomas of old, condemned not to believe, lest I see. Alas, a time would come when mine eyes would see and mourn because of it.

Why did that story come to mind in those lonely moments on the north bound train from Arkham? Why did it leap to my mind, unbidden and uncalled? Fate's foreshadowing perhaps, as fate's hand was constantly upon me that night. Fate, or perhaps the power of the Book.

The train chugged north, through the darkened countryside, over the Miskatonic River and into the river valley itself. It passed sturdy rock walls and ancient gabled barns; thick, untouched forests and domed hills. Then the dark, churning wilderness gave way to what looked in the shadow to be an endless flat plane — we had reached the sea. The combination of the black night and thick snow made it impossible to see the tempest no doubt rocking its surface. I saw the lighthouse of Anchorhead before the dimly lit houses came in view. Its powerful beam swept across land and sea like a single, great eye casting its gaze upon all within its sight.

The train jerked and spasmed as it pulled slowly into Anchorhead station, a desolate edifice consisting of no more than a platform and a darkened shack. I was the only person to alight from the train, and there was, to my eye, no living soul in the vicinity. This might have bothered me at another time, but the north winds were now roaring fiercely from the sea with such violence that none with a sound mind would have ventured into their midst. There were, of course, no stagecoaches to be had either, and so I began what I hoped was a short walk to the nearest inn.

I found it not fifty feet from the station. I entered quickly, pressing the door forcefully closed against the now raging wind outside. I turned to see an elderly woman glaring at me from behind a solid oak desk.

"Good evening," I lied.

"You need a room, I suspect?" she snarled.

I told her that I did, and she begrudgingly obliged me. I paid her for two nights with the promise I would likely stay for more. She spoke little, using the minimum amount of words necessary to show me the location of my room and its arrangements. I realized as I placed my bag upon a bedside table that I was quite famished. I hesitated to venture back into the howling maelstrom rocking the panes of my windows, but it was evident that either I must or go to bed hungry. The innkeeper brusquely indicated there was a tavern only a short walk away, a quaint place located on the shores of the sea. I took her up on this suggestion and stepped out once again into the swirling darkness.

I was immediately buffeted by the wind. I would call it a gale, but it was too constant in its fierceness for that appellation. As I turned down the road, it seemed as though the direction of the storm shifted. It was now blowing in my face, every fleck of snow stinging like the sharp prick of so many needles. The road curved sharply right and after passing between two rows of wooden and brick houses, the pungent aroma of the ocean surrounded me. Even with the blinding snow and darkened skies, some unknown glow illuminated the oily sea as it roiled and undulated under the ever gathering barrage.

The tavern sat on a ledge at the ocean's edge. The sign hung lower on one corner than the other, and its violent swinging on the metal chain holding it indicated it was not long for this world. I could barely make out the name etched into the ancient wood: The Kracken. I took a moment, despite the howling gale buffeting me, to smile.

I pushed open the heavy door and stepped inside, letting it slam behind me. The room was lit by oil lamps hung haphazardly from the ceiling. The gust of wind pursuing me had rocked them to and fro, and now their pale light cast grotesque shadows that seemed to gibber and dance on the tavern walls.

I looked around the room. It was built like the bow of a ship, the center portion lower than its sides. There were several denizens, regulars of this establishment I would have wagered, spread here and there about the place. But it was a particular table, the only one in the center depression that was occupied, that stood out to me the most.

At it sat four men, incongruous for their diversity of dress and the mien with which they held themselves. They sat quietly, each man seemingly more interested in his ale than those around him. One was an ancient man, dressed in a thick, but grizzled, fur coat and an unkempt beard obscuring his face. His warm dress was the most appropriate for the evening. Next to him was a man who had the look of a scholar or professional, as if perhaps he were the town magistrate. There was yet another man, who while attired in a similar manner to the previous fellow, I took immediately for a doctor of some sort. And finally, another bearded gentleman, though he was more thoughtfully trimmed and kept. He wore a dark blue coat and pants with black boots. And he was the only one staring directly at me. There was a light in his eye, not of welcome, but of knowledge and recognition.

I walked down the three steps into the central depression and past the table. The three men never looked up; the fourth never looked away. I stepped up three more steps and found myself at the bar. The man behind it, a heavyset older gentlemen who, in his day, would probably have been considered a ruffian, stared at me without word or welcome, and so I felt compelled to lead the conversation.

"Excuse me, good man. I wondered if you might have some food available."

"Fish stew's all we got," he said with a deep New England accent. "But I reckon a fella' from Boston-way would frown on that."

"Why, certainly not," I said, trying to save a first impression. "A bowl of soup and some bread, please. And a pint to wash it down."

For a moment he only glared. But then eventually he turned and walked to a large pot sitting over a fire, raging hot and wild, in the hearth. As I waited uncomfortably for him to return, I felt a hand on my shoulder.

Chapter

4

Turning was only the work of a moment, but in that moment several thoughts ran through my head. I realized this could be an aggressive move by the unknown possessor of the hand now on my person, and a fight might prove imminent. I also knew I was in a place where such a fight could very well turn deadly. I considered the possibility I was already undone, that some stranger had recognized me as Thayerson's emissary, in which case this journey might be all for naught. Before I could ponder the consequences of such a disaster, I was looking into the green eyes of the blue coated, bearded fellow I noticed only a few moments before.

"You sir," he said, "have the look of a man who doesn't belong."

It was a phrase that, were it not for his general demeanor, could have been taken as a threat. But there was a smile on his face and, more importantly, in his eyes, and I was immediately aware he meant me no harm. I tried and failed to place his voice as he spoke. It lacked a defining accent, but deep within it rolled the salt sea.

"And by that," he continued, "I mean you must be a visitor in these parts. I've always been a man to welcome those who wander, as I've done quite a bit of wandering myself."

The barkeep had returned by this point, loudly dropping the bowl of soup, bread, and ale in front of me. "Ah, now that Tom has got you your food, please, join us at our table. We have much to say, but I fear the years have tired us of the listening. Perhaps a fresh set of ears would bring some of that old joy back."

On the surface the offer was a friendly one, and, in fact, I had judged the man to be sincere from the moment he began to speak to me. But there was something else there, an ulterior motive that lay beneath. It wasn't that he was lying, or even that he was concealing. Just, there was something beyond that I couldn't quite place. But in any event, I never considered rejecting his offer. This was an unexpected chance to ingratiate myself with some of the locals, and I had vague hopes this man might be just the sort of person who could direct me to the location of the book. And so, at his behest I gathered up my food and drink while he pulled a fifth chair to his table. I sat down, and my new host began to introduce me to his companions. He started with the heavily furred man to my left.

"This is Jack," he said. "Jack, in his day, was a master trapper. Isn't that right, Jack?"

The man smiled weakly at me and said, "I guess that's so."

"Daniel, here," he said, already moving to the man I had pegged as a magistrate, "is a solicitor of some renown in these parts."

"In better days," the man said with more than a modicum of sadness and regret.

"William, here, is a doctor. Before he joined us in our little town, he spent his early years with those poor souls whose minds have been lost. The insane, the demented. The truly damned of this world."

The doctor took a long drink of his beer. He did not speak. It struck me, then, as I looked at them, their worn faces, and their dark shrouded eyes. These were broken men. All except the one who spoke first and last.

"And I am but a simple fisherman." I saw Daniel smile and cough out a laugh. "Spent damn near all of my life on the sea," the man continued. "But now I'm retired," he said, grinning. "Jonathan Gray," he offered. "Captain Jonathan Gray."

"It is a pleasure to make the acquaintance of you all," I said. "My name is Carter Weston."

"And what, if we may ask," spoke the Captain, "is a fellow like yourself doing here, especially on such a night. Not that we would mind, of course. We consider ourselves a hospitable people," he said, politely but inquiringly. "But the wind has blown up a storm tonight the likes of which we have seldom seen, even here."

As if on cue, a particularly powerful gust shook the brittle panes of the tavern with such ferocity I feared they might shatter. But then the wind calmed, and the Captain turned his gaze to me again.

"Well," I replied, somewhat withered beneath his eyes, "I am a student at Miskatonic."

The captain's countenance did not change, but I noted the man I now knew as William, the doctor, shuddered at that name. It was not a reaction I was altogether unfamiliar with. "I am a folklorist," I continued. "I have been traveling about these parts collecting the stories of its people."

"And what drives a man to do that?" Captain Gray asked.

"Well, to preserve them," I answered. "And to better understand from whence they came. I, of course, did not know of the coming storm, not being a man versed in reading the weather, that is. But I'm here now, and here is where I suppose I will ride it out."

"Ah," the Captain offered. "So you say you want to understand where these stories come from. Do you ever suppose perhaps they are true?"

I smiled back at the Captain, and a little bit of the old skeptic took hold.

"Why, of course not. Things such as I have heard exist only in the mind of the teller."

Then, unexpectedly, the three men who sat around me chuckled. Captain Gray only smiled. But there was no joy in it, neither in the smile or the laughs.

"Ah, my dear boy," Captain Gray said with a solemnity that betrayed the smile he wore, "there are, indeed, more things in Heaven and Earth than are dreamt of in your philosophy. Let me ask you this," he continued, "the people with whom you spoke, were they personal witnesses to the substance of the stories they told?"

"Why, no," I replied. "First-hand stories are most welcome, but people in my profession rarely receive such a treat."

I saw the Captain glance quickly to his companions. Then, there was a flicker of recognition in his eyes as if they had communicated something to him without words.

"Well, my friend. The night is young, and we are all very thirsty. So perhaps there is time to share with you some stories of our own. And then, upon the hearing of them, you can judge for yourself their worth to your studies."

I smiled politely. An opportunity to relieve myself of the burden of the task I faced was welcome.

"I think I would enjoy that," I said.

"Then, I will begin," said the man I had come to know as Jack. I turned to him, and behind his grizzled beard and beneath his thick, fur-lined hat, his eyes burned with a new intensity that had been absent from them only a few minutes before.

"It's been now on 50 years ago," he began, growing wistful. "And yet when I see it in my dreams, it's as if he were upon me again."

"It was," he said in a deep, sonorous bass not uncommon to the western woods of Massachusetts, "as these things always are, I suppose, long ago. So long ago now."

He looked down at his glass, and for a long moment I wondered if he had the strength to continue. A life, no doubt, flashed before his eyes. But then he spoke again, and I felt myself carried back to those days so long past.

Part II

Chapter

5

Jack:

I was, if you don't mind me sayin', not much older than you, I guess. Maybe even younger, by the look of you. I was a fur man by trade, as my father was before me, and as his father before him, all the way back to when my ancestors came from the old country. They were Huguenots, they were. Fled from one persecution to the next. I guess it was only fitting they should find a home in the woods and the wilds.

I had learned the trade from my father, but this was to be my first time on my own, as much as I ever would be. You may not know this, but a fur man never travels alone. We work in teams, you see. Trackers and trappers, a man who is handy with a pot and some pans and, if he is worth anything, a hammer and saw. Even a doctor if, per chance, we could find one.

I was in Monterey in those days, a wild bit of country in the Birkshires. There were to be five of us on that trip. The leader was Tom, a big man who looked like he was cut from marble. Tom was a friend of my father's from back in their wilder days, and he had agreed to take me on that trip as his apprentice.

Then, there was Dr. Stanley. We never knew if he was a real doc or not, but he had a reputation in the hill country as a man who could be counted on and knew how to treat a fever or a sickness. And, he could fix a wagon. We hauled one behind us as we went. We'd skin the animals as we caught them and, then, line that thing with as many pelts as we could carry. Once the supplies ran out and the wagon was full, we'd make our way back to the outposts along the rivers. But that was always the worst part of the trip. Wheel would break, wagon would get stuck. Without a man who knew his way around some carpentry, we would be lost. I had some of that knowledge, but the doc was the best with a knife, whether he was cutting on a man or a pine board.

Andrew was another trapper, a skinny fellow, that one. He struck me as a bit skittish straightaway, and I marked him as a man you couldn't trust. Joe was our scout. He was a bit of a mystery. He was a tracker by trade, though he could probably trap better than the rest of us, too. They said he was part Indian; I never learned the truth of that. He died too soon. And he was quiet. Spoke barely a word.

And then there was Travis. Travis was an experienced hand. He knew the woods, knew the secret paths, the dark places where the best fur would hide. There was something about that man, something missing from his eyes. I know that sounds strange. But that's what I felt. Like he was empty somehow. But Tom wanted him. Between Tom and Andrew, Travis, and me, we had a pretty good team goin'. There were no doubts we would make good coin on that trip. And so I guess we got a little wild, as men like us were wont to do. On the night before we were supposed to leave, the wine, the whiskey, and the rum flowed hard and fast.

Tom had a rule on the trail — no liquor, no exceptions. It bein' the last night in town, I guess we drank a little more than we should. There was a girl who worked the bar that evening, an Indian girl. Travis watched her all night long. She was shy and a tiny bit of nothin'. Dark haired and dark skinned. Young, no more than 16, I'd wager. Every time she'd walk by, Travis would grab her, pull her to him, tell her she was "a pretty little thing."

It boils my blood to even think about it. There was a sickness in his voice then, a nasty, godless quality. Depraved, he was. Just depraved.

Anyway, she obliged him at first, as any good girl in that trade would. But then it was too much even for someone who made her money off men like Travis. She began to struggle, to try and get away. Andy told him — that's what we called Andrew — Andy told him to leave her alone. Travis just glared at him. He scared me, then, with that look. I wanted no part of that.

I left the bar and found Tom outside, smoking his tobacco. There was the hint of coming snow that day, but it wasn't cold.

"You ready for tomorrow?" he asked between puffs. I wasn't really sure. I had only gone with my father before, never with anyone I didn't know.

"Sure, I am," I said, mustering as much confidence in my voice as I could manage.

"Good, I'm going to need you," he said. He didn't say how or why. I simply nodded. I had learned not to question men like Tom too often, and then to ask only the questions that really needed answerin'. But I'd be lyin' if I didn't say there was something about that night that scared me. I don't know how I knew it then, but the trip already felt foul, as if it was marked from the beginning.

I stumbled through the darkness, the haze of the whiskey thick on my brain. I don't know how long passed before I found my way to my bunk, but I do know my head had barely hit the pillow when I was asleep.

I had strange dreams that night, nightmares filled with flashes of light and thunder. I was in the forest, but I was alone. I still remember, even as I was dreaming, that I was struck by my own loneliness. "Never trap alone." That was my father's cardinal rule. But there I was, without another soul in sight. It was a familiar forest, and I felt I knew it, but in that familiarity there was also great fear, as if something wasn't quite right. The forest was like Travis's eyes. It was missing something, something basic and good. It was quiet, too. A stillness as unnatural as it was complete. Nothing moved there. Nothing.

And then it was night. I can't explain it, but just as suddenly as you could strike a match, the sun vanished from the sky. Darkness and silence. Isolation, loneliness. Those were the things that overwhelmed me. But there was a voice in my head, too.

"Steady on Jack, steady on. You have a job to do. If you don't finish it, no one will."

And so I began to move. But then came the thunder. Then came the light. It roared and flashed throughout the wood, and it was all the more horrible because of the silence it shattered. Then a single roar over all others — the screeching of a bird, a great and terrible beast unlike any flying thing you ever saw. A great black shadow covered me so thick even the flashes of lightning couldn't lift it.

I woke, then, drenched in sweat, screaming. I sat bolt upright in my bed. Joe was sitting across from me, just a-starin', his black Indian eyes as impenetrable as the meaning of my dream.

"What did you see?" he asked. If he had spoken a word to me before that moment, it's not one I remember.

"Nothin'. Just a dream," I said.

"No dream. What did you see?" he asked again, this time more forcefully. He scared me, but I wasn't going to relive that, no matter what he did.

So I just said, "I told you, nothin'."

I'm old enough now to know something I didn't know then — an angry man, or a scared man, he's liable to turn in a moment. To snap, as they say. And Joe snapped then. He leapt from his bunk clear across the room to mine and grabbed me around the throat. His mouth made sounds, but if they were words I could understand, I sure as Hell didn't then. I think he would have killed me. Well, I damn sure know he would have killed me, but then I felt him fly away from me. I looked up and through my near-on blacked out eyes I saw Tom sling Joe across the room like he was a bag of dirty laundry.

"Enough!" I remember he thundered like Zeus himself. "You two get your gear. We've already overstayed our welcome here."

There was anger in his face, but I knew despite my youth that it wasn't directed at us. He stood there for a moment longer and, then, turned to go, saying, "Be at the wagon in five minutes."

Three minutes later I emerged into the morning sun. Tom was at the wagon with Dr. Stanley loading the last bit of supplies. Travis was there, too, sitting on the buckboard smoking a rolled cigar. He was smirking, and like everything else Travis did, there was no joy there. Just a cruel, cold sneer. Joe and I walked over together, but I kept my distance. Whatever had come over him earlier, now he was as implacable as the grave. That same flat, stone-faced look I guess he always wore. I could see Tom and Travis were talking, and I could tell it wasn't a pleasant conversation.

"Damn it, Travis!" I heard him say. "You're bringing bad luck on us, bad luck already."

I heard Travis curse in response. "I make my on luck, Captain," he growled in that toneless voice of his. Where he was from, I didn't know, and his voice didn't betray it, either. I just knew it was a place I didn't want to visit.

"That's right Travis, you do," Tom replied. "And that's the fear, isn't it?"

I didn't know what they were on about, but I was sure it had something to do with Tom's sudden desire to get out of that place as soon as he could. I loaded up my gear in silence and climbed aboard. Joe and the doc followed. Andy skulked about, doing his best to stay invisible. It was his way, I guess. Tom had the reins of the horses, and we were about to leave. I suppose, if we had been a little quicker, I might not be sitting here today. But that's the way of the world, right? For just as Tom was about to lead us out of that place, there was a shriek, a howl really. It stopped us dead in our tracks. Then, it turned to a word.

"You!" it thundered. We turned as one, turned and saw an old Indian woman, older than I am now I would suppose. She had that little girl from the pub by the arm and was dragging her along behind her. But she wasn't pretty then, probably wouldn't be pretty for a long time after that. Her face was shattered. That's about the only way to put it. Her lips were busted, and her cheeks bruised. One eye was so swollen she couldn't have opened it for King Phillip himself. She was crying, though. I guess that must have hurt quite a bit.

I gaped at her, mouth as open as it could be. I had never seen nothing like it. I followed the old woman's eyes to Travis. He didn't look shocked. He just sat there and smiled, smiled that same awful smirk he always had. This was nothing to him. Tom just looked from the woman to Travis and struck the horses. He didn't take his eyes off of the road until we were clear out of town. But the woman didn't stop. She dragged that girl until they were running alongside the wagon.

"You did this!" she screamed at Travis in a thickly veiled tongue I could barely understand. Travis just smiled even broader and shrugged his shoulders. Then, the woman threw the girl to the ground and pointed at Travis. I couldn't understand some of her words, and I have come to believe they weren't all English. But I did hear one sentence, the most important one.

"A hex on you, you black-hearted beast. The Wendigo will have you. He will have you yet!"

Travis chuckled. And that was it. The wagon rolled along, and we sat in silence except for the creaking of the wheels and the crinkling of the tobacco in Travis's cigar as his breath ignited it. I looked around the wagon. Tom was emotionless. Doc Stanley was not as disciplined a man, and if Travis had cared to look he would have seen a snarl of disgust on his face. Andy just looked scared. But it was Joe that interested me the most. He looked off through the forest, peering really, and mumbled to himself.

Despite our earlier encounter, my curiosity got the better of me. I reached across the wagon and tapped Joe on the shoulder. He spun around, and when he looked at me, I knew the face of terror.

His skin was ashen, his dark hair drenched with sweat. The eyes were the worst, though. They were opened wide, pupils as big as saucers. He grabbed me on the shoulders.

"He will come for us now!" he screamed. It was as if he had gone mad. Out of the corner of my eye, I saw movement. Travis landed a swift kick right to Joe's midsection.

"Shut it, you damn fool," he spat. "Superstitious bullshit, that is. There ain't nothing out here but what we're gonna kill. Should have left you behind with the rest of your kind."

"Silence!" Tom yelled, the veins in his neck beginning to throb. "One day in, and I don't need this!"

Travis leaned back and returned to his cigar. Joe just rocked back in forth in the floor of the wagon, while Andy looked the worst of the group. We rumbled along, deeper into the woods. We didn't stop till night fall that day. When I felt it was safe to speak, I moved quietly over to Andy who still looked as though the fear of God was in him.

"You alright?" I asked.

"No," Andy spat. "And you ain't either. You're just too stupid to know it."

I let it pass. "What's wrong? What was Joe all up about?"

Andy looked at me with terror-filled eyes and said, "The Wendigo."

Chapter
6

For the second time that day I heard a word that had never met my ears in my previous 18 years of life.

"What," I began to ask, swallowing deeply before I continued, "is the Wendigo?"

The voice that answered me was not Andy's. It was deeper, stronger. I turned to see Joe had pulled himself up and leaned against the side of the wagon. Whatever panic had covered him before now seemed to vanish as he spoke. His voice was melodic. On the surface it was steady and firm, but I sensed the fear still lurking beneath its seemingly calm waters.

"The Wendigo," he began, "is the whisper in the darkness, the voice in the night. He is the wind that shakes the forest, the thunder in the blizzard, the lightning flash that follows. The Wendigo is death."

Andy whimpered audibly and then curled himself into a tightly wound ball. I looked from him back to Joe's now-bloodless face. Then Doc Stanley interrupted.

"All superstition and myth," he said. "None of it's true." He cut his eyes to Joe and in that look there was a none-too-subtle command to end this talk now. The forest is no place to lose your head. Joe, however, did not keep his peace.

"No myth," he said. "My ancestors came to this land long ago, and they brought with them wisdom that your kind has long since forgot.

Our histories speak of a book, more ancient than man, written in a language that all can read. In that book is the legend of the Wendigo.

"Long ago, before the age of man, there walked this Earth a race whose name is now lost to us, if it was ever known. My people speak of them. These are the Great Old Ones, creatures of legend who for eons ruled the forests and the plains, the sea and even the sky from whence they came. Some say they were gods, but I do not believe it. They were cruel and cold-hearted. They reveled in pain and their hearts were filled with hate. The world was covered in darkness then, and if men had been there to see their cruelty, the agony of it would still be burned into our memory, even now.

"There was one who ruled over them all, one who made them and formed them. We do not speak his name, and I will not speak it here. The Old Ones were his spawn, and thousands they were, but he loved one above all others — a daughter, Lilitu. Lilitu was as beautiful as she was depraved. She gave herself freely to her brothers, the sons of the dark one. But unto one of her kin, Witiko, he who lusted for her most fiercely, she refused. As his desire burned within him, Lilitu mocked Witiko until finally he took her by force. But it was all part of her ploy, you see, all part of her game. She went to her father and cried out for his vengeance on Witiko. In a mockery of all that is holy, Witiko was brought before his father to face his 'justice.' Witiko was not killed. Instead he was stripped of his authority and power on this Earth, stripped even of his name.

'You shall be Wendigo,' his father roared. 'You shall walk the Earth alone. Off it you shall gain no sustenance. You shall eat of neither the plants of the forest nor the plain, nor of the animals that now swarm about us. Pain will be all that you know.'

And so the Wendigo was banished from his brethren, and in pain and darkness he traveled the land, his skin stretched tight over his bones, his hunger burning as bright as his hate. But the age of the Old Ones passed, and only the Wendigo remained. A new creature arose then, one that had not been refused to the Wendigo, one unknown to his father. This was man, and he the Wendigo could eat. Since then, the Wendigo has haunted the north woods, devouring whomever he finds as prey. From him, the Wendigo takes his knowledge and his skill, but never gains sustenance, never fills his hunger, never quenches his hate. This is the Wendigo, and now, he comes for us."

"Bah!" Doc Stanley spat. "No more of this! There is no Wendigo."

"What of the stories then?" Andy muttered through his creeping fear.

"A disease of the mind," the doctor responded matter-of-factly.

"Wait," I said, breaking my silence for the first time, "you mean to tell me there is some truth to this?" Until that moment, Joe's ravings, though frightening in their power, struck me as nothing more than a myth from the old days. But now the doctor appeared to give them some weight.

"Well," the doctor replied, stuttering, "the legend, such that it is — absurdities all, of course — is not merely that the Wendigo devours his victims. You see . . ." He paused then, studying his hands. "Oh, it's rubbish. We shouldn't talk any more of this."

"He takes you," Joe interjected. "His spirit is strong, stronger than yours. But his body was imprisoned long ago, along with all the Old Ones. They speak to us only in dreams now. But the curse gave the Wendigo power beyond even theirs. But though he lives, he must take the form of a man to partake of this world. Whomever he takes is doomed to feast upon the flesh of his brothers, to watch through eyes that are no longer his as the Wendigo devours all before him."

"It's a mental defect," the doctor spat, showing both his own frustration but also a hint of doubt. "Certain of the Indian tribes around these parts are known to succumb to it. To explain their sudden insanity and . . . cannibalism, the legend of the Wendigo was invented. That is all. These are mad men and nothing more. And if you persist in this kind of talk, we are liable to lose our own minds over these next few months."

I suppose it might have gone on like that for a few more hours, but at that moment Tom pulled the wagon to a stop. We had arrived at the first of our campsites. The next few hours of work made us forget quickly about the curse that had been laid upon us, about the Wendigo. But as I lay in my tent that night, I couldn't help but hear whispers on the wind as the first snows of winter began to fall in earnest.

* * *

Without notice our duties consumed us. The life of the men of the forest is not one of leisure. As the air grew colder, the work got harder. I was used to a more lenient taskmaster — my father. But Tom was relentless. He was the best in the western woods, no doubting that. But there was a growing gloom above us as well, and as the moon waxed brighter, as a steel-gray curtain of clouds rose, and as the icy cold wind cut through our tents and our clothes, it was clear to all that the season's worst was near.

"We should close up early tonight," Tom said. He had a wary eye on the dim light of the setting sun. It was an hour yet until twilight, but thick clouds had rendered it night already. "Everyone, make sure everything is double secure tonight. Trust me when I say night in a snowstorm is no time to try and pitch a tent."

Tom's point was well taken, but it was advice we didn't need. We had already begun the work and were well underway before the first burst of snow. Joe was our cook, but he had a hard time getting anything together that night. The winds and the snow were such that the fire would barely stay lit, no matter how much wood we fed it.

We bedded down early. I stood at the opening of my tent and watched as the snow began to fall in ever greater quantities. I glanced back at the dying fire and saw Joe still sat at its edge. The waning embers did not give much light, but he had drawn near to their warmth, and the rays that remained illuminated his face. Perhaps it was the light or the shadow or the snow, but I noticed for the first time that Joe had aged over the past few weeks. The lines were deeper, the skin more leathery and pulled taut across his face. His eyes were simply empty. There was no fear, no worry, just nothing, a cold resignation that frightened me more than anything else possibly could. That may sound strange, but I know no other way to describe it.

They say man is an animal, and that may be so. But most men don't know nature. They are like you, my young friend. They live in the world of the city, and when they come to the wild it is for leisure and peace. They do not see the cold killer lurking in the darkness, the hunter red in tooth and claw. But we saw it that night.

The blizzard came hard and fast, falling upon us like the eagle strikes its prey. I lay listening as the wind buffeted my tent, and the snow struck its sides like grapeshot fired from a distant cannon. I know I slept that night, as strange and unbelievable as it might sound. Yes, the work had exhausted me, but my senses were so heightened, my fear so deep, that sleep should never have come. I was as a man taken by opium, and my eyes grew heavy, my mind grew cloudy, and I drifted in and out of consciousness.

I cannot know how much of what I remember was real or imagined. But I heard things that night. Not just the wind or the snow. It started with a howl, a low and distant whine. I wasn't sure it was there at first, thought it might just be something from a dream. Soon it was joined by another and another. It was as if all the wolves in the western wood had suddenly been called to a common purpose.

But it wasn't the howl itself that sent a chill through my bones. No, it was the message of that call. It was pain and fear from an animal that rarely knew either. At one moment the sound was all about, as if we were surrounded. Then just as quickly it seemed to be coming from within my own mind. And then it changed, my God, did it change. No more the call of a wild dog. Now it was the pitiful cry of a woman. So deep was her anguish, so terrible. As if the world had been taken from her, as if a child had been ripped from her bosom and slaughtered before her very eyes. Oh, the pain in that cry. But it was not the worst I heard, no, not at all. Vile sounds followed, sounds that are beyond my meager education to describe, but I wager the greatest poet in the world couldn't write a line for them. Demon haunted the forest was that night, and in my dreams, I heard and felt the darkest and foulest beast that ever gibbered its wail from the depths of the pit.

There was thunder that followed lightning, the mark of a summer storm in the heart of winter. In those flashes of light, I saw figures outlined against the thin skin of my tent, figures that danced outside my vision. And then, even in the night, even in the darkness, a shadow fell upon me, that of a great bird, a flying beast never before seen on this earth by the eyes of man. Its cry rent the night air, and in that moment my mind snapped, and I sunk into blessed black oblivion.

* * *

I awoke the next morning to the brilliant, blinding light of the morning sun shining through my now open tent. Outlined in its gleam was Doc Stanley. If the bitter night had shaken him, the blank expression on his face did little to reveal it.

"Get up," he commanded. "Joe is missing." And with that, he turned and was gone.

I pulled on boots and rushed outside to find the entire campsite covered in snow. I remembered the wolves and immediately walked around to the back of my tent. I expected to find paw prints, fur, something. But there was only snow, thick and as untouched as a lamb that had never been sheered. I told myself it had been all a dream or that, at worst, the snow had covered whatever markings the beasts had left behind. I told myself that, but even in those early days I didn't believe it.

Then I heard my name. It was Tom. I walked back to the center of the campsite to find the entire group gathered around the spot where the fire had been before. Tom was serious, Doc Stanley's expression remained as impenetrable as the grave, and Andy looked like he wanted to crawl into a hole and hide. Travis merely seemed irritated.

"What's going on?" I asked.

Tom sighed and said, "Joe's gone. He should have been up making breakfast by now, but he never even started the fire."

"Maybe he needed some wood," I offered.

"We cut some yesterday," Doc Stanley replied. I knew this. I had helped break it up.

"Maybe something was wrong with it." Tom sighed again, and I saw Doc cast a weary look his way. When Tom didn't speak, Doc Stanley did.

"He didn't go for wood," Stanley said. "His tent is empty, and there are no footprints. No footprints anywhere. Not going to it, not going away. Nothing. It's like . . ." Andy whimpered, and for a second Doc Stanley paused. He looked at him with less contempt than I expected and then said, "It's like Joe disappeared. Just up and vanished. We looked in his tent. Everything is in place. Nothing messed up, nothing broken. And, nothing taken. It looks like he just walked out of camp with nothing but the clothes on his back."

"Oh, God," Andy stammered, "Joe knew this trip was trouble. Knew it was trouble from the start. And now it's got him."

Doc Stanley jerked his head towards Andy and fixed him with one of the most hate-filled gazes I've ever seen.

"Who's got him?" Tom asked.

"The Wendigo!" Andy cried, oblivious to Doc Stanley.

"Oh, not this rubbish," Doc Stanley said as he turned and walked towards his tent.

"Look." Now it was Travis's time to talk. "Ain't nobody here who put any stock in Joe. I don't even know why you brought him along," he spat, pointing a long narrow finger at Tom. "He was always liable to run off, and now he has. He probably left last night. He probably got spooked by the storm and struck off into the woods. The snow covered his tracks, and he's gone. If the wolves haven't gotten him, the snow damn sure did. He's probably buried under three feet of it now."

"You heard the wolves too?" I asked instinctively.

Travis's eyes went from mine to Tom's, and as I followed them I saw the answer to my question in both their faces.

"No, kid," Travis lied. "I was just sayin' is all. There ain't no wolves in these parts. But Joe is dead either way."

Tom still hadn't spoken, and I knew given how he guarded his words, he wasn't likely to.

Then Travis continued. "Look, we got dry wood. You clean off a spot," he said to me, "and I'll get a fire going. I think I can round up something for us to eat. And then we can go look for Joe."

When I heard that I lost my words. Travis didn't do anything for anybody. Now Tom did speak. "You don't cook," he said.

"Yeah, well, looks like somebody has to learn, huh?"

With that he turned and walked away. I went to work clearing a spot for a fire, and soon we had a pretty big one going. Before the sun had risen too far in the sky, Travis had cooked up some of the rabbit we had trapped the day before. For a man who had no way with food, I remember thinking to myself that it wasn't half bad. I had never thought much of Joe's cooking, and I reckoned what Travis had made was just as good. I ate more than I was accustomed to. I was hungry, and Travis, though he had cooked it himself, obviously had doubts about his ability as he ate almost none.

"Not hungry this mornin'," he said. Something with his stomach.

We ate quickly. If Joe were still alive out there, we needed to find him and find him fast. Tom gave us our orders.

"Each man take a line and walk it. Don't wander off. We'll cover the forest close by as good as we can, but I don't want nobody else gettin' lost. You walk straight out and then you follow your tracks and come straight back. You got it?"

Each man nodded his assent, and we were off. Before long, the camp was far behind me, and I could no longer see the man to either my right or left. The forest was thick, and if Joe had climbed under a bush or a tree for cover in the storm, there would be no finding him now. With the snow as thick as it was, I doubted I would spot him unless I damn near stepped on his chest. I began to think back to the night before, the things I had heard, seen. The thought of it made me stop in my tracks. If any of it were real, even a fraction of it, then Joe would never have left his tent. Never willingly, that is. No man would, and especially not one as superstitious as he. Joe was no coward; I would never claim that. But I wouldn't call it courage that would lead a man to have stepped into that maelstrom. And that could mean only one thing — someone had taken him. Someone big — Joe was a strong man. His attacker had done it without making a sound, without knocking a single thing out of place, without leaving any evidence of his having been there.

The forest changed. I noticed every sound, every twig snapping and every creak of every tree. Something, and I didn't know what it was, was out there, and suddenly I felt the cold stare of an unknown pair of eyes on me. I spun around, peering into the blinding white wilderness that surrounded me. That's when I saw Joe.

He was standing a couple hundred yards from me. His arms and legs were spread wide, like he was trying to hold up the two trees on either side of him, or like he was trying to hug the world. His mouth was slightly open, his head cocked to the left. He was completely naked. At first, I didn't know what to do. He had clearly lost his mind, and I knew he must be freezing. But I started towards him anyway. He was alive, and I would do my best to save him.

But as I walked towards him he never moved, even though I knew he had to see me. Then I began to notice something was wrong. Joe was a big man, but he didn't look big anymore. He looked thin. He looked small. He looked . . . empty. Then I saw the ropes, one tied around each hand and each foot. They ran to the trees on either side, and there was another rope running to the branch above his head. I recognized the purpose immediately and wished I could not. I had done it a thousand times. Each time I had stripped a raccoon and laid out its hide to tan the pelt. At that moment I saw the blood, the pool that dripped down from the seams where Joe's skin had been ripped from his body.

I didn't scream. I just turned and ran. I ran blindly. I smashed through branches, slashing my cheek so deeply the blood flowed down my face. I fell no less than three times, but by some miracle I found myself back at the camp.

Tom was the only one there, and I quickly fell at his feet. He looked at me like I had lost my mind, and part of me wondered if I had. He grabbed me by the shoulders and pulled me up.

"What's the meaning of this, boy!" he screamed in my face. There was fear in his eyes, and that was an emotion you didn't often see from him.

"It's Joe," I said through gulps of breath. "I found him."

"Then why didn't you bring him back?" Tom asked.

"He's sliced up," I remember saying. "Skinned like an animal."

"Skinned?" Tom whispered. The anger and excitement had vanished from his voice. He didn't know if he should believe me, but he had no doubt he didn't want to. "Show me," he commanded.

I led him, reluctantly I might add, back down the path made by my boots in the snow. It had seemed so far before, and now my fevered mind wanted nothing more than to never reach my destination, yet it came more quickly than seemed possible. Then we arrived, and the thing I feared most to see met my eyes. There was no body. But fortunately, if you can use that word, the once pure white snow was stained a dark crimson red. Tom stepped forward and knelt down where the red snow began. He then looked at me.

"So the body was here?" he asked.

"Yes."

"Only a few minutes before?"

"Yes."

"Then, where is it now?"

"I don't know."

Tom sighed deeply and stood up.

"Well," he said calmly but to no one in particular, "it was definitely here before. No doubt about that." He turned back to me. "You sure it was Joe? You sure it wasn't just an animal?"

"He wasn't just lying there. He was tied up to the tree. He was tied up liked you'd tan a hide. He was here, Tom. He was here, and now he's gone, and that means somebody took him. Ain't no animal done this."

"No," Tom said decisively. "No animal did it. And that means we are all in danger here. Let's get back to the camp. With any luck, the others will be there, too." He turned and took a couple steps. Then he stopped. "Look," he said, "it's good enough to tell them that Joe is dead, and someone took his body. That's enough. They don't need to know how you found him."

I nodded my head to show him I understood, and we turned and hurried back to the camp. Tom was in front, and I noticed that he constantly glanced from side to side as we moved along. If whatever had taken Joe was around us, he at least wanted to see him coming. We found Doc Stanley, Andy, and Travis huddled around the fire.

"About damn time," Travis grunted. Tom ignored him.

"Did you find anything?" Andy asked, his voice shaking. I could only imagine how he was going to react to what he was about to hear.

"Joe is dead," Tom said matter-of-factly.

"Dead?" Andy stuttered.

"Mountain lion?" Doc Travis asked nonchalantly.

"No, he was murdered." Tom let his pronouncement sink in.

Doc Stanley went pale while Andy looked like he might pass out. Only Travis kept his cool. "And his body has been taken." Now Andy did fall to his knees. No one seemed to notice.

"Who could have done this?" Doc Stanley asked. "There were no footprints, no signs of struggle."

"The Wendigo," Andy muttered as he rocked back and forth.

"He must have heard something, saw something," Tom answered. "He left camp, and somebody got him. Then, the snow covered his tracks. It's as simple as that. No ghosts. It's a man out there, or men."

"We should hunt 'em down and kill 'em," Travis spat. "I got no love for Joe, but he was one of ours."

"No!" Andy wailed. "We gotta get out of here. No man did this, and we can't kill what did. Let's go. Let's go now!"

Tom waved his hand as if to dismiss him. "We ain't going now, and we ain't going to hunt down who did this. The day's already burnt up. We're going to stay here tonight, and then at first light we start heading back to town. I don't want to hear nothin' else about it. We'll take turns tonight keeping watch. They won't trick us again, and anybody who shows up won't be walkin' out."

"Who's goin' first?" Andy moaned.

"I'll go, I'll take the first watch," Doc Stanley said, casting a contemptuous glance at Andy. "But you will damn well have to do it at some point, by God."

"Right," Tom said. "Jack, can you take second watch?"

"Yah," I muttered. I would say I wasn't scared, but that would be a lie.

"I'll take next, then Travis. And Andy, I think you can handle the last watch till sunrise."

Andy didn't look too confident, but he didn't complain. It was the best he could hope for.

"Good," Tom said, looking to the west. The sun had fallen below the horizon, and soon it would be dark. "I suggest you all get some sleep," he continued. "It's going to be a long night."

Chapter
7

As I walked to my tent, I noticed Doc Stanley pulling a crate close to our fire. He held a rifle in his hand, the same I knew I would have to bear in only a few short hours. I hoped I would not need to use it. He rubbed oil along the stock, and I could tell he was trying desperately to remain calm. I grabbed two logs and walked over to him. As I threw them on the fire, he looked up.

"Thank you, Jack," he said quietly, rubbing a thick rag back and forth along the rifle. I simply nodded and took a seat on the ground next to him. For a moment, I just sat there. He didn't speak, and I didn't know what to say. I couldn't know, of course, what was coming or when it would hit, but I had a feeling that whatever it was, Doc Stanley had the best chance of seeing it first.

Finally he broke the silence. "You should go on," he said. "You won't get much sleep, and there's no telling what you might see."

I simply nodded in reply. But I had a question before I went.

"Doc, I saw Joe. I saw him today out in the woods. Tom didn't want me to say anything, but I saw him, and ain't no man did that. No animal, either."

Doc Stanley held up his hand. "I know," he said simply. "Tom told me about it. Didn't want you to say nothing cause of what it would have done to Andy."

"Then, you know we ain't dealing with nothin' you can kill with that gun?"

He turned and looked at me then, and I saw fear in his face. He knew all too well.

"We survive the night, then we get out of here. He has power in the forest, but not in the cities. He is the lord of a lost world. He draws his strength from the wild."

"He?" I asked stupidly, as if I didn't know.

"The Wendigo," Doc Stanley replied matter-of-factly. "No question of that now."

"But I thought you didn't believe in that?"

"Oh, I believe," he said. "Seen too many things out here not to. You would have come to believe, too, even if this had never happened. But now it has. We are at the mercy of the Old One now, and there is no power we possess that can stop him."

There was a haunting call in the distance, as if to punctuate the doctor's words. I saw his eyes narrow and then, "Whippoorwill," he said. "Bad sign. They should be long gone by now. But they follow death, so I suppose we shouldn't be surprised."

"Is there any way to stop it? The Wendigo I mean?"

"You ever met anybody who has seen the Wendigo?" Doc Stanley asked.

"Well, no," I stammered, "but I had never even heard of it 'til this trip."

The doctor allowed himself a chuckle. "Fair enough. But I will just go ahead and tell you that I've been wandering these woods for thirty years, and I've not met a soul that saw him and came out of it alive. So, I don't suppose there is a way to stop him." Then, he paused. "Of course, the legends do speak of a weakness."

Doc Stanley looked up from his work and furrowed his brow. "They say he was the most beautiful of them all, the Old Ones. But when he was cursed, his beauty was taken, and he was rendered hideous to behold. And perhaps if you were to show him his own image, you might have a chance. But, like I said, that legend has been around for as long as I can remember, too, yet I've never met a man who used it to his advantage."

I looked out into the now darkening forest, and in my mind's eye I saw the Wendigo in every tree, in every swaying branch, in every rustling bush. "So, he's really out there," I said.

Doc Stanley just smiled.

"There's nothing out there, Jack." I looked at him and didn't understand. After all this, I thought there was no question.

"What do you mean?" I asked. Doc Stanley looked up and off into the distance, and I saw him make a decision.

"You should know," he said, turning to me. "Tom didn't want to tell you, but you should know. The Old Ones have passed from this Earth, at least in their physical form. The Wendigo is a spirit, a powerful one, yes, but not strong enough to act in this world. Not without a body, at least." Doc Stanley looked at me, seeing if I understood. I did not. "The Wendigo, my friend, is one of us."

I sat there a second, not believing what I had heard. Then, I turned slowly, looking back at the tents behind me, wondering about the men who lay within.

"But if it's not you, and it's not me," I began, but Doc Stanley held up his hand to stop me.

"We don't know that is true."

"What?" is all I could manage.

"The curse of the Wendigo is upon us. Whoever he has taken, he will soon take completely. Only the dead are above suspicion. The true horror of the curse is that he who has been chosen does not know it at first. The Great Old Ones are the masters of dreams, and in those dreams they will possess you. To he who is Wendigo, the possession will begin as nothing more than a nightmare, a horrible flash of color and pain. But, eventually, the power of the Wendigo will overcome him, and he will live the life of the undead, locked in his own mind, seeing through his own eyes as he does unspeakable things, but having no power to control it."

I thought back to the night Joe disappeared, to the fevered and demon-haunted dreams that filled my mind. I shuddered at the horror that might be before me.

"So, tonight," Doc Stanley continued, "I will be watching the others. It is not the things of the forest I fear. It is what lurks in our own midst. Now, it is late. Go sleep, if sleep will come."

I left him then, and something inside of me knew two things: I would not sleep that night, and I would never see Doc Stanley again.

* * *

I didn't sleep. My fevered mind raced from dark thought to darker. It seemed to me there could be only two choices. Either I was the Wendigo or I would die at his hands. That one fate was more horrible than the next offered no comfort. And that death was the preferable choice . . . These were the thoughts that filled my mind, and my troubled soul found no respite.

After several hours, I decided there was no point, and I arose to relieve Doc Stanley. The fire still burned, but Stanley was gone. He had not disappeared without a trace; in the flickering firelight, I could see blood dripping from the box on which he had sat. The area around it was stained crimson with the same blood. The rifle lay in the snow. I could see something else was beside it, something that shimmered tan against the red blood beneath it. But I ignored whatever it was. I needed the rifle. That was my primary concern.

I ran to where it lay and offered a glance to the thing that sat beside it. And then I fell backwards. It was Doc Stanley's face — just his face — as if it had been ripped clean from his skull. Empty black holes stared up at me where his eyes should have been.

I reached down and grabbed up the gun. It was sticky with dried blood. Then I heard quick footsteps behind me. I spun around and shouldered the rifle, but it was only the others. It was then that I realized I had been screaming the whole time.

"What happened here?" Tom yelled.

"I don't know. I just found him like this."

Tom stepped forward and saw the face that still sat upon the ground. He stumbled backwards and looked at me. It was then that the wind picked up, and in that wind was a voice — that of Doc Stanley.

"Help me!" it cried, begged. Oh, it was a horrible voice, a moaning shriek that rent the air and my soul. We all heard it, each man. We turned about ourselves trying desperately to place it. But it was to our left and, then, our right. It was in front and then behind. Finally it was everywhere, all around, all at once.

"Tell us what happened," Tom commanded above the voice in the wind.

"I've told you. I got up and found this."

"You didn't hear anything? You didn't see anything?"

"No!" I screamed. "Nothing!"

"How is that possible, Jack?" Tom stated more than asked.

"How is any of this possible?" I screamed.

"Give me the gun, Jack," Tom commanded. His voice was too calm, too under control. He was struggling to keep it that way. Then suddenly I realized — he thought it was me. We stood there in silence for a second as Doc Stanley's wale echoed around us, sometimes louder, sometimes not.

"No!" I shouted, as firmly as my feeble heart could manage.

"That's an order, son," Tom said calmly.

"I think we're beyond orders now, Captain," I replied.

"Enough of this foolishness!" Travis growled, taking a step forward. "Give me the gun!"

I shouldered the rifle and leveled it at Travis's heart.

"I'll shoot any man who tries to take it from me."

"You can't kill us all," Travis spat, taking another step.

"But I can damn sure kill you, Travis Walker. Damn sure. It was you who brought this down on us. Two men are already dead for what you done. And, if I am going to die tonight, you sure as Hell are going with me."

"Look, Jack," Tom said, "it's one of us. You know that. It could be you. Can you live with it if it is?"

"It could be you, too, Tom. You don't know any better than me."

"It was you who found Joe," Travis said. "And you who found the Doc, or what's left of him, at least. You think that was a coincidence?"

I turned back to Travis. "And what about you?" I said. "Never cooked a day in your life, and then Joe dies, and all of the sudden you can? I noticed you didn't eat any of it either. Was it 'cause you couldn't?"

"Now, wait one minute," Travis said, backing up and putting a hand out to Tom who was now eying him suspiciously. "I was sick, you know that," he said, pointing at Tom.

"I don't know anything, Travis. All I know is the boy is right."

"And where were you when we found Joe's body? Huh?" Andy stammered. "We came back to the camp, and you were still gone. It had to be you that took it."

Travis turned to me. His face contorted into a snarl. He took a step toward me. I raised my rifle back at him and started to pull the trigger. But before I could, there was a thud as Tom smashed a piece of firewood against the crown of Travis's skull. His eyes rolled back in his head, and Travis collapsed to the ground.

"Tie him up!" Tom commanded.

We pulled Travis up to the wagon and lashed his hands and feet to its side. It was no easy task. He was all dead weight, and Andy was little help. Eventually he was tied fast. We waited for him to awaken. Only then would we find some answers.

Chapter

8

For many long minutes we stood there, our eyes on Travis's limp body. The fire was roaring behind us. We had built it up to a blaze, whether to provide light or buoy our sinking spirits, I don't really know.

"So, what do we do with him?" Andy asked. "Maybe we should kill him now."

Tom pursed his lips, thinking on Andy's suggestion. "No," he said, "no, we won't do that. We don't know for sure it's him."

I turned from Travis and stared at Tom. "You don't still suspect me?"

"I don't know who to suspect," Tom answered firmly. "I know what you said about Travis, and that seemed pretty right to me. But we can't know. We just can't know. And, until we do, we can't kill him."

"I hear you, Captain, I really do," I said. "But something tells me, if he is the one, those ropes won't hold him."

No one said anything else. Hours passed, and the night deepened. And then Travis awoke. It was slow at first. His eyes fluttered, then were filled with confusion. He strained for a second against the bonds that held him, and then he knew. Now he was angry.

"You sons of bitches!" he screamed. "What the Hell are you doing? It's him you want!"

"Is it Travis? Is it?" Tom asked, stepping in front of me. "You're going to talk, and you're going to do it now. These men," he said, gesturing to me and Andy, "they think we should kill you now. I said we wait. But if you don't answer me, I may just let them."

Travis simply spat at Tom; it was his way I suppose. Tom didn't react. Instead, he turned to me and said, "Give me the rifle." For a second I hesitated, so he simply grabbed it from me. He could have done it at any point, I guess. And I guess he knew that, too. He raised the gun and pointed it at Travis's head.

"You will answer my questions, Travis. The first one you don't, I pull the trigger on this rifle and put another hole through your face."

"You got it, Captain," Travis snarled.

"You had any dreams lately? Any you can't explain?"

"I don't dream," he said. "Ain't never, ain't startin' now."

"How'd you know how to cook that rabbit?"

"Hell, Captain, it's meat. You put it in the pan and watch it burn. How hard can it be? But I damn sure wasn't gonna eat any of it."

Tom lowered the rifle and turned to me and Andy.

"He sounds right, and he sounds like himself."

"You can't know that, Tom," I said.

"Yeah, Captain," Andy added. "Was him was cursed. Was him the old woman wanted. I say we give him to her."

"I don't know," Tom said.

"Tell him, Jack," Andy begged. He was shaking, and I thought he might cry. He wasn't fit to take much more of this. "Tell him. You're the one who found Joe. You're the one who found him all emptied out, skin off of him like somebody was making him into a suit."

"It's true, Tom," I said, but even in the saying it, something wasn't right.

Tom creased his brow.

"I suppose," Tom said. He looked as if he had made a decision. But now I wasn't thinking about Travis anymore.

"Wait," I almost whispered. "Andy, that about Joe, how'd you know that?"

Tom and Andy both looked at me funny. "What are you talking about, Jack?" Tom asked.

"How'd he know that? I didn't tell him. You told me not to."

Tom still looked at me like I was crazy. But then his eyes showed some recognition. "Yeah," Tom said, his mind starting to clear, "yeah, I did. How did you know that Andy?"

"I don't know," Andy said. "What's this all about?"

"I only told Doc Stanley, and I was the last person to talk to him," I said. "Come on, Andy, how'd you know that?"

"Well," Andy stammered, looking pale and thin, like he was scared to death, "I just . . . just . . ." And then his voice changed. "Oh Hell," he growled. He grinned, wider than I thought a man's face should go. Then he started to laugh. As his laugh grew deeper and louder, his face began to split. Where his smile should have met his cheek, the skin began to crack, like a man had taken a knife and sliced him from the corner of his mouth to his ear. I fell back in sheer terror. His head was literally flapping back and forth on his laugh, and his eyes had grown as red as fire. Tom fell back beside me, but to his credit, he raised his rifle and fired it at Andy's heart. Andy stopped laughing. He cocked his head sharply to the right, and then he let loose an open-mouthed howl, a roar from some ancient, horrible world that shook me to my very core.

No shame in saying it, I turned and ran, and Tom was running right beside me. We ran until the howl was only an echo, until we were deep in the forest. If I hadn't tripped on a root and fallen, with Tom stumbling over me, we might still be running today.

We lay there like that, not wanting to move, not wanting to believe what had happened. All around us still echoed the now distant howl, the roar I suspect few men on this earth have lived to describe. The night was thick and dark. Only the pale, now waning moon provided any light. The trees shook though there was no wind, and just beyond my sight seemed to move creatures and phantasms from another world, one long past if it ever really was. Finally, I spoke.

"God, Tom, what do we do?"

"We run, Jack. We run, and we don't look back."

He was right, of course. But at seemingly the same moment I made that decision, a scream came ringing through the forest — it was Travis's voice, though not in any form I had ever heard before. I looked at Tom, and he looked at me. I had no love for Travis, and neither did Tom. But that scream. I knew at that moment that it would be a mortal sin to leave him behind. It was death or damnation now, that was all there was. Tom exhaled deeply. He had come to the same conclusion.

"We go back, then," Tom said. "But I don't know what we do when we get there. I hit him right in the chest, right in the chest at point blank range, and it didn't faze him. Didn't even slow him down."

"There's a mirror in my tent," I said, "that I use for shaving. It's small, but it might work."

Tom's eyes brightened. There was no need to explain. As I have come to learn, the men of the woods all know the legend of the Wendigo in full.

We made our way back to the campsite. Even in the dark, it wasn't hard to find our way. Travis's ever-loudening screams served as the perfect map. When we reached the edge of the woods along the clearing where our camp was set up, a horrible sight met our eyes. Only the fire still burned where we had left it. Our things were strewn about the ground. The two horses were dead, whether from an attack or fright, I couldn't tell. But it was Travis I will never forget. He was still tied to the wagon wheel and still alive, though barely. His stomach was sliced open, and his bowels spilled out onto the ground. Andy, or the thing that had been Andy, was on its hands and knees, shoveling Travis's intestines into its mouth. That Travis was still conscious made it all the worse. I looked over to where my tent once stood. It had collapsed, and I couldn't be sure that anything was where I had left it. Given Travis's state, it was surely an empty gesture anyway.

"Well?" Tom asked.

"I don't know, Tom. Travis is dead. His body just hasn't caught up to the fact. Maybe you were right before. Maybe we should just go."

I saw Tom purse his lips in thought.

"Naw," he finally said, making a decision. "Naw, I was wrong before. We can't run. He'd track us down. No doubt about that. Even if he couldn't before, Joe was the best tracker I ever met. And he has his talents now. No, we got only one choice, and that is to stop him here. You think you can still get that mirror?"

I looked back at my wrecked tent. I couldn't be sure.

"I can try, Tom, but I can't promise it."

"Well, then," Tom said firmly, "that'll have to do. Let's get down there. If he doesn't notice you, all the better. If he does, I'll distract him as best I can. You get that mirror, and do what needs to be done."

I nodded. Tom held out his hand. I grabbed it, and he shook firmly. And then reluctantly but quickly, we made our way down the hill and into the camp.

Chapter 9

We stopped at the edge, and Tom motioned for me to go on. He would remain in the shadows. If we were lucky, he would stay there. I stole quietly across the grounds, taking cover behind a lonely tree whenever I could. But it didn't take long till there was nothing but open ground between me and my tent. It was still ten yards off. Not a long distance on most days, but an eternity with a beast like the Wendigo in your sights.

I sat there for a good minute, watching him. He was oblivious to me, his hands working a string of Travis's intestines like it was a line of sausage. Travis wasn't screaming any more. He just moaned. I doubt if he was in his right mind. I thought about what I would do, what was the best I could hope for. That thought sent a chill to my bones. Even if I found the mirror, it would mean confronting that thing. And if it didn't work, death, and probably not a quick one, was assured.

Now I could wait no longer, I took a deep breath and moved towards my tent as fast as possible while still staying silent. It was no easy task. Seven yards away. There were pots and pans, traps, boxes, and everything you could imagine you might need on that kind of trip, strewn about all over the ground. I dodged them as best I could. If he heard me then . . .well, I didn't want to think on it.

Now I was five yards from the tent. I looked back at the Wendigo. He was still hunched over, still consuming his meal. Three yards. What was left of another tent had been thrown clear across the field and lay in between me and my destination. I walked around, but it just meant more time I was in the open.

Finally, I reached the remains of my tent. But the ordeal wasn't over. I crouched at the side where my shaving kit should be. I sat there, for God and all his angels to see, feeling blindly under the canvas, trying not to make a sound while also looking with my hands for a small object I didn't even know was there.

I could hear the sickening sound of the beast, not more than fifty feet beyond, his teeth ripping through flesh. I looked over at him. Still he continued to feed. The sound of his mouth working bloody meat grew louder and louder till I thought it would steal my mind. On I worked, feeling about, trying to find the one thing that might save me. That noise continued, like a drumbeat in my brain. Then, finally, blessedly, it stopped. I said a quick prayer of thanks and searched on with new vigor.

But then I felt cold fear fall over me. I looked over at the Wendigo. There it sat, blood and muscle hanging from its mouth and hands, its demon red eyes locked on me. I froze, but the low growl that started deep in the pit of its flesh-gorged stomach spurned me into feverish action. I made no attempt to be quiet now, feeling desperately for my mirror.

The roar grew louder until finally it burst from what had been Andy's mouth in a hellish, deafening sound. It loped toward me, running like some primordial beast, pushing with its legs and thrusting with its knuckles off the ground in great bounding leaps. All the while it screamed at me in a voice no human mouth ever made. It was upon me, and I knew it was the end.

Then there was a flash in the corner of my vision, and the beast, in mid-spring, was thrust to the side. It let out an almost pitiful yelp, like a dog kicked in the gut by an angry master. I sat there frozen, staring at the ax blade protruding from the side of Andy's contorted and barely recognizable face. I looked to the side to see Tom standing next to the fire, a flaming log in one hand and another ax in the other.

"Don't just sit there, kid! Find it!"

I jerked back into action, feeling madly for the mirror. The Wendigo lay still for a moment, but then it began to push itself up. I began to give up hope. What if I had moved it? What if it were somewhere else in the wrecked camp? Panic set in. My vision became blurry. Tom's cries as the Wendigo righted itself and ripped the ax from its head began to seem more and more distant. It was as if I was falling into a deep well, far from the world around me.

I was shocked back to reality by a sharp pain that shot through my hand. In any other situation, I would have jerked it out, and all hope might have been lost. But I was so close to being gone that I just sat there, wondering what it could mean. Then it struck me — my razor! I had cut my hand, and that meant the mirror was close.

The Wendigo was up now, advancing on Tom. He held his ground, swinging the flaming log, but he couldn't hold the beast long. Then, salvation. My hand felt smooth, polished glass and the cold kiss of metal. I grabbed the mirror and pulled it out. I leapt to my feet, running towards the spot where the man and the beast were circling each other. But I was too late. With a brutal strike, the Wendigo, avoiding the torch, ripped open Tom's leg with a quick slice of his claws. Tom fell to the ground with a cry. The Wendigo poised itself over him, ready to make the killing blow. But at that moment, I jumped on his back, thrusting the mirror in his face.

I felt the demon shudder beneath me. Then, it let out a cry unlike the ones before, for this was a howl of pain. I fell backwards off of him, and he fell to his knees, hands clasping his face. Tom, despite his injury, looked at me with a face beaming in triumph. But then, from where the Wendigo lay, came an unexpected sound. He was laughing.

It was a guttural laugh, a courage-stealing, soul-crushing laugh. It was a laugh that seemed to come from Andy's broken body and all around at the same time. It was a cruel, cold laugh, a rumbling, rolling laugh. The Wendigo lifted itself from the ground. It turned around, not even noticing Tom lying not more than a few feet from him. It turned and glared at me, and Andy's split face seemed to smile.

"Pitiful child," it said, in a voice that was not Andy's, one I seemed to hear in my mind rather than in my ears. "Superstitions and petty tricks do not harm me."

I stumbled backwards, nearly falling over a burning log. I stooped down and picked it up, swinging it wildly at the loping beast before me. It laughed again.

"I do not fear fire or flame, the gift of my race to your primitive fathers. We, who walked among the stars and will again. The ancients are not dead. No, they sleep only, but the time is coming of their waking. What is your life against ours? A blink, a whisper in the night, a flash that fades into darkness. So, do not fear your death. You will serve a grander purpose."

I continued to fall back, but he matched me step for step.

"Do not run. Your pain will feed me, your flesh will be my sustenance, and in your death, I will live. What is your end? Will you feed the worm? Or a god?"

It hit me, then. I would not survive. I could not run. There was simply nowhere to go. I stopped backing up. If he was to take me, I would face him. He took another step towards me and another. And then, I felt myself transported back, back to something my father once told me. I was a young boy of twelve. My father had taken me aside.

"Jack," he said, "this is dangerous business, and a man who lives by the forest may well die by it."

My father was not an educated man. I guess he never had any schooling at all. But he was wise, wise in a way that a man only gets through hard experience. He knew one bit of Latin I suppose. Just one bit. And he taught me it that day.

"Always remember this, Jack. If the breaks go against you, if you are staring death in the face, *in hoc signo vinces*. In this sign, you will conquer. Remember it Jack, always. And if death comes, you'll die in His bosom."

The Wendigo was on me now, so close I could smell death on his breath. I looked down at the log next to me and accepted my fate. I took it, raised it in the air and brought it straight down. Then, I moved it from my left to right. In the darkness, the cross of flame I had cut into the night shimmered in front of me, though the flaming brand was now at my side. The Wendigo stopped, grinning at what I had done. He laughed.

"More foolish superstition?" he asked. "I wager this one will serve you no better."

Then, he took another step forward, his chest passing through the spot I had marked. I closed my eyes and prepared for death. But nothing happened. I ventured a look and saw the Wendigo standing in front of me, his blood red eyes peeled back, his mouth hanging open in what can only be described as shock. He took a step backwards, and his knees began to shake. He grabbed at his heart.

"No!" he cried, in shock as much as pain. I stood there dumbfounded as flame burst from his chest. I watched as it spread, consuming the beast before my eyes. In haunted cries, he broke from one unknown language to another, speaking words whose meaning I do not wish to know.

The beast fell to his knees. But then, as the flames threatened to consume him, he looked at me and said, "The body dies, but the spirit lives on."

I saw his eyes change, saw the red drain from them. In the instant before he died, I saw the eyes of Andy. And though he was in unimaginable pain, they were filled with gratitude and joy.

I suppose that is the end of the story, though it was not the end of the ordeal. The horses were dead, and Tom could barely walk. I took a bear skin and made it so that I could pull it behind me. Tom rested inside, and I began to drag him through the snow, back through the forest to the town that lay miles beyond. We had no supplies, no provisions. But I was not concerned. I could trap something, find something. But as we moved on, it was as if every animal in the forest had vanished, as if we were cursed. There was no food then, nothing to eat, nothing to catch. A man can go a long time without food, but not in the cold, not when he is dragging another behind him. Things happen in times like that, things you try and forget, things you don't talk about. Five days later, Tom died. Seven days after that, I stumbled into the village. Alone, but not starved.

That was fifty years ago now, fifty years in which I have made the forest my home. I never saw the Wendigo again, not in the flesh at least. But there were times when the night was dark and cold, when the moon was full in the sky and the icy wind would cut through flesh and bone. In those times, I would hear a voice on the wind and my dreams would be filled with flashes of light and peals of thunder, of dark shapes moving in the distance, and the screeching cry of a great bird seeking its prey.

Part III

Chapter

10

Carter Weston:

The howling wind continued to roar outside, and even the flames in the fireplace seemed to shiver as the strongest gust yet shook the very walls of the old tavern. I looked around warily at the ancient structure, but my companions showed no signs of concern, and so the moment passed.

Jack had leaned back in his chair now. His ale was in his hands, but though his eyes peered into its amber depths, something of the way they shimmered told me he was far away, somewhere still in the past of which he had just shared.

"And what of that?" asked Captain Gray. "Here is a story from the mouth of a witness. Can such a story, as fantastic as it may seem, be seriously doubted?"

I looked from Gray to Jack. I thought at first I should choose my words carefully. But it was evident to me Jack was no more present for the conversation than if he had been a thousand miles from that place. Outside in the snow, the rare sound of thunder echoed in from the sea.

"Well, Captain," I began, "I believe Jack here must have endured a terrible ordeal. Of that I have no doubt. But being alone and hungry in the cold and the dark, I'm sure one sees all number of things. That he believes it, that it is a memory in his mind, I am sure. But I hesitate to give full credence to such a tale, given the circumstances."

"Ah, the consummate skeptic," the Captain said.

"And I would wear the name gladly," I replied, "for it's only the skeptic that gives value to the truth."

"Yes," the Captain said nodding, "but only when he is open to the truth. The skeptic with a closed mind becomes the worst kind of believer."

To that bit of wisdom I could only nod and raise my glass in acknowledgment. At that moment, another traveler opened the door of the pub and threw himself in, a great gust of wind following behind.

"I fear the storm will not abate for some time," the Captain said. "But I take that as a blessing. The night is young, and there is so much more to tell."

"Of this there is truth," said the lawyer Daniel. It was the first time he had spoken since our introductions. "And if our young guest can spare yet more of his night, I suppose some of that story is mine."

I nodded my head in agreement, and he began to speak.

Chapter
11

Daniel:

I was a younger man then, probably not much older than you. I was born in Boston and had only recently completed a course of study at college in Cambridge. For some time, it had been my intention to enter into a career in the legal profession. My father, a man who built his fortune in the years following the war, had made it his purpose that his son should live a life better reflecting that of his more established peers.

It was a classic case of new money. My father had wealth, but wanted respect. So, he would attempt to purchase it. I saw the inherent flaw in his thinking. Respect is a thing earned, not bought, and a man who lets it be known that he seeks respect will probably never see it bestowed. But I digress, I suppose. It is important only that his son had no intention of refusing his largesse. And so I departed on a steam ship bound for the old country.

Oh, those were heady days. To be on a transatlantic ship, in the middle of the ocean, nothing but great blue water as far the eye can survey. I know, Captain Gray, why the sea calls. But less than a fortnight passed before I reached the shores of England. It was there I met the man who was to be my guide across an unknown land — Lawrence.

Lawrence was an interesting fellow, a burly, muscular man who, through many years in the service of Her Majesty, had seemingly learned the languages and customs of most places in the world.

"Served in India once," he would say. "Met a beautiful girl there. As spicy as the food, she was. If you want to know a culture, the best classroom is the bedroom, if you take my meaning, sir."

There had been a girl in every country, apparently, or maybe more than one.

"Your father laid it out how he wants this to go. Culture, history. Classical antiquity. All of the things one would expect."

"Sounds terrific," I lied. "But perhaps we will leave some room for imagination?"

"Perhaps," Lawrence responded tentatively. "But your father isn't paying for imagination."

Lawrence was true to his word. After a brief stay in London, we left the White Cliffs of Dover behind, setting down in the port city of Calais. From that idyllic spot, we rented a coach which carried us from the channel to the grand city of Paris, the City of Lights.

There we remained for some weeks. I was directed in the various accoutrements of fair society — fencing, riding, even dancing — all while I tried vainly to acquire some semblance of the French language. On the latter I failed, though not for want of sampling Lawrence's own particular brand of cultural exchange.

From Paris we made our way to Geneva. I could have stayed among the Alps until the rivers carried them away, but Lawrence was determined. No, we must press on, through the mountains and into Italy. And so we made the climb, though the men we hired to carry our baggage greatly eased our burden. Then, to Turin for a spell and on to Florence.

In Florence was spent the days and weeks that I had wished for in Geneva. A beautiful city, a blessing to visit, but one can only have so much of cathedrals and the treasures of the arts. It was among that whirlwind of marble statues and priceless paintings that I met Charles.

Chapter 12

I first encountered Charles in a dark and dusty corner of the Uffizi. He was admiring one of the many semi-clothed statues of some unnamable Greek goddess, peering intently at an exposed breast. I was standing beside him, as I had stood by any number of other young men of rank and class on similar excursions. What made Charles different was he deigned to speak with me.

"It appears modesty was not one of the foremost Greek virtues. Don't you think?"

I looked at Charles and smiled. With the exception of Lawrence, I had found the "Grand Tour" to be anything but. In America, I had lived my life in excess. Thus I had never been so keenly aware of my own relative poverty as in those few months. But these were not just men of wealth. No, they were of title and position. These were Von's and Van's, dukes and earls. Even the occasional prince.

"Apparently not," I replied.

"Oh well," the young man continued, "I suppose if you have seen one stone breast you've seen them all." He looked at me and grinned. "Charles Cawdor," he said, sticking out his hand. I took it with a smile.

"Daniel Lincoln," I said with a laugh.

"American, I presume?"

"You presume correctly."

"Any relation to the late, great president?

"Ha!" I exclaimed, rocking back on my heels, "No, no relation." I wondered if my ever-declining prestige would bring this conversation to a quick end.

"Good," he said blithely. "I hate politicians."

"How about yourself? English?"

"Oh," Charles coughed, throwing back his head as if he had been struck, "Scottish, my good man. But I forgive you your Yankee ignorance. Now, where does one get a bloody drink around here? Being called English has me as dry as a parson's wit."

I didn't know what that meant, but I had immediately taken to the young Scot. Lawrence was initially thrilled to find I had made a friend, particularly one who was apparently noble. His opinion was changed after a night of drinking, smoking, and singing a passel of songs I had never heard and could barely understand.

"The young master would do well to avoid Lord Charles," Lawrence was heard to say the next day.

I say he was heard. The thundering headache that pounded between my ears was heavy on the listening. But it wouldn't have mattered. Charles was an oasis in a desert of tediousness. We left Florence together when it was time. From there, we traveled to the canalled city of Venice, the crown jewel of Renaissance Italy, the decadent heart of a dying culture. Yes, Charles was a godsend. Oh, that I had never met him. How much different those next few days might have been.

* * *

Ah, Venice. Even now I long for its narrow, winding corridors, its floating villas, its streets of cool water. Even our tired and restless minds found succor there. We played amongst the ancient churches, the lion-crested palaces of the doge, the thousand islands that formed the heart of the city. In that magical place we found, for not a small time, true joy and peace. But alas, the young mind easily grows weary of even the most extraordinary things. Soon that grand city became as elegant Florence had — a general bore. So, we took to the other great treasure of Venice — its wine.

That night was not unlike the others that preceded it. A warm spring evening, a little cafe along the Grand Canal, our second, or perhaps our third, bottle of sweet, gently bubbling Prosecco. Even the conversation was repeated.

"The 'Grand Tour,'" Charles sputtered as if addressing a person he did not like. "Grand, indeed. I hope you don't mind me saying, Daniel, but I find nothing grand about it. I expected adventure," he said, thrusting his glass in the air and spilling a few drops of wine as he did. "But, instead, nothing more exciting than a trip down to London." He caught my eye and for a moment faltered. "Oh, you must think me quite the fop. I am sure this has all been most intriguing for you."

"No," I replied candidly, "No. I did not think it possible to grow tired of such wonderful things. But I have, nonetheless."

It was then that I noticed a man eyeing us from an adjacent table. He was an older gentleman, one of some wealth, no doubt. He wore a bright madras coat and fondled an ivory-handled cane. As he moved it about, I could see he held it by a bone-white carving of a great sea beast. I stared at it, transfixed. My mind was transported back to a day from my childhood in a classroom far away, a voice of a teacher in rhyme.

> *Below the thunders of the upper deep;*
> *Far, far beneath in the abysmal sea,*
> *His ancient, dreamless, uninvaded sleep*
> *The Kraken sleepeth.*

I have often thought back on him, whether he was a figure of good or ill, how and why he came into our lives when he did. I have since concluded he was an innocent — our encounter was random and banal, the consequences of which could not have been foretold.

But in any event, there he sat, and his attention was drawn to us. He seemed to be considering whether to interrupt. But once it was clear I had noticed him, he made his decision.

"Gentlemen," he said as he approached, spinning his cane between his thumb and his index finger, "I hope you don't mind the interruption."

His words said he was friendly. The way he spoke them, English. Charles gestured to a seat beside us and said, "Of course, please join us."

"Why, thank you. I did not mean to intrude, but on a cool and quiet night, one can't help but partake in the conversations of those around him, even if he is not one of the participants."

"Oh, it's no bother," Charles said. "We were merely complaining amongst ourselves. Maybe you can help to shake us from the doldrums."

"Yes, I heard. I take it you two gentlemen have brought yourself to Venice as part of a tour of the continent, no?"

"That would be correct," I said.

"Ah yes, I remember those days. I followed your steps myself when I was young. A peculiar thing. Such a grand adventure in theory, but far more tedious in the doing."

Charles and I chuckled.

"Yes," I said, "that would be precisely the problem."

"Well, have you considered a deviation from your present course?"

His words came almost as a blow. It had been so far from my mind not to follow the preordained route that this was the first I had considered it.

"Well," I began, speaking for us both, "what do you mean?"

"It is on to Rome after this, I expect?" he asked.

"Yes," Charles answered. "On to Rome, and then Naples."

"Well," the man said again, "have you considered going east?"

"East?" I exclaimed.

"Yes," the man said enthusiastically. "East through Austria-Hungary. Across the Carpathians. To Russia even. Perhaps down to Constantinople on the shores of the Black Sea. Many men will see Rome, but the jewels of the East, those are precious stones, indeed."

Charles looked at me, and I saw the sparkle in his eyes. I hadn't known him long, but that look was universal.

"What do you say, Daniel?" he asked.

"Well," I replied, "it's all rather sudden. Are you sure we should? What of Rome? And what will Lawrence . . ."

"Oh, fie on Lawrence," Charles interrupted. "Old man needs a break from you, anyway. And besides, Rome can wait. We have nothing but time."

This was true. Time was a luxury we possessed.

"So?" Charles said, his eyes demanding.

I looked at him for a moment, unsure. But it was adventure I had sought, and he would brook no answer but yes.

"Yes," I said, forcing a smile, "Yes, let's do it!"

"Excellent!" Charles exclaimed. "Then we shall," he said, raising his glass for a toast.

I suppose we should have taken pause there, but the euphoria of change had overtaken us. We would go east. To what place and what destination we did not know, but at that moment, neither did we care.

* * *

"I forbid it!"

I had expected this.

"Your father would never approve."

"Lawrence," I said calmly, hoping some of my reserve would accrue to him, "the decision is already made. You cannot stop me."

"I most certainly can!"

I held up both hands and said, "Lawrence, please. You have been so good to me on this journey. Please, let me do the same for you. I will be fine. I'll be with Charles. You can stay here in Venice until we return. You were saying only yesterday how much you love the city. Now you can enjoy it without having me on your conscience. Look, I know if you put your mind to it you can prevent me. But I'm asking you not to. As a friend. Just stay here. My father need not know. And if he finds out, I will take all the blame. You have my word on that."

Lawrence eyed me uneasily for a second. Then, he sighed, lowering himself into a chair next to the bed. I knew then I had won.

"Fancy lot of good that would do," he said. "But I suppose you have earned a diversion. I'll wait here for your return. Just promise you won't be long."

"Oh, Lawrence, you saint you," I said cheerfully. "You have my word we will return post haste."

"Yes, yes," Lawrence said. "I'll be lucky to see you in three months," he moaned with a smile. But then his face turned stern.

"There is one thing, Daniel. And I want you to promise you will listen to me and heed my counsel. Can you promise me that?" I saw resolution in his eyes, and when I gave him my word, it was not vainly that I did so. "In Europe," he continued, "the sun rises in the west and sets in the east. There is darkness there, darkness you have never seen. That land can be a wondrous place, no doubt of that. But promise me you will take care you do not stumble out of the light."

I looked at him for a moment, and it was no doubt clear to him that, while I had heard his words, I had no way to fully comprehend them. Still, he gave no further explanation.

"Yes, Lawrence," I said. "I will be careful."

His eyes betrayed the doubt that was in his mind, but he obscured that uncertainty with a smile, nodding his head once and covering my hands with his.

"Yes," he said. "Yes. But I hope you will not begrudge an old man a prayer for you daily?"

"Never," I said, now covering his hands with one of mine. "In fact, I will count on it."

Chapter
13

Our plan was simple. We would travel mostly by train, switching to stagecoach when necessary. We would go east to Trieste. Then, on to Vienna and to Budapest. From there, the Carpathians would stand in our way. We would cross them to Czernowitz and from that city travel to Odessa. Our travels on land would end there. A ship would take us down the Black Sea to Istanbul and through the Bospurus into the Aegean. Then the Mediterranean, the Ionian, back up the Adriatic, arriving in Venice from whence we came.

Trieste was the port-city jewel of mighty Austria-Hungary, the beating heart of an empire, a crossroads between two worlds. There gathered the peoples of Asia, Africa, and Europe, all tossed together, mixed up and splattered across a canvas, like Van Gogh at his wildest. Such was the exuberance of that city I was loath to leave the bustle of Trieste behind.

We arrived next in Vienna, the imperial city on the shores of the crystal waters of the Danube. It was here I began to doubt Lawrence's warnings. Vienna was so European, so Western. It was palaces and opera houses, cathedrals and museums. It was the essence of the West. But then to Budapest we went. It was just a little bit darker, a little bit dirtier, a little bit more Gothic. Vienna was the setting sun of Europe, and Budapest was its gloaming. But it could not compare to the unpronounceable little town we came upon in the foothills of the

Carpathian Mountains, Kryvorvni, if memory serves.

It was a village, if ever a place deserved that moniker. Muddy roads instead of paved streets, thatched roofs on moss-covered stone walls. Proud-faced people, but poor, cautious, quick to suspect and slow to trust. A fog hung over the place and the mountains beyond, an unnatural mist seemed never to lift. And hiding, just beyond its shroud, were mysteries I was none too quick to discover.

"I will say this, my new friend," Charles said as he stepped down from the stagecoach into one of the muddy streets, "it is at moments like this I am most pleased I made your acquaintance."

"Yes," I said, as I took my first look around, "I would not want to travel to such a place alone."

The stagecoach that brought us from Budapest would take us no farther. As it turned back down the rain-soaked path down which we had just come, it was left to us to find a way over the mountain. We had been assured by the driver that the local tavern owner could provide us with transportation to Czernowitz.

We found the tavern shortly, a sturdy stone building with thick, wooden beams holding up the roof. Other than the Orthodox Church, it was the only building in the village that showed any indication of permanency. The heavy oaken door provided much resistance to our entrance. But with a hearty shove from Charles's shoulder it gave way, revealing a sparsely populated hovel. It was dark inside, made darker by the soot-stained windows and low burning lamps hanging in no great number from the ceiling.

Behind the bar, pouring an unknown liquid from an ancient bottle, stood a large unkempt man, one whose face had not seen a razor for many years past. I looked at Charles and him at me. This was apparently the man we sought.

Charles strode confidently to the bar, in the way that becomes a person who has always known lordship, and spoke to the man in the broken German by which we had navigated this latter part of our journey. The man simply stared back, unblinking. Charles glanced over at me with some unease, but then the man said, in the thick, guttural accent I had come to know from that region, "You are English, yes?"

"Why, yes," Charles replied somewhat giddily, "and you speak English?"

"I speak enough," the man replied. "But you should not expect the same from others in the village. We not see many outsiders."

"Why no, I wouldn't expect," I said. The man looked at me strangely for a moment, and it struck me he had likely never seen or heard an American before.

"What do you want?" he asked, turning back to Charles.

"Transport, if it is available, over the Carpathians to Czernowitz."

"Czernowitz?" he exclaimed more than asked, changing the pronunciation ever so slightly. He waved his hand in front of his face dismissively. "No Czernowitz. You should ask to go to the moon. You more likely to find someone take you there. No Czernowitz."

Charles turned and glanced at me and then said impatiently, "But sir, we have traveled from Budapest for this very purpose. We were told we could acquire transport here to Czernowitz."

"No, no, no," the man said, as one speaking to a child, "You had best go back to Budapest. Take train there south, through Transylvania and Wallachia. Then, go north. That will take you to Czernowitz."

Charles chuckled, but without humor. "That would add a good three weeks to our trip. No, sir, if you would just direct us to the local stagecoach man, I am sure we could persuade him."

Now, the man laughed. "I drive stagecoach," he said. "Stagecoach is mine. I no go over mountains. Mountains very dangerous for young gentlemen. Wolves, thieves. If stagecoach break . . ." he said trailing off, raising his right hand in a gesture to indicate he would not complete his thought, but rather leave notions of what atrocities might befall us to our own imagination.

"We are willing to take that chance," Charles continued, spreading out a line of gold sovereigns across the counter, "and we will make it in your interest to help us, as well."

The man raised his eyebrows and pursed his lips. A man should keep his faith, but there are times when it takes gold to move mountains.

"So be it," the man said, clearing the coins from the table in one swipe of his hand. "You may stay this night in my inn. We will leave at first light. The journey over the mountains will take two days. We cannot avoid traveling at night, but best to begin in the morning. Whatever we may face, young masters cannot say I led you there unawares."

"Then we have an agreement," Charles said, thrusting out his hand. The man simply looked at it, reached down below the bar, and threw down a skeleton key.

"Your room will be upstairs, the first door you see. I have only one."

"Right," Charles remarked, pulling back his hand and taking the key with it.

"We leave tomorrow, first light. If you are late, we no go."

And with that, the man turned back to his work. Charles and I gathered our things and made our way to the ill-equipped room we had been provided. As he threw himself on the large, lumpy, feather-filled bed, Charles looked up at me.

"Well, Daniel, I do believe we have found what we were looking for."

The no-doubt aged old ropes beneath him groaned under his weight. I wondered if they would simply snap, plunging him and his make-shift mattress to the floor. Given that I would be joining him that night, I hoped they were stronger than I thought.

"Yes," I replied, "but I am starting to miss the luxuries of home. What did you make of all that down there?"

"Ha!" Charles coughed. "That was a ploy for more money, my friend. And as you might have noticed, it worked. I wager these people do not see our kind too often. When they do, they are sure to get their share."

I looked out the grime-covered window of our room. In the streets below, nothing moved, save for a lone women pushing a primitive wheelbarrow filled with random trinkets. The fog still hung tightly around the mountains, the very cliffs we would ascend the next day. For the first time, I began to wish we had simply stayed in Venice.

Chapter
14

I awoke early with the rising of the sun. Charles and I gathered our things in silence, and as we did, I began to feel a sense of general foreboding. I was not a superstitious man, but on that day, I felt as if there were a hex on our journey, as if we were doomed to some ill fate before we even departed.

We descended the stairs to find the inn keeper waiting on us. He was dressed in a heavy brown leather overcoat and black boots. He had a wide-brimmed hat on his head and a black whip in his hand. He struck a frightful figure, but given the fear I held for the journey, a not altogether unwanted one.

"Well, old man," Charles said, "you look as though you expect some trouble."

"I do not expect it," the man said as he led us to the door, "but I am ready for it, nonetheless."

He held the door open wide, and we exited through it. The stagecoach was waiting outside. I followed behind Charles. He reached up and jerked open the stagecoach door. But then he paused and, cocking his head to the side, said, "Well, hello. How very rude of me to not announce my entrance."

I peeked around Charles' shoulder and in the darkness of the cabin saw the figure of a woman, though in the early morning haze I could not make out her features. But the voice that answered Charles was not that of a lady.

"It is of no concern, sir," a man's voice answered, in the deeply accented English common to the few of that land's people who spoke anything more than their native tongue. "Please, do join us."

Charles reached up and pulled himself in. I followed. As I sat down next to Charles, I took a moment to glance at the two people seated across from me. One was a young woman, I would say no older than twenty. She was a strikingly beautiful girl, firm in all the places that required it, but with a softness that immediately soothed me. It was her hair that stood out most to me, though – her long, straight, raven-black hair. Next to her was a man, much older, weathered, like leather that has spent too much time in the sun. I could tell immediately his life had been hard, but his finely tailored dress disclosed it had been a successful one nevertheless.

"I apologize for startling you. I am Vladimir," he said, raising his top hat slightly. His hair was as long as the girl's beside him and had been, at one time long ago perhaps, as black as hers. But now it was streaked white in places, more places, in fact, than it retained its previous luster. "And this is Anna," he continued, gesturing to his right with a hand on which sat a large gold ring. It was then I noticed in his other he held a thick black cane, the handle of which was molded in the shape of the bowed head of a large wolf.

"Hello," Anna said shyly, bowing her head with a blush as she did. She had the lilting voice of an Easterner, though the accent was not one I had previously encountered. She did not look long at me, though. She had eyes for Charles. At about that time the stagecoach shook with the weight of the innkeeper as he ascended to the driver's box. After only a moment, I heard him cry something in his native language, and I felt the sudden jerk of the coach as the horses began to pull.

As we began to roll along, Vladimir said, "You must be the two young gentlemen who took the only room in the village last night."

Charles chuckled. "I am afraid so," he said. "A place such as this rarely sees visitors. I doubt it has ever had a lodging shortage before."

"Yes," Vladimir replied with a smile. "So you go to Czernowitz as well?"

"Briefly," Charles replied, "on our way to the Black Sea."

"Ah, the Black Sea. It will be beautiful," Vladimir said with a wave of his hand. I glanced out the window and noticed that the houses had ended. We had entered the forest.

For a moment, there was silence, but then I broke it. "So Anna must be your daughter then?" I asked. Vladimir looked at me for a moment with mouth agape. Then, he began to laugh.

"No, my young friend," he said gently. "Anna is my fiancée. We travel to Czernowitz to be married."

"Oh," I said quietly, trying to cover the embarrassment of my social faux pas. I could feel Charles's disapproving glance. No doubt at some point in his extensive social training he would have learned not to ask such a question unless the answer was sure. I had received no such instruction.

"Czernowitz must be special to you, then," Charles said with a smile.

"Oh, it is. It is my home, or it was, many years past. Before I came over the mountain to seek my future and fortune. My fortune I secured long ago, and now that I have Anna," he said, turning to stroke the young girl's cheek, "my future is in hand, as well. So I will return to the place of my birth, and there I shall live until I die."

"Wonderful," Charles said with a smile, pulling out a cigar and lighting it with a match from his pocket.

I glanced from Vladimir to Anna. Vladimir had the look of a man who pursued what he wanted relentlessly and tended to get it. Anna simply looked empty. I wondered what had brought her here, with him. I had come from a place where people married others of their own choosing, where little girls grew up expecting to fall in love. Anna probably never had that dream. She grew up waiting to be sold. And Vladimir had bought her. No doubt a girl of her beauty had fetched quite a price.

I looked over at Charles. He was listening thoughtfully as Vladimir described his business as a merchant. I wondered what Charles thought of all this. He came from a different world than I, and no doubt such things were common there. Vladimir was just another powerful man in a long line of powerful men he encountered, and his ways were, no doubt, common to them all.

I turned again to the window of the carriage. Something struck me then, struck me as clearly as a bell ringing at noontime. This was a dying land. While the world moved on, this place remained, falling slowly behind, growing more decadent, more decrepit. Even nature had followed suit, and I knew as I stared out into the dead forest beyond the road with its chalk white trees driven into the ground like the bones of some ancient race of giants, that I should never have come here.

* * *

We rolled along like that for several hours, sometimes talking, sometimes in silence. The sun had climbed high in an empty sky when I felt the coach jerk to a halt. The sound of our driver's heavy footsteps as he exited the box preceded the sudden opening of the door.

"We stop here," he said. "We will eat now. The mountain climb begins here. Eat well. We will not stop again until the morning."

The driver gathered wood from the edges of the forest and then, with apparently no fear that anyone would be following, built a fire in the middle of the road. Drawing water from a stream that ran just at the road's edge, he brought a large pot of water to boil. I watched as he added vegetables and slices of meat from the large knapsack he had carried from the tavern. It wasn't long before we had a thick, hearty soup to eat. It was filling, and it needed to be. If our driver truly did not intend to stop until we had descended the mountain, it would be long before we would eat again.

As I finished my soup, I noticed our driver standing at the head of the coach, staring up the road. I wondered what was in his mind, what he was considering, what dangers lay ahead. But there was little time for such thoughts, as shortly he had turned back and commanded us to re-enter the coach. Before he closed the door, he handed us a bag.

"Some bread and some cheese for the journey. Sorry I not have more, but this will do. We climb the mountain now. We will go straight through, up and over. We will not stop until first light. It will be long night for all. Here, take these," he said, handing two pistols to Charles. "Perhaps we will not need them. But better to have." Then he slammed the door, and we felt the weight of the stage shift as he once again returned to his perch above.

Charles handed one pistol to Vladimir and then offered another to me.

"You should probably hang on to that. I'm a lousy shot," I offered.

"Oh, I have two in here," he said, patting the bag that sat beneath his seat. "I try not to put my trust solely in local hospitality."

"So," Vladimir said as I took the gun from Charles and the horses began to pull again, "what compelled two young gentlemen such as you to come by this way to Czernowitz?"

"Well," Charles began with a smile, "we simply pulled out a map and drew a course. You might say we are wandering with a purpose. We have a destination, but no set path by which to get there. The transit over the mountain seemed to be the most logical road."

"Ah yes," Vladimir said, nodding his head knowingly. "I suspected as much. Few who knew this place would have chosen this course willingly. Too much legend, too many superstitions."

"What do you mean?" I asked.

"Oh, this is a witch-haunted land, my young friend," Vladimir said solemnly, his dark, hooded eyes reinforcing that this was no idle talk. "This mountain is the source of much fear in this country, and none born here would follow the course you have set. And at this time of the year especially. Walpurgis Night is upon us, a little less than a week away. The stories the people below would no doubt tell of the things that transpire on this peak, when the sons of Satan and his servants dance and gibber beneath the Beltane moon. Ah, yes. You are most certainly strangers here."

"And what of you, then?" Charles asked with a sly grin. I could see by the fire in his eyes he was both enjoying this and believing none of it. "Why have you come?"

"Oh," Vladimir said after a pause, "I am not a superstitious man. Just stories all. And my Anna was eager to reach my homeland. The way over the mountain is fastest, as I am sure you are no doubt aware. I was prepared, obviously, to pay a handsome price for transport. Pay it I did, though I would like to believe that your contribution helped lighten my load a bit."

Charles chuckled. "Believe it all you will, then," he said, "but I doubt that will make it so."

Vladimir smiled. "Yes. But I do not begrudge the workman his wages. They are very poor, and I have prospered greatly. And if my eyes did not deceive me when we stopped earlier, he will earn his pay tonight."

"What do you mean?" I asked.

"A storm is building," Vladimir replied. "In here, we will be safe. But not so for our friend."

I glanced out the window of our carriage. Vladimir was right;

there were dark clouds swirling about. In fact, night was upon us, as the light of a dying sun provided little illumination. We had been gaining altitude for some time, but the air was thick and warmer than I would have expected, even for a late April evening. Then, a rumble in the distance.

"Does anyone live upon the mountain?" Charles asked. Vladimir chuckled to himself.

"No, my friend. As I have said, the mountain is bathed in superstition."

Now, Charles smiled. "Yes, I understand that. But surely there are some who don't believe the old tales, some who defy them and build a life here."

"No," Vladimir replied. "None." As he spoke, the first drops of rain fell on the roof of our coach.

"Well there must be more to the story than you have told," said Charles as the rain began to tap-tap-tap above us with more authority. For the first time since the trip began, Anna looked interested in the conversation. Vladimir stared blankly at Charles for a moment but then, apparently making a decision, he nodded.

"Are you a religious man, Mr. Charles?"

"Of course," Charles replied.

"And the great dragon was cast out," Vladimir quoted, "that old serpent, called the Devil, and Satan, which deceiveth the whole world: he was cast out into the Earth, and his angels were cast out with him."

"Revelation," Charles said. Vladimir nodded once.

"It is the conceit of man that Satan is not among us, that he is locked in his prison in Hell, and that we are free from his devices. But the devil was not cast into Hell. No, he was banished to the Earth. When Satan was cast down, when he fell, where do you believe he fell to?"

Charles smiled. "I never gave it much thought."

"No, and most do not. But the people of this land believe Satan did fall to Earth. And when he did, he came to rest on this mountain. It is an ancient belief, older than that of the Christians or the Mohammedans. Some say Satan sleeps in the heart of the mountain, waiting for the day he will be awoken. And on that day, he will plunge the world into a second darkness, not seen since the Lord split the void and called forth for light."

I glanced out of the carriage and into the night beyond. Through the driving rain and swirling darkness, my eyes saw, or my mind created, movement in the forest, darting to and fro between the trees. It was then we heard the first howl, the call of a lone wolf in the night. It would not be the last.

"The wolves are vicious here," Vladimir said with a grin I would describe as cruel. "We would do well to pray our carriage comes to no harm on this night."

We sped on up the mountain, faster and faster if I judged correctly.

"If no one lives here, who built this road?"

"It was built," Vladimir said casually, "during the many wars between the Turk and the Wallachian princes."

The conversation died away then, and for many minutes, hours perhaps, we spoke little. The rain continued in torrents, and the thunder and lightning that followed filled our ears and gave our eyes the briefest glimpses of the world outside. In those flashes, I saw amazing things, impossible things, and always the wolf, following our path, marking our trail.

*   *   *

It must have been well on past midnight when it happened. We were moving along, traveling at some speed, and I would learn later we had nearly reached the summit of the mountain. It was then that Charles spoke.

"Vladimir," he said as he gazed out of the window and into the darkness beyond, "I thought you said no one lived on this mountain."

"They do not," Vladimir replied, with the look of a man confused.

"Then what is that?" Charles said, never taking his eyes off of the coming road. The rest of us all crowded over to one side. Though I could barely see, it was still apparent to me what Charles meant. In the coming darkness loomed a massive structure, a fortress built of solid stone, seemingly cut from the very side of the mountain. And it was not abandoned; through its windows, the flickering light of torches shone into the night.

"I do not know," Vladimir said, amazed. "I must admit," he continued, "that I have never come this way before."

The gigantic structure loomed ahead, growing ever larger as we approached. I slid closer to Charles to get a better look, until finally he gestured with one hand that I could trade places with him. It was a Gothic castle with a central tower rising from the middle of four smaller redoubts. A high wall surrounded it, and as we approached, I could see the gate was open. It was then I felt my eyes deceived me. To them there appeared a figure, dressed in a long black cloak, standing on the side of the road. A hood obscured its face.

The carriage thundered by so quickly I glimpsed it for only a second. But in that second the lightning flashed and I could see it was a woman, her long dark hair as black as the night that surrounded her, with green eyes that burned into my soul. I will see that image for the rest of my days every night when I close my eyes to sleep. But then the flash was gone, and so was the woman. The coach rolled on up the mountain.

No one spoke. Although we had traveled far in wilderness, it was this glimpse of civilization that shook us the most. I suppose we might have gone on like that for the rest of the journey. But suddenly, jarringly, we came to a halt. I looked from Vladimir to Charles. It was the look on Vladimir's face that froze my heart: that of sheer terror. Vladimir knew these lands, and though he professed not to give credence to many of the stories surrounding them, he believed enough to fear.

We felt the shifting of our driver's weight as he climbed out of the box, heard his boots as they splashed along the ground. Then, the door was wrenched violently open. What we saw would have been humorous in a different setting. He stood there drenched in the rain, water pouring off of his broad-rimmed, leather hat.

"You should see this," he said. Then, he turned and walked towards the front of the carriage. The three of us looked at each other, silently questioning whether any would follow him. Finally, Vladimir spoke.

"Stay here, Anna. We will go see."

No other words were necessary. One by one, we filed out into the pouring rain. What we saw was as shocking as it was disheartening.

Our driver stood at the front of the carriage, one hand on the lead horse's halter. Beyond him was the road. But then the road suddenly came to a sharp stop. Where it should have continued sat what looked to my darkened eyes as a sheer rock cliff. I followed it up to the sky, but in the night, I could not see how high it went. It was unimaginable, impossible. The road had been built to go over the mountain, and at some point previously it had. But now it ran directly into a wall. I would have questioned my own sanity, but it soon became clear it was my eyesight that deceived me. A flash of lightning revealed the truth.

It was a wall, indeed, but not the sheer stone cliff I had first imagined. Rather, it was made up of boulders of varying sizes, some merely pebbles, others the size of the coach itself. It was not incredibly high, and a man would have had no trouble traversing it. But to our coach, it was as impenetrable as if it stretched all the way to the heavens. Our driver released the horse he held and walked back to where we stood.

"Impossible," he said simply.

"What is this devilry?" Charles asked. The innkeeper looked at him as if he were a fool.

"A rock slide, of course. The road is useless. We have no choice. We must go back."

"Go all the way back?" Charles exclaimed more than asked.

"There is no other way."

"What of the castle we passed earlier?" I asked.

The other three men turned and looked at me. None answered, so I continued.

"Well," I said, "it is occupied. And I think none of us cherishes the thought of traveling all the way back down the mountain at this time of night. And more importantly, perhaps there is a way around this impasse. If so, they may know."

It was the last thought that captured Vladimir and Charles, that bit of hope the journey was not all in vain that made them forget their fears and embrace my plan. To this day, I do not know why I suggested it. Even then, I feared that place. Even then, the vision from the road had begun to haunt me. But I pressed anyway, as if I had no choice.

"No," our driver replied, apparently not convinced.

"It is a good plan," Charles said.

"No, we should keep moving."

Vladimir joined the fray. "Let us at least try. Perhaps we can ask if our young friend's supposition is correct. If so, we can stay. If not, we can continue." Vladimir punctuated this thought by placing several more gold coins into the man's hand.

He still looked unsure, but finally said, "Alright. We try. But we go if no way around." Before anyone could answer, a wolf howled somewhere not too distant from where we stood.

"We go now," our driver ordered. On this point, no one challenged him. We climbed back into the carriage, suddenly aware of the water that had filled our clothes. We felt the coach turn and the horses pull, and then we left that rock wall behind and rode to an uncertain future.

Chapter 15

The feeling inside the coach was a strange mixture of excitement and fear. None spoke, but as we descended the mountain, I found myself eager to see what mysteries lay beyond the walls of the fortress we had passed earlier and perhaps learn the identity of the woman I had glimpsed only briefly. But I was afraid as well, afraid of the secrets and legends that surrounded that plutonian peak and of what person or persons would make their home on its slopes.

But there was little time to think, as the quick movement of the horses had already brought us to the gates. The carriage jerked as the horses hesitated, but a sharp word from the driver and a sharper strike of his whip forced them forward. The carriage then rolled into an open courtyard before coming to a stop.

This time we didn't wait for our driver to descend. I threw open the door and hopped out. Charles and Vladimir followed with Anna close behind. We stepped into a walled space, the gate behind us and a stone fortress in front. The cobblestone was slick with new rain, but the fall of it had slacked, leaving a cool, crisp night behind. There were none about, but the burning torches along the wall — clearly lit after the rain no longer fell — told us one had been here not long before and perhaps our arrival was expected. A pair of great wooden doors stood before us. I looked at Charles to gauge his interest in knocking, but he was already looking at me.

"So, what will it be my friend? Should we announce our presence?"

"We should leave this place," spat the innkeeper. "There is an unholy feeling about."

"More superstition," Charles said with a chuckle. "Well, if no one else is going to take the lead . . ."

Charles didn't get the chance to finish. His words were interrupted by the clanging boom of a large bolt being withdrawn somewhere beyond the wooden door. One of the doors swung slowly open, and the light from a large chandelier hanging over the entryway streamed out into the night. Outlined by that light was a figure, one that looked to my adjusting eyes to be an unnaturally large person, bigger and bulkier than seemed possible. But then I realized that it wasn't unnatural at all. In fact, it was a woman in the thick, enveloping dress and hood of a monastic.

She stepped out into the night with the confidence and poise of a leader. Then she spoke.

"May I help you gentlemen?" she asked, in a sing-song timbre I couldn't trace but felt instantly entranced by. For a moment we just stood there, mesmerized both by her voice and by the glowing light that seemed to surround her. She was as out of place as she could possibly be. Finally, as was his wont, Charles took the lead.

"Yes, Abbess, I believe you may be able to help us. We are travelers. We have come from the village at the base of this mountain on our way to Czernowitz. But at the pass beyond here, the road has been blocked."

"Yes," she said. "A landslide blocked it only a few weeks ago. Our convent priest, Father Kramer, left us some time ago on his way to Czernowitz. I imagine that he will return soon with help from the city to clear the way."

"Abbess," Charles said, "we have been traveling for some time. It appears, based on what you have told us, our travels are all for naught, and we are need to return from whence we came. Could we trouble you to stay the night?"

"I suppose," the woman began, "it is not wise of me to allow four unknown men to stay within the walls of this abbey. But I see a kindness in your eyes, and I judge your intentions pure. You may stay not only the night, but if you desire it, you may stay until Father Kramer returns. It shouldn't be long, certainly no longer than any alternative route to Czernowitz."

"Please, excuse us," Charles asked. He turned to us and said, "Well boys, what will it be?"

"I not stay," the driver said. "Not here, not in this place."

"Is this a play for more gold?" Charles spat.

"No money. This is a cursed place. You should go with me."

"Gentlemen," the sister spoke from behind us. We all turned to her. "I am sorry to overhear, but I notice one of your number has no desire to stay with us. We have a coach here, and upon Father Kramer's return, we can arrange for your travel to Czernowitz."

Charles looked to me. I shrugged my shoulders. Vladimir simply nodded. Charles turned to our new hostess and said, "Good. Then, we will stay."

Our driver said not another word. He walked back to the stage, removed our bags, and climbed into his driver's box. With a quick flick of the reins and an unintelligible command, the horses began to pull. He turned them around and led them out of the gate. As he disappeared into the darkness, it struck me we were now trapped there. We had no way to escape.

Charles turned on his heels and faced the woman who remained in the doorway. "Well, Abbess, it appears we are in your hands."

"Yes," she said, stepping into the night. "I am Sister Batory. I am the Abbess of this convent. The young women within are my charges. I expect you will treat them with dignity and respect."

The friendly tenor of her voice had changed, the kindness drained from it. Now she sounded colder, less welcoming. It was apparent she did not trust us.

"Of course," Charles replied with a bow.

She nodded subtly, and then turned and entered the castle. We gathered our belongings and followed.

"The abbey, as you can probably tell," she said as she walked quickly across the vast chamber beyond the door, "was once a mountain fortress. It is, therefore, quite vast, with the advantage that we have plenty of room."

"So how did the convent come to possess this edifice, if I may ask?"

The sister turned on one heel facing Charles. The gleam in her eye indicated this was a tour that expected no questions, but she answered it nonetheless.

"When the wars between the princes of Wallachia and the Turk ended, there was no more need for a place such as this. The wide world moved on, leaving this mountain behind. A traveler, a man of God, came upon this place in much the same way as you. That the Church has managed to find some use for it is a blessing upon us all."

I took this pause in what had been our hasty crossing to study my surroundings. The ceilings were high and vaulted as was to be expected. There were corridors surrounding us that lead off in many directions, most of them dark. There were a great number of sturdy wooden doors, all closed and, something told me, all locked. We appeared to be heading towards some sort of grand staircase at the end of the room. It led up to a second floor where I presumed our lodgings would be.

"In any event," Abbess Batory continued, "the castle is large as I said, and much of it is still unused. I advise you that we keep many of the doors locked. If you come to a door and find that it will not open, I would ask you to leave it be, for your sake as well as mine."

"Whatever do you mean?" Vladimir asked, somewhat concerned.

"Well," Batory continued, "it is simply that many of our sisters have taken a vow of seclusion. I would have you not intrude upon that. But also, this structure has stood for many centuries. Much of it still lies in disrepair. We wouldn't want any of you to lose yourselves within its depths . . . and become injured."

There was a certain menace to her voice, as if her statement was more in the nature of a threat than a warning. I noticed Anna shiver beside me. Apparently Abbess Batory noticed, as well.

"I am sorry, dear. I do not mean to frighten you. But it is better to know the dangers you face, of which there are few I assure you, than to leave you in ignorance."

We began to climb the staircase. It was winding and stone, as was most everything else in the once-fortress.

"Your rooms are located on the second floor," Batory continued. "There are four of you, but we have only three free chambers. The two young gentlemen will stay together. You, sir," she said, speaking to Vladimir, "will have your own room, as well as the young lady."

Vladimir said nothing, though I could tell a part of him strongly wished to object. Whether out of fear for the young woman's safety or out of some basic lack of decorum his impoverished upbringing had bequeathed upon him, I couldn't say. In any event, I doubted Abbess Batory had any intention of allowing two unmarried persons to stay together overnight. So, it was probably the better part of discretion that made Vladimir hold his peace.

The sister escorted us to our rooms and said, "Of course, once you have entered your rooms, I will lock the door behind you. I hope you understand."

Charles apparently did not. "But, Abbess," he began, "that seems most unusual."

Batory turned to him, her thin, bloodless lips drawing taunt across her bright white teeth. "Yes," she said, drawing out the word, "I can see why a man such as yourself, might feel that way. You must understand my responsibilities. You are, as I said, unknown to me. I will allow you to stay here, as is my Christian duty. But faith and good sense are not exclusive of one another. I cannot allow you simply to roam about the halls at night unsupervised. Not until I get a better feeling for you, at least."

Charles began to object, again, but she held up one hand.

"This is not open for debate, sir. There is no purpose in arguing. You may do as I say, or you may go. This is a point I cannot concede. You will enter your rooms, and I will lock them behind you. In the morning, when your breakfast is prepared, I will return. At that point, you may join us, and I will introduce you to the rest of the sisterhood." Then she paused, staring intently at Charles. "But let me say again, any attempt to leave your rooms once I have locked them would be most unfortunate."

Charles looked at me, and I at him, but we said nothing. It was a Hobson's choice. The truth was there was nowhere else to go and no real decision to be made. We had one option, and that was to stay, whatever Abbess Batory required.

Anna and Vladimir entered their rooms, and we did the same. But as I turned, and before Abbess Batory could close the door and lock it, I noticed in the corner of my eye a young woman, standing at the end of the hallway. I saw her only for a moment, just as I had seen her before. For it was the same girl I glimpsed in the night, the same girl I saw as we had passed by the fortress earlier. But then as quickly as she was there, the door was closed, and she was gone. I heard a key enter the door's lock and a tumbler turn, followed by the steady steps of Abbess Batory as she walked off into the darkness. For a while we simply stood there. Then, Charles stepped forward, putting his hand on the door. He looked at me, but I simply shrugged. He jiggled the door handle a couple times and then pushed against it. Nothing.

"Well, old boy, I guess we are stuck here for the night."

"It would appear so," I said.

I looked around the room. To say that it was sparsely decorated would be an understatement. There was a large bed in the corner. Of that, I was thankful, as it appeared we would be sharing it in the night. Other than that, there was a desk and a chair, several candles, a lantern which was lit, and a window with a ledge just large enough to sit upon. It struck me I saw no crucifix, no icons, no images of Christ or the Saints, and no Bible. Apparently this room had gone unused for some time.

"Well," Charles said, "I doubt anyone would call these luxurious accommodations."

He pushed gingerly down on the mattress on which he would sleep. It creaked and groaned, even with his gentle prodding.

"Could you expect more from a convent?"

"I suppose not," he said, sitting on the edge of the bed. "I wonder how long it will be until the Father returns."

"I don't know," I replied, walking to the window ledge. I peered off into the night. If there were a moon, it was hidden, and in the darkness I could see nothing. "We can hope it will be soon."

"Yes, though I suppose we are here for the duration. So," Charles said, and I could tell he was changing the subject, "what of Anna?"

"What *of* Anna?" I asked.

"I find her . . . intoxicating," Charles said with a grin.

I leaned against the window sill and stared at him.

"She is quite beautiful, Charles. But as you are all too well aware, she is also engaged. And Vladimir does not strike me as a particularly honest man."

"How so?" Charles asked, as if he did not know.

"Well, let us say he is a man who knows what he seeks and is ceaseless in the seeking of it. And, if I had to wager on the point, doubtless not all of his gains were made honestly. He is a dangerous man, Charles. I know you are accustomed to getting what you want when you want it, but we are not in England."

Charles nodded absentmindedly. I knew, as he knew, all I said was true. But I also knew, despite the danger involved, he would not shy away from Anna when opportunities presented themselves. It was merely my hope that in doing so neither he nor she would come to any untoward end.

Oh, what a predicament we were in, I thought. Here we were, in a foreign land, in a more or less abandoned fortress, on top of a mountain shrouded in darkness and myth, in the hands of strangers, with no means of escape should we need it. At that thought, I chuckled to myself.

"What?" Charles asked.

"Nothing," I replied.

I knew even as I felt them these were irrational thoughts. There could be no place more secure than here. I knew I should feel safe in a place such as this, a holy place, a place I could lay my head down knowing no danger could come to me. And yet, while my rational mind told me this was true, there was something else. Something preternatural, something left over from the oldest age of human experience, which told me as long as I was within these walls, I would not be safe.

I did not dwell on this thought long. Charles turned to me and said, "Well old man, it is late, and I am tired. As our options are limited, shall we turn in?"

"Yes," I replied with a smile. With that, our strange night was ended. It would be only the first of many.

* * *

The night passed without event. The journey had drained me physically and mentally, and I was very tired. Despite the rather cramped conditions, sleep came quickly. I slept deeply and cannot say I remember my dreams, not really. I awoke with only the barest glimpse of them, like a shadow that moves in the water. That something is there is undoubted, but your eyes cannot see it. I remember only flashes of color and of sound, and the figure of a woman. But the more I sought to focus, the further away those images would drift in my mind.

We awoke to the bright light of day. I suppose that should not be surprising. But the night before, I believed darkness would always cover that mountain, that the light of the sun could be nothing more than a distant memory on its peak. As the gleam of morning streamed through our open window, I felt my spirits rise.

I had not been awake long before Charles also roused himself. "Well, it would seem we've made it through one night intact."

I heard a key slide into the door and a bolt turn. The door was opened, but it was not Abbess Batory as I would have expected. Instead, it was a younger girl with a kind face and dark hair.

"Breakfast is prepared, sirs," she said shyly, never lifting her eyes to see where we lay. "If you will, kindly join us downstairs." Then, as quickly as she had come, she was gone.

"Well, she is quite the pretty thing," Charles remarked. He looked at me and no doubt was surprised at what he saw, for I am sure I was visibly dumbfounded at that moment. It was the same girl I had seen twice before, the same girl who had been outside the gates, the same girl whose outline I had glimpsed as the door closed last night.

"Are you alright, Daniel?" Charles asked with some concern.

"Of course," I almost whispered. "We should go."

In only the briefest of time we were clothed, and we made our way quickly down to the dining room below. We needed no guide as the sounds of activity carried us along. The castle was a brighter place in the day, and one could feel the energy pulsing through it as if it were a being come to life.

As we entered the dining room, it became evident to the both of us that, indeed, this was a convent. The sisterhood was gathered around various tables, eating what could only be described as a sumptuous meal. I immediately wondered from whence they received their provisions. No doubt the citizens of Czernowitz were less superstitious than their compatriots across the mountain and did a brisk trade with the abbey. I suspected there was also a garden somewhere nearby tended by the sisters. It was even possible wild game was gathered to add meat to their diet.

Anna and Vladimir were seated at a table alone. The sisters had shunned them, whether out of some negative feeling or out of modesty and fear, I could not know. Charles and I sat across from the pair.

"Good morning," Vladimir said.

"Good morning," I responded. "I trust you spent the night well?"

"If I have ever been more tired than I was last night, I do not remember it."

Plates had been set out, and there were bowls of various breakfast foods on the table. Charles and I took generous portions. Apparently, he was as hungry as I. For a long while we sat there, more or less in silence, eating our food. But then one of the sisters I did not recognize approached.

"Monsieur Vladimir," she said. "Abbess Batory would like for you to join her briefly. She is curious to learn of your travels."

"Of course," Vladimir responded. "Anna?" he said, apparently ensuring she would be fine without him. She merely nodded. He arose from his seat, leaving his empty plate behind, and made his way to the front table where Abbess Batory sat. Charles glanced at me, slyly. I knew what he was thinking. He had made his affection for Anna clear, and this would be an opportunity for him to get to know her better, no longer under the stone-cold gaze of Vladimir. As I glanced at the head table, though, I noticed, although he was engaged in conversation, Vladimir's eyes often found us. And I knew to whatever extent Charles would have preferred to keep his affections secret, Vladimir was no fool.

I knew Charles would prefer I leave him alone, but there really was nowhere for me to go. As I pondered this quandary, I failed to notice the approach of the young woman who had so struck me only a night before. When she sat down beside me, it came as a complete surprise.

"Hello, sir," she said.

"Oh! I'm sorry," I exclaimed. I must have looked a fool, as she chuckled lightly when I spoke. I was not Catholic, and I admit the young women who choose to give their lives to Christ were a mystery to me. I had often noticed the modest dress that marked their sacrifice stole from them whatever natural gifts they might possess. But in spite of the ungainly clothing she now wore, the softness of her face and the light in her eyes revealed the beauty beneath.

"I'm sorry, sir, I didn't mean to startle you," she said through a glowing smile.

"Oh no, of course not," I said quietly. I have never been a man of great boldness, and now I felt as though this pretty little girl sitting beside me had sapped whatever courage, whatever confidence, I would normally hold.

"It's just," she said, "I saw you last night, and I admit my curiosity has gotten the better of my manners. But, I can leave if you would rather. . ."

"Oh no," I interrupted, putting a hand on her wrist. "Please stay, I am as curious as you."

"Thank you, sir," she replied, blushing slightly from my lack of decorum. There was, in her face, innocence, peace, joy. I wondered where it came from. I wondered where she came from. How she had come to be here. Perhaps she would tell me.

"I judge," she said, "by the sound of your voice, you are not of this country."

"No," I said, "I am an American."

"American!" she exclaimed. "Why I've never met an American before."

I had heard that often but still was not sure what response was expected. So, I merely smiled.

"Will you tell me of America?" she asked, with a smile on her face filled with both the innocence and eagerness of youth.

"Nothing would make me happier," I replied. "But first tell me your name."

"Oh," she said. "I'm sorry. I'm Lily."

"Lily," I replied. "That is a beautiful name."

"Well thank you, sir," she said, blushing again.

"And how long have you been here, Lily?"

"Not long. I am a novice, you see. I only joined the order a little less than a month ago."

"And what do you think of it?"

"Well," she stuttered, her countenance falling ever so slightly. "It is different than I expected. I suppose I was not so prepared for the isolation, the being alone. Oh . . . perhaps I speak too openly."

"No, please continue," I implored her. "You have my confidence."

She looked at me for a second, judging me, weighing me in her balance. For the first time in a long time, someone found me worthy.

"I do not know what it is, sir. But there is something in your face. I trust you."

"Good," I said, nodding.

"Well," she continued, "I do love the sisterhood. But like all things, I suppose, this one has been difficult in the beginning. Perhaps once I know the other sisters better, things will improve."

"I am sure they will," I said.

"Now," she said, her face brightening, "tell me of America."

I smiled. So breakfast continued, longer perhaps than I would have expected. Charles chatted freely with Anna beside me. She had struck me immediately as a shy girl, one closed to outsiders. She spoke little, and often it seemed as though she would prefer just to fade into the background. But as I talked to Lily, I could not help but notice the giggles, the smiles, the little sighs of the girl beside me. Vladimir couldn't help but notice either. Charles, oblivious, was apparently employing all his charms. As for me, I told Lily all the stories I could muster, most of which were less than entrancing. But to her hearing, they were all the highest adventures.

Undoubtedly, Abbess Batory was also fascinated by her guest. Though Vladimir probably would have preferred to return to the table and retake possession of Anna, Batory kept him there long after the food was finished. Had I not known better, I would have said she was enjoying this spectacle.

But breakfast could not last forever, and soon Vladimir had freed himself from Batory's grasp and returned to our table. Charles changed like a chameleon, immediately turning to me as if he had been involved in my conversation all along. Lily was not impressed. She looked from Charles to me and said, "Well, Daniel, I hope we can continue our conversation later." And then she was gone.

Chapter 16

"Oh, Daniel. Anna is a dream."

The rest of the day had been a bit of a blur. Dinner and supper had come and gone, with Batory stealing Vladimir away on both occasions, much to his dismay. Charles had taken advantage of each opportunity. Sadly, Lily had not returned, though her absence did more to whet my appetite for her charms than her presence ever could. Now, Charles was leaned against the once-again locked door, purring over his newest love.

"Yes, Charles, she is a dream. But I cannot imagine Vladimir has many more stories to tell Batory, and even if he does, what exactly do you propose to do? Steal two horses and ride off into the night with her?"

"Perhaps," Charles said with a grin. "But enough about me. What about you, old boy? I saw you talking to that young girl at breakfast."

I couldn't help but smile. "Yes," I said. "Lily."

"Lily," Charles repeated. "Well, Daniel, it would appear we are both sunk. At least mine has yet to take her vows."

* * *

The night passed, once again without disturbance. But we were more restless, less apt to give in to slumber. The fears of the last few days had dissipated, replaced with the eager love of youth. We lay there, both trying to sleep, neither admitting sleep would not come. I suppose it was nigh on midnight when we heard it. It was, as most sounds are when they begin, unremarkable at first, but slowly built into something one would notice. At first, I heard it but wasn't listening. It was a shuffling sound, the movement of cloth across stone. The muffled sound of soft, quick feet.

"Do you hear that?" I asked Charles.

"They're moving," he replied. "Look!" he said, pointing. Light was streaming in from underneath the locked door. I watched for a moment, and nothing happened. But then a shadow moved across the floor, then another and another, as if person after person was moving down the hallway.

"Midnight Mass?" Charles asked.

"What else could it be?" I said. But even in the asking of it, I somehow knew that was not the true explanation. Charles didn't respond, but he knew it, too. I stepped quietly out of the bed and walked silently over to the door. I was sure what would happen, but I tried the lock anyway. Nothing. The bolt was still fast. I turned and looked at Charles. I could see the disappointment in his face. Even as I stood there, shadow after shadow continued to pass underneath.

* * *

The next day began much as the last, except that morning Lily was waiting at the table when we arrived.

"Good morning, Daniel," she said with a smile. "Sir," she continued, turning to Vladimir, "Abbess Batory has requested your presence, once again."

Vladimir frowned. "Of course," he replied with the frustration of a man who could make no other response. "Anna, gentlemen," he said with a bow. A glance at Charles revealed he was positively ecstatic. I sat down across from Lily.

"Did you sleep well last night, Daniel?"

It was an innocent question, but it cast my mind back to the night before, to the shadows that passed silently beneath my door.

"Lily, last night, around midnight I would say, we noticed a, how to say it, a procession of some sort. Down the hallway past our room. As we were locked in, we were unable to see what the commotion might be."

"That's the Midnight Mass," Lily said brightly. "It is supposed to be beautiful."

"Supposed to be?"

"Oh, I've never seen it," Lily replied. "Novices are not allowed."

I gave her a puzzled look. "That seems rather peculiar."

Lily shrugged. "It is simply a rule of the Order. I never thought to question it."

"No," I replied, looking off to the head table where Vladimir still sat. "I don't suppose you would."

I thought for a second about what to say next, but my curiosity had the better of me. I judged the girl had immediately taken to me, and I decided to prey upon that good will.

"Lily," I began, "I would very much like to explore this castle. It is very beautiful, and part of my purpose in my travels is to investigate places such as this."

"Yes, of course!" Then, she paused. Lily looked around, as if seeing if anyone was listening. Sure that we could not be heard, but dropping her voice to a whisper nonetheless, she said, "There are many wonders to be found in the castle. Abbess Batory keeps all of the doors locked. She says that a wondering mind is the Devil's workshop. But I am curious," she said with a mischievous smile. "She keeps an extra key in her office. I have taken it several times."

"Could you get it for me?" I asked.

Lily's smile faded. For the first time, I think she realized perhaps she had spoken too freely.

"Well . . ." she began. "I think I could get it, but I would want to go with you. It is not that I don't trust you. But it would be most unfortunate if you were to lose it."

"Of course," I said with a smile. I was determined to have that key for myself, but now was not the time to argue the point.

"Anyway," Lily said, "I have chores to attend to." Then, looking around, she said, "Meet me after dinner. I should have the key by then." With a smile, she was off.

I was left alone. Well, more or less alone. Charles and Anna were now whispering down the table. This was not a place I wished to be, so I stood up and wandered about the high vaulted expanse. There was little to attract the eye. I had never been in a place of God with less to recommend it. Less architectural beauty, less in the way of art or sculpture.

I supposed the fortress's history had much to do with its starkness. I leaned myself against a column and began to think. I suddenly hoped we would not be here much longer. I found it to be cold and unfriendly despite my growing affection for one of the young women who had sentenced herself to a life here. I had begun to think on whether that was an unfair judgment when I felt a presence beside me. I turned and was shocked to see it was Vladimir.

"The Abbess," he began, "seems never to tire of questions." He smiled at me, and then turned his head to look at Anna and Charles. "Apparently, neither does your friend. He appears to have taken an interest in my Anna. Do you think," he continued now turning his gaze back to me, "that I should be concerned?"

I stared dumbly back at him, unsure of what to say. Vladimir chuckled.

"She is a very beautiful girl, of that I am sure. So I do not envy a man if he admires her. As long as it is at a distance, of course. I am an old man, and I realize Anna may find she has more in common with a younger set. I do not begrudge her the friendship of others. But you would be wise to ensure friendship is all that it remains."

"Of course," I said, with a slight bow. We stood there like that in silence for a few minutes. Then, Vladimir deigned to break that silence.

"I hope the priest returns soon with help from Czernowitz. I do not wish to remain here any longer."

"Vladimir," I said, determined to ease his mind and possibly save Charles' health, "you have nothing to fear from Charles. His intentions are pure, I am sure."

Vladimir laughed, but without humor. "It is not Charles I fear. It is this place. Can't you feel it? The sisterhood may have taken it, but they do not own it, not yet. There is still something unholy about it. And two nights hence . . ." His voice trailed off. He did not finish.

"What?" I asked

He squinted at me with a queer look. "Your people have forgotten the old ways," he said. "You would do well to remember them." I simply said nothing. He frowned and continued, "We should not be here, my young friend. And in two days, it will be May Eve. Walpurgis Night. We should not be on this mountain on such a night. I have seen many things in my life, enough to not be superstitious, enough to know most can be explained. But there are some things for which one would be wise to maintain a healthy respect. This place is one of them."

"What if he doesn't come?"

"If the priest doesn't come," he said, "then we will wait it out the best we can. And hope the blessing of the sisterhood will keep us safe."

It was a dark assessment from a man who I felt held few sentimental thoughts. I, for one, knew nothing of May Eve, of Walpurgis Night, nothing more than I had discovered in the most recent days of my travels. But the more I learned, the less I wanted to know.

Dinner came and Lily appeared, but she had no key. She apologized profusely, but the Abbess had remained in her office all morning, and there had been no opportunity to obtain it. The same story was told at supper. Charles and I returned to our room to be locked inside. At midnight the procession began again, as silently and stealthily as before.

* * *

The next morning at breakfast, Lily was nowhere to be seen. My initial reaction was to worry; there was a danger she may have been caught in the midst of our crime. If she confessed, then our conspiracy would be uncovered, and Abbess Batory might choose to banish us from the castle.

Charles was similarly put-out; that morning Batory had not sent for Vladimir. And so there he sat, hovering over poor Anna. The timid girl, so boisterous and talkative the past few days, did not dare to speak now. The mood was one of overall gloom, and the longer Lily's absence continued, the gloomier it got. But then I saw her, standing next to a column on the edge of the room, beckoning to me. I excused myself from the table and met her.

"I was beginning to think something happened," I said.

"Such as what?" she asked with a smile.

"Well, I thought you might have been caught."

"Not quite," she said, holding up a steel gray skeleton key.

"You got it!" I said, perhaps too loudly.

"I got it," she replied. "Meet me in the outer chamber after breakfast. I have some free time before dinner, and the others will be busy. There is something I want to show you."

"I will meet you," I said as she stood there smiling brightly, the darkness lifting that had been hovering over me. For the first time, the first time really that is, I wished we had met in a different place.

* * *

I waited as she had asked in the outer chamber just beyond the hall in which we ate. I stood in the shadows as several groups of sisters moved about on their way to their sundry duties. Finally, there was Abbess Batory walking confidently, with purpose, through the chamber to some unknown destination.

I watched her as she went, but when she reached an outer door, I saw her stop. For a moment, I thought she would turn and find my hiding spot. I immediately began to concoct a dozen different excuses, sure in the knowledge she would see through them all. But after only a moment's pause, she continued through the door and was gone. I stood in the hall alone for a few more minutes, but then Lily arrived.

"Come!" she commanded in a whisper. "We must hurry, and we must not be seen."

She led me through an open hall to one of the many locked doors in the corridor. Lily produced the key and unlocked it with no difficulty. The open door revealed a long corridor. I had little time to study it before I was hurried in by Lily who quietly closed and locked the door behind us.

The hallway immediately fell dark, the only light provided by windows placed high upon the wall near the ceiling. Lily handed me one of the lanterns she carried with her, opening the vents to allow light. The corridor was blacker, dirtier, older than the one we had just left. I could tell immediately this was not an area of the castle that was often visited.

"They had planned on opening this all up," Lily said. "To give the Order more space. You are lucky there were rooms available when you arrived. Normally, each sister would have her own cell, but here most share rooms. Yours were being prepared for sisters when you arrived. If you had come but a day later, they would not have been open. Lucky for you, I guess. I am actually lucky, as well. I am one of the few sisters who has her own room."

We walked down the length of the hallway. There was a stairway leading down and curling back around the wall at its end. As we descended, Lily continued, "As I was saying, they had planned to open all this up. But then they found it."

The stairway continued to descend before dead-ending into yet another doorway. But this one was different from the others. The walls around its edges were rougher, as if the once smooth stone had been chiseled or beaten away. The door itself was not the same as those we had already passed through. I would have sworn those doors had been in place for hundreds of years, but this one was new and looked as if the wood had been cut and planed only a few months before.

"When they found this chamber," she said as she slid the key into the lock, "it was entirely blocked in. It was bricked up," she continued, turning the key, "and beyond that were boulders, as if the roof had fallen in or someone had tried to forever fill the hallway beyond. They had to use dynamite to blow through the wall. The other sisters say it shook the castle so, they thought the whole roof might fall in!" she whispered with a mischievous smile. Then she flung the door open.

A black, gaping hole was before us. It seemed to leer out at us, like the empty smile of a toothless skull. I looked at Lily and she at me.

"Shall we?" she asked. I simply nodded. We entered a narrow, downward-sloping corridor. Its walls were different, more ancient, less chiseled, more rough-hewn. I was immediately interested in the method of its construction, of whether it predated the castle. But then it opened up into a high chamber, and all my previous curiosities were forgotten.

"Oh my sweet Lord!"

"Incredible, isn't it?"

So many thoughts entered my mind at that moment, and I must concentrate if I am to relay them in any coherent way. My first thought, after the shock of what I saw had passed, was the distinct and overwhelming certainty I shouldn't be there. Not then, not ever. It was the sort of place no man should see. No Christian man, at least. A fearful place, a horrible place. It then struck me how young Lily must be, for only a youth could see such a thing and not recoil instantly from the sight of it.

It was a chamber, as I have said. High vaulted and massive. A great inverted bowl, seemingly carved out of the depths of the mountain. At the far end sat a table. No, not a table. An altar. That is the only word for it. A single piece of stone. Four feet high and six feet long, made out of a single block of marble, smooth at the top. It was darker in some places than others, and though it may have just been a trick of the light, at that moment I could almost see the bloodstains as black and sinister as if the slaughter perpetrated upon that slab had happened only moments before.

On the walls were symbols, runes, drawings: some older than others, some so ancient they had faded to mere outlines of the horrors they had once represented. There were winged creatures, men with the heads of animals, paintings of dead bodies, tortured men and women, decapitated children and babes.

And in the rear of the chamber was a great painting of a throne, seated in which was a familiar image. It was a winged beast with the body and arms of a man and the legs and head of a goat. Etched into his forehead was a pentagram and in his hand he held, perhaps most bizarrely of all, a cross. Opened before him was a great book, one of arcane and tenebrous lore no doubt. The golden letters seemed to shine in the dark twilight of that cavern, and I was glad the words they formed were of a language I did not understand, even if they were somehow oddly familiar.

"God, Lily . . ." I whispered. She barely seemed to notice. "Lily, we shouldn't be here," I said.

"No, you shouldn't," a high, cold voice echoed from behind us. We both turned. Abbess Batory was standing in the doorway, holding a lantern. I felt Lily move close beside me. We stood there for a second, starting at the Abbess. I felt Lily's hand slip into my pocket, and when she removed it, my coat was heavier than it had been before.

"Lily, leave us," the Abbess commanded. "I will deal with you later."

"Yes, Abbess," Lily said with a bow. She exited then, never looking up from her feet as she went, never glancing back at me or the Abbess. For her part, the Abbess never took her eyes off of me. I waited for the worst.

"Well, Mr. Lincoln, it appears your corrupting influence has taken hold over the youngest of my charges."

"Abbess Batory, I . . ."

She lifted her hand quickly to indicate no explanation was desired. In any event, none would suffice.

"She is a child, Mr. Lincoln. And, doubly that, she is a child of God. Thus, your corruption is doubly damned. Of course, I should not expect a wanderer such as yourself to respect her commitment."

"Is that so, Abbess?" I said, more boldly than perhaps I should. "What of yourself, then? What is your view on commitment? Or is your sudden interest in Vladimir's travels to the exclusion of the rest of us as innocent as you feign?"

For a moment she merely stared at me, a penetrating gaze of death she had apparently perfected over her years of command. But then, surprisingly perhaps — or perhaps not — she smiled. The smile was as steely cold as her icy, pale blue eyes.

"There are," she said, stepping down from the stairs and into the pit, "a multitude of commitments. Some holy. Some not. I do not know if I approve of your Lord Charles, but he is no Vladimir. And of Vladimir, I have no use."

She now stood in the center of that ungodly pit, a symbol of holiness in a most unholy place.

"Well, Mr. Lincoln, I suppose this is my fault," she said, her demeanor softening. "Your curiosity was bound to get the better of you eventually. So I will answer your questions now, to the extent you have them."

"I suppose I would start with the obvious."

"Yes," she said with a smile, "I suppose you would." She walked around the chamber looking with evident disgust at the paintings and engravings on the walls. "Every place," she said, turning to me, "has its superstitions, its secrets. But in some places, those superstitions and secrets are true. Such it is with this mountain. This is an old place, Daniel. Where you stand now was carved into this mountain long before the birth of Christ. From it, evil has long emanated. Do you know what this is?"

"A temple of some sort?" I said.

"That is partly true, but it is more than that. The name of it is whispered amongst Christian men, and even those who serve the darkness do not speak it lightly. It is the Scholomance."

I knew nothing of the occult then, but even I had heard the dark tidings of that place. The stories were so outrageous they couldn't help but contain some kernel of truth. A school of the blackest, foulest magic, taught by the Devil himself. It was a focal point of evil, a den of sin and iniquity. I shuddered to think I stood in that place at that moment and such an innocent as Lily had led me there.

"I see from your face you have heard of this place," the Abbess said as she walked along the outer wall. "Ten at a time they would admit, the scholars who would learn the Devil's ways. But only nine would leave. That is the price of immortal knowledge. One would be sacrificed to the dark lord of this chamber."

She rubbed her hands along an indentation that had been carved into the far wall. "They kept the books here, you know?" she said, almost wistfully. "Ancient tomes, scrolls. I wonder where they went. Burned, I hope. Burned away into dust, burned with their owners. But probably not," she said, whipping around to face me again. "Do you know your Bible, Daniel?"

That question seemed to have become common. "Better than some," I said. "Not as well as others."

"Then I will quote it for you. 'And when the thousand years are expired, Satan shall be loosed out of his prison, and shall go out to deceive the nations which are in the four quarters of the Earth, Gog, and Magog, to gather them together to battle: the number of whom is as the sand of the sea.' Gog and Magog," she said. I simply stood there, waiting for explanation. "That all the Scriptures are truth cannot be denied, but not all truth is revealed in scripture. Do you understand now?" she asked.

I shook my head as I still did not.

She sighed, leaning against the wall. Then she said, "Revelations speaks of two great beasts, one to rule the Earth and one to rule the sea." She quoted again, "Then I saw another beast, coming out of the Earth. He had two horns like a lamb, but he spoke like a dragon." The ancients speak of these two beasts, as well. That this is the Scholomance is truth, but what is also true is we stand today in the Temple of Gog. Gog, the beast of the Earth, and Magog, the beast of the sea. They worshiped him here, long before those words were written. They awaited his return here, and Magog's, as well."

"Gog and Magog," I repeated.

"Gog and Magog, though not always by that name," she said, stepping close to me, so close I could feel her breath on my face and taste the fire of her words. "Perhaps here, perhaps then, he went by another name. They have a thousand names, yes? Some are lost. Some are still remembered. They ruled this world in days gone by. The darkness covered the Earth once, in the days before days, before God said, 'Let there be light,' and it was good. They sleep now, or so some say. Waiting to wake, waiting to retake the world that was theirs."

She stepped back. "And we stand in their way, you and I and the builders of this fortress. We didn't know when we arrived, of course. We found the corridor to this chamber blocked off. It looked as though the roof was caved in, but it was too methodically done to be an accident. And so we brought in dynamite and blasted our way through. It was then we found this. You can see now why we keep these corridors locked?"

"Yes, yes I can."

"And now that I have told you these things, I will ask you again. Please do not wander aimlessly through this castle. You never know what you might stumble upon. We should go now," she said, turning her back and climbing up the stairs. I followed her. As I did, I put one hand into my coat and felt cold metal. In the confusion, Lily had slipped the key into my pocket.

Chapter 17

"The Scholomance? Here?"

It was night. Charles and I had only been locked in our rooms a few minutes when I began to relay the events of the day. Charles had listened with growing interest, but when I mentioned the Scholomance, he could no longer remain quiet.

"And even better," I said, pulling the key out of my pocket. "We are free."

"Excellent, Daniel!" Charles said, plucking the key out of my hand. "How?"

"Lily," I said, taking it back. "And I'll hold on to that."

"Oh, Daniel, you devil," he said with a wolfish grin.

"Stones and glass houses, my friend. I propose," I continued, "that once the Sisters take to their Midnight Mass, you and I do some exploring."

* * *

The next two hours seemed to last two days. Charles and I sat on our bed, trying to pass the time through conversation.

"It's April 29," I said.

"And that is significant how?" Charles asked.

"Vladimir thinks it is significant. Tomorrow night is Walpurgis."

"Ah, yes. Vladimir is rather superstitious, don't you think?"

"He claims he is not."

"He claims he is not, but his thoughts betray him."

There was no more time for talk when the shadows of the nightly procession once again began to pass beneath our doorway.

"Shh!" Charles commanded, as if I needed the warning. We sat there in silence for several minutes, until long after the last shadow had disappeared down the hallway. Finally Charles said, "Let's go."

I walked quietly over to the doorway, sliding the key into the lock. At first the bolt resisted, and I began to wonder if the key would work. But then, the familiar sound of metal on metal, followed by the thud of the bolt withdrawing. I opened the door slowly, quietly, and looked into the corridor. It was empty and silent. The lit lanterns hanging from the wall cast shadows that danced down the hallway.

"Come on," I whispered.

We walked as quietly as possible down the corridor, though my heart thumped against my chest every time our shoes made a click-click-click sound against the stone floor.

"The chapel is down the stairs and to the right. We'll take the left side. Be very quiet," I said, as we prepared to descend. It was impossible to be silent, but I hoped the sounds of the Midnight Mass would mask any noise that we made. But despite the ongoing service, not a sound emanated from the chapel. We redoubled our efforts at stealth and crept across the open chamber, our most exposed and dangerous position, finally reaching the locked doorways along the other side.

"Which one?"

"Does it matter?" I asked.

We started at the end of the wall, determined to investigate all we could before retreating back to our room. I slid the key into the lock. We stepped inside a hallway and let the heavy wooden door close lightly behind us.

We were immersed in complete darkness. I took the lantern I had brought from the room and opened the shutters on its sides. We were standing in yet another long corridor. Tools littered the floor. Hammers, chisels, saws: all the necessities of a workman's trade. Half of the hallway had been refinished, but the rest looked as if it hadn't been touched in a hundred years.

"It's as if they started working and then one day just dropped their tools and left."

"Yes," I said, a cold chill passing through me, "that's exactly what it's like."

We walked down the hallway, past where the refurbishment had ended and opened some of the doors. They were simply empty rooms, untouched by human hands. We exited again into the main chamber. We did so quietly, although it was as deserted as before. The next door down revealed yet another corridor; the architectural plan of the castle was becoming obvious. It was the same as the last. Work had obviously been underway here, but it was never completed. The tools here were discarded as well.

Three more corridors, the same result in each. We opened the final door and slid inside. There was no corridor here. Instead, we were in what can best be described as a closet. There were crates on the floor. The lid of the one nearest us was off and sat askew on its top. Charles walked over and lifted it, placing it gently on the ground.

"What is this?" he asked, reaching inside and pulling out what looked like a perfectly round, red candle.

"That," I said as he stood up, "is dynamite."

"Dynamite?" he replied, tossing the stick nonchalantly into the air.

"Don't!" I almost yelled. It was then we heard a sound from the outside. I looked at Charles and he at me. We threw ourselves against the wall, and I shuttered the lantern. There was the sound of shuffling feet coming from just beyond where we stood.

Suddenly the long shadows we had come to know were passing underneath our door. Fortunately, none stopped. We stayed there, in the dark, for another thirty minutes or more. No sounds came from outside, and no more shadows were seen.

"Well?" Charles finally asked.

"Let's go," I replied.

We opened the door and stepped outside. Nothing. We walked quickly across the open chamber and up the stairs. In what must have been only moments, but what seemed like hours, we reached the door to our room. I unlocked it, and we stepped inside. The door closed and securely locked, I turned to Charles.

"Exciting!" he said with a smile.

"Yes," I replied, but my mind was somewhere else. I walked to the desk and thought for a second. Something wasn't right.

"What?" Charles asked.

"I'm not sure," I replied. "You know," I said, turning back to face him, "we picked the far side of the chamber for a reason. The sisters were all in Mass, right?"

"Yes," Charles replied, not seeing my point.

"And the chapel, such that it is, is across the way."

"It is, though I will say I've never seen a more sparsely decorated chapel before in my life. Not a cross or statue in that place. It's not much more than a big room."

"Yes, yes," I said, literally brushing his comment away with my hands. "But the point is there shouldn't have been any of the sisters anywhere near us. All of their rooms are upstairs. So if they were in the chapel, why would they be walking anywhere near that door?"

Now Charles understood. He furrowed his brow and said, "And, if they weren't in the chapel . . ."

"Then where were they?"

Somewhere in the mountains, a wolf howled.

* * *

We slept fitfully that night, and although I was tired, I woke well before any of the sisters came to bring us to breakfast. I was surprised to see Charles sitting at the table across the room. If he had slept at all, I couldn't tell.

"We can't stay here, Daniel. We can't stay here any longer."

"Charles, let's be reasonable," I said. "The priest will be back soon, and when he does, they'll clear the road, and we can go."

"Wait? For the priest to come back? Do you think he will bring the workers back with him? What happened to them, Daniel?"

"Look. They found the Scholomance. The people here are superstitious. It's no surprise they fled."

"No, I think it's more than that. This place has a strange feel to it. You and I both know that. Vladimir has felt it, too. I don't trust the Abbess. Everything is wrong here. Where were they last night? They weren't in the chapel. Where are the crosses? The saints? Stained glass?"

"Stained glass?" I said. "Charles, it's a fortress. It's a place of war. One day it may have all those things. But not yet. As for last night, I can't explain that either. But let's take a moment. Where would we go? We can't cross the pass."

"I don't care about that anymore, Daniel. There's more. I've been talking to Anna."

"Oh, Charles, please don't tell me you plan on taking her with us."

"That's exactly what I intend!" he said, looking up at me. "I've come to know her, Daniel. Vladimir is a cruel man, an evil man. She's afraid of him and with good reason. I can't just leave her behind. Even if what you say is true, even if the Abbess is everything she says she is, one day that priest will return. And when the road is clear, they will travel on to Czernowitz, and then she will be lost forever."

I sat on the bed and Charles at the desk. We didn't speak for some time. What could I say to that? No matter how foolish I might think his relationship with Anna, it didn't take her words to convince me Vladimir was a man to be feared. So, though this was insanity, I could think of no other option but to help Charles all that I could.

"Fine, fine. What do we do?"

"I've thought about that. Tonight is Walpurgis Night. I expect Vladimir will be more distracted than usual. That will help us. I say we wait until the Midnight Mass has begun. Then we go to Anna's room and get to the stables. We take some horses and ride all night. By the time anyone knows we are gone, we will be well on our way back to Budapest. From there, we head back to Venice. You go to America, and I to England. If Vladimir finds me, if he even bothers to follow, at least it will be on my ground."

In a hundred ways, it was an insane plan . . . but a sound one nonetheless. There was the danger, of course, that we would be discovered in our escape. However, given our success the night before, that was unlikely. Once we had the horses, we would have only the wolves to fear. And as long as we kept moving, I was fairly certain they would not dare to challenge us.

"Alright," I said finally. "Alright, let's do it."

Now Charles smiled. "Thank you, my friend, thank you."

"I don't know if it will work, Charles. But we will do what we can."

"There is another complication, isn't there?"

"What is that?"

"Lily."

Yes, Lily. I had thought of her myself. Could I take her? Should I? I wasn't sure, but there was little time to think.

"I will speak to her," I said at last. "If she wishes to come, I will take her."

"Can you trust her?"

"Yes, she is trustworthy," I said, although I was not convinced. "She may not come with us, but neither will she reveal us."

"Good," he said. "Then we ride at midnight."

* * *

Breakfast came quickly that morning, pressed forward by the dread we both felt at revealing to the women who only recently came into our lives our plans for escape. I wondered what Anna would say, and I was entirely unclear as to what Lily's reply would be. Were it not that she had already shown herself to be a rebel, I would have fully expected her to alert Abbess Batory to our plans.

Things went as well as could be expected. We arrived. Lily was waiting. Abbess Batory called for Vladimir. He went. We sprung into action.

"Good morning, Daniel," Lily said with a smile. "Did you sleep well?"

"Lily," I said sternly. She heard in my voice that not all was well, and the smile faded from her face.

"What is it, Daniel? Whatever it is, you should tell me."

"We are leaving tonight, Lily," I said. I saw her countenance fall and the blood drain from her face.

"No," she said, almost falling into tears. "You can't leave me." With that she grasped my hand. I immediately looked around, but no one was watching. I pulled my hand away, nonetheless.

"Shh, it's alright. We want you to come with us."

Now she was simply confused. "What? Me?"

"This is all coming out wrong," I said. "We must leave tonight. Vladimir is an evil man, Lily, and we have to get Anna away. She's coming with us. Your fate is in your own hands. I'm not telling you to come. But if you want to leave, we want you with us."

For a moment, she paused. It was so much for her young mind to process. So much. But I suppose it all came down to one question.

"Daniel," she said solemnly. "Do you want me to come with you?"

I started to answer, but she put up her hand. "Do *you*, Daniel, do you want me to come?"

I didn't hesitate, lest she see in that hesitation the doubt I felt. "Yes, Lily. I want you to come with me."

"Then, I will come. When do we leave?"

"Tonight, after the Midnight Mass begins. That's our chance. That's when we go."

"Alright Daniel, midnight it is."

* * *

The remainder of the day crawled by at a maddeningly slow pace. Anna agreed as heartily to our proposal as Lily. Now, it was merely a matter of waiting.

"We cannot take our baggage," Charles said, going over our plan yet again. The sun had long sunk behind the mountain top, but midnight could not come soon enough. "We'll take my pistols. One each. I intend no confrontation with Vladimir. But, if it comes, we will be prepared, and it will be his last."

It was only then I truly began to comprehend what we were doing. This was to be a daring escape, despite the ease with which I still believed it would occur. Even if Vladimir became suspicious, he would be locked securely in his room. The sisters would never notice our absence or Lily's. Yet we were stealing four horses from an Abbey, debasing a novice, and robbing a man of his fiancée. If we were captured, the consequences could not be imagined. And if Charles were to murder Vladimir, as he seemed quite willing to do, we might both hang for it.

I dreaded the coming of midnight as much as I wished its arrival. But time is inexorable, and come it did. We waited quietly in our room, the lantern shuttered as if we were asleep. As the hour arrived, like clockwork, the procession of shadows past our door started. One after another, they floated silently by. And then, as quickly as they had begun, they stopped.

Now we sprang to action. We tried to stay quiet, but there was no time to lose. We took very little, dressing quickly and throwing on our warmest traveling cloaks.

"Daniel, here," Charles said, pushing a pistol into my hand. "Use it only if necessary."

"Of course," I said, taking it with more than a little unease.

"Shall we?"

I simply nodded, pulling the key from my pocket and opening the door, as quietly as such a thing would allow. We stepped out into the corridor. Nothing moved below, or if it did, it was silent in the moving. I looked at Charles. He simply nodded. We moved along the corridor, tiptoeing past Vladimir's room and on to Anna's. She was to meet us there, ready to travel, and then we would pick up Lily.

We reached Anna's room with no trouble. Vladimir was either

asleep or had not noticed us. I slipped the key into the door and opened it. The room was empty.

Charles looked sick. "Anna!" he whispered, though louder than he should have. There was nowhere in that small chamber for her to hide. Her overcoat was laid on her bed, as if she had been ready to leave at a moment's notice. Yet she was gone.

"Where could she be?" Charles asked, desperation sneaking into his voice.

"Could she be with Vladimir? Perhaps he grew suspicious."

"No, Daniel, Batory would never allow it. And besides, she knew we were coming for her tonight. If she could have been here, she would have."

Charles was shaking now, and I put my hand on his shoulder in a vain attempt to comfort him. "Let's go get Lily, Charles. Then we will find her."

For a second he stood there, and I knew he didn't want to go. "Yes," he said finally. "Let's get Lily."

We exited back into the corridor, closing the door behind us. We crept on down the hall to the room in which Lily slept. I knocked gently on the door. Three quick raps, as I told her I would. Then I slid the key in the lock and opened the door to her room. It, too, was empty. Everything was prepared for her departure. There was even a letter on her desk, explaining to the Abbess her decision to leave.

"What devilry is this?"

"God, Charles, what do we do?"

"We go to Vladimir's room," Charles said.

"Are you sure?"

"The doors were locked. The girls are gone. Something is amiss, something more serious than we imagined. We go to Vladimir's room, and we move on from there. The time for discretion is at an end. We must be men of action now. Whatever may come."

Charles would not be denied, and I was not the man to deny him in any event. We left Lily's room behind, not bothering to close and lock the door. When we reached Vladimir's room, Charles pulled out his pistol and glanced at me. The silent command was obvious. I removed the gun from my coat pocket. Charles nodded to me once. I stuck the key in the lock, turning it quickly. At the click of the tumblers, Charles threw open the door and leapt into the room. Like the two before it, the room was empty.

Chapter

18

"Impossible," I muttered. "Where could he have gone?"

Charles didn't answer. He simply stood there, clutching the grip of his pistol.

"There's only one answer," he finally said. "How many keys, Daniel?"

"Keys?"

"To these doors? How many keys?"

"Two, or so Lily said," I answered.

"And you have one, and Batory has one, correct?"

"Yes, correct."

"Well, all the doors were locked. Anna's, Lily's, and now Vladimir's. You didn't lock them, and you didn't take them. Batory must have."

"Batory?" I asked, still confused.

"Don't you see?" Charles said, taking a step towards me. "Vladimir talks to her every morning. What do you think they discussed? Vladimir saw this coming. He knew what we would do. She is in league with him. We must find them now and take Lily and Anna. I'm sorry, Daniel. I know you didn't want it to come to this. But we have no other choice."

"No," I said, still trying to comprehend it all. "No, we must act. We have no other choice."

"No other choice," Charles said. "Come, it's time we went to Mass."

For a moment, that old smile returned. But there was little time for such sentiment. Charles led the way. We rushed into the corridor and down the steps, no longer attempting to disguise our movements. We ran to the chapel and threw open the doors. I suppose we should have expected it. The chapel was empty. Charles was dumbfounded.

"Impossible," he said. "Impossible!" he repeated this time in a yell. "Where could they be?"

We stood there in silence. They were not in the dining hall; we could see it from the chapel doorway. None of the other rooms could hold them all; none we had seen, at least. A thought began to creep into my mind — a terrible thought, an impossible thought. But there was no other real possibility, none we knew about.

"Charles," I began softly. "What about the Scholomance?"

Charles looked at me as if I had gone mad. "The Scholomance?" he whispered. But then I saw him work it out in his mind, saw him consider the other options and realize there were none. "Daniel, what have we done?" he asked, looking up at me.

"I don't know, Charles. But we are in it now. We might as well see it through."

"Yes," he said slowly. And then more surely: "Let's go."

We walked now, down to the corridor that led to the Scholomance. I allowed myself a moment to realize the storage room we had found ourselves in only a night before sat beside that door. It was clear to me where the shadows came from while we were locked inside.

We walked down the hallway to the winding staircase, and in no time at all we had reached the portal to the Scholomance. We pulled out our pistols once again and braced ourselves for combat. I slipped the key inside and threw the door open. We rushed into the corridor beyond, leaping into the high vaulted chamber of the Scholomance. As I had expected somewhere deep in the recesses of my mind, it was empty.

Charles slumped against the outer wall, uttering the most pathetic sounding "no" I had ever heard. I stood in the middle. Somehow, I wasn't concerned. Something was working in the back of my mind, something that had been there since the first moment I had entered this room.

"All is lost!" Charles wailed.

"Shh!" I spat violently. "Hush your whining, Charles."

For a moment I regretted the tone, but then my mind went back to work, and Charles's silence was a blessing. I looked around the chamber. I looked at the unholy etchings on the wall, at the indentations in the stone where unnamable books had once sat. My eyes scanned the room, finally resting on the massive mural of Lucifer on the far wall. Then, I saw it.

"Charles," I said.

"What?" he asked tersely.

"Have you seen a crucifix? Anywhere? In this whole place?"

"No," he responded, obviously surprised. "Why?"

"I see one now."

He stood up and walked over to me. "What do you mean?"

I pointed, and his eyes followed. It was something that had stuck with me, subconsciously, an incongruity that made no sense but wasn't so obvious as to invoke my conscious mind. There, in Lucifer's left claw, was a cross.

"Why would you put a cross here, of all places?"

Charles simply shook his head. I walked up to the mural, running my hand over the wall. The cross was not painted; it was raised ever so slightly. I grasped it with my fingertips and, as I suspected, it began to turn. I spun it clockwise. And then, when it was fully inverted, it clicked into place. I heard a rumble beside me. The stone slab on which the image of Lucifer had been etched slid aside, revealing another winding staircase leading further down into the heart of the mountain. From somewhere far below, the faint sound of chanting could be heard. I looked at Charles and him at me. The fire was back in his eyes. Without a word, we began our descent.

This time we moved carefully, slowly, down the winding staircase. I found my eyes drawn to the walls. There, written in crimson, were words. Some I recognized, some I didn't. Dark words they were, names of demons and whispered works some would say were written by their hands. I remember some of them: *Saducismus Triumphatus, De Praestigiis Daemonum, Clavicula Salomonis.* Apollyon, Semiazas, Moloch, Belial.

There were many more, but they have escaped my memory now. One step at a time we went, the sounds from below growing stronger as we descended. I would tell you what they said, but it was in a language I didn't understand, an old language, an ancient tongue. Then the stairway turned sharply to the right, and the scene was unveiled before us.

* * *

I will describe the scene as I saw it, but even now I think it must have been something out of a dream, nay, a nightmare. The stairway opened into yet another cavern, this one larger than the one above. It lacked the other's decoration, but there was something about it, the smell, the look, the feel, that was sinister, evil. It was ancient, eldritch. There was a gaping hole in its center, a deep pit that, judging from the darkness that seemed to emanate from it, ran on to the very center of the Earth. But it wasn't the chamber that struck me the most. No, it was the semi-circle of women who surrounded that gaping maw.

It was, I suppose, the entire sisterhood. But you wouldn't know it. They were locked in some sort of demonic ecstasy, swaying and jerking in time to the rhythm of their own chanting. They were led by Abbess Batory who stood before them, leading them as a conductor might an orchestra. And they were all, to a woman, naked, save for long black cloaks that hung from their shoulders.

But that was not the worst of it. Were it so! Anna and Lily were there as well. Both women were tied to thick stakes that had been driven into the ground before the pit, their eyes covered by blindfolds. At least their clothes had been left to them. The same could not be said for Vladimir, whose fate was so horrific I hesitate to describe it. He had been crucified, but the cross on which he had been nailed leaned over the mouth of the pit, held back from the plunge by a single thick rope tied to the rock behind it. Vladimir's skin had been slashed, and the blood flowed in torrents from his body down into the void below him.

For minutes we stood there, shocked into silence at what we saw. The ritual continued before us. Finally, Charles pulled out his pistol and fired a shot. The roar of the gun rent the air, and the rhythmic chants screeched to a halt. All eyes were suddenly on us, all that is, except Abbess Batory's. She stood, back turned to us, before slowly turning to face where we waited. She looked at us, her cold, dead stare boring a hole in me. Then, she smiled.

"Daniel!" Lily screamed.

"What in God's name!" Charles yelled.

"God?" Batory said with a sinister grin. "There is no god here. Not yet."

"Free them," Charles commanded, leveling his pistol at Batory. "Free them now!"

Batory jerked her head to the right, and two of the women advanced. They did not release the girls, but they did remove their blindfolds.

"Look upon your lovers. Look upon them before they die."

"I said to free them," Charles spat.

"Ah, Lord Charles. So used to command. So used to getting exactly what you want. Not tonight, not tonight. Tonight is Walpurgis, and they are my guests. You may not have them."

Charles cocked his pistol. At that moment, the sisters who had removed the blindfolds of the two women pulled sharp, curved blades from their cloaks, pressing them tightly against the girls' throats. I shuddered as the point of one drew a drop of blood from Lily's neck.

"No!" Charles screamed.

"It appears we're at an impasse. But it is no matter. Stay, and witness the rebirth of he who walks in shadow."

"You are insane," Charles spat.

"No, my ignorant child. The insane live in a world that is not. We see the world as it will be. You will see it, too."

"Free her!" he commanded, once again.

Batory merely smiled. "Certainly," she said. "She is not needed. Vladimir will suffice. Place your weapon on the ground and come for her. Daniel, you do the same. Leave your weapon behind, and free the one you love. You have my word I will not harm you."

"No," I whispered.

"Alright," Charles yelled to Batory, ignoring me. "Alright," he repeated, as he knelt down to place his pistol on the ground.

"No!" I said, grabbing Charles by the arm. He turned and looked at me, his eyes determined, yet resigned, to whatever fate would come. "I must, Daniel," he whispered pitifully. "I will either save her or I won't. I'll either live, or I won't. But without her, there is no point in escaping."

He was irrational, but at that moment, argument was useless. I released his arm. He nodded once to me, giving the best half-smile he could muster in that moment. And then he was gone, walking gingerly around the pit in the center of the chamber. I reached down and grabbed the pistol he had left on the ground.

Batory watched Charles as he walked, but none of the other women moved. As he approached the pole to which Anna was tied, the woman who stood behind her removed the knife from her throat, stepping back into the group surrounding them.

Charles ran to her, ripping the bonds that held her to the stake, speaking to her as he did, but in words I could not hear. Then, she was free. I saw them embrace. For one golden moment, I felt the love between them. But then I saw one of Anna's hands fall to her side. When it rose again it wasn't empty. There was a flash of light as fire glinted off steel. Then it was gone as her hand fell again, this time with purpose.

I saw Charles jerk backward, saw the look of shock in his face, watched as Anna seemed to drag her hand along his back, and finally felt myself sicken as the blood poured from the gash she had carved to the stone floor below. Charles collapsed to the ground.

Batory's cackle echoed throughout the chamber.

"Foolish," she said, looking from Charles's writhing body to me. "We tried before, you know. A year ago today. We read the ancient rights, made the sacrifice as it was prescribed. But, you know, the storybooks are wrong. The darkness does not call for the blood of a virgin; it does not seek the life of an innocent. So when we sacrificed Father Kramer, our offering was rejected. No, the darkest magic calls for the darkest soul. But how to attain that? How to harvest one such as this?" she said, gesturing toward Vladimir who still moaned and bled from his perch above the pit.

"Do not mourn for him," she said, seeing my eyes drawn to Vladimir's dying body. "How many lives has he snuffed out? How many have given their blood so he could have his fortune? You will never know, but believe this — there are few souls as dark as his. Anna was our hunter," she said turning to the girl, "and she did well to bag her quarry."

"And what of us?" I asked. "Why are we here?"

Batory turned back to me and arched one eyebrow. "Well, Mr. Lincoln, I don't know. Why are you here? We did nothing to draw you. You came of your own accord. Fate alone brought you."

"What now?"

"Yes, what now," she repeated, as she walked over to where Charles lay. "Your friend," she almost moaned, "his was always to die. Too noble, this one. His breed is too single-minded, too unbending. Death was always his muse, and death has come for him. But you," she said, looking up at me, "you, Daniel, are different. I sense in you a desire to seek the truth, whether it be in the light or the darkness."

"What is the truth?" I asked, tightening my grip on my pistol as I spoke.

"The truth?" she asked. "The Christian age has ended. When John wrote Revelation, he did not see a vision of the end of the world. Not the physical one, at least. No, his was a story of rebirth. Long have they slept, Daniel, the ancient lords of this world. Too long. But their return is upon us. Accept that now, and stand with us. She can be yours, Daniel," she said, pointing to Lily. "I can make it so. He can make it so."

I stood there in silence as she spoke. There was something in her voice, something that drew me, despite all of my being crying out against her words.

"I was once like you," she said. "Afraid, enslaved by those who came before. But when I arrived here, he came to me in my dreams. I saw this place, buried deep beneath the mountain. We found it. The workers, they ran. Their superstitions told them to fear this place. But I wasn't afraid. No, I embraced it. Now I will bring him back. The lord of the Earth. Gog, Lucifer, Temeluchus, Vaspasian, Marluk, and a thousand other names in tongues long dead. When he is risen, he shall call forth the Great Old One, he who sleeps beneath the waves in the City of the Dead, the City of Darkness, until death itself passes away.

"He shall rise, and the shade will cover the Earth again, as it did in the old times, before the slave God split the darkness, speaking light into the night."

"No," I stuttered in reply, breaking from the web she wove around my mind. "No, this is all insane. You've gone mad and taken them with you. But I'll have none of it. Release her!" I commanded, once again leveling my pistol at Batory. She began to laugh.

"Would you kill me then, Daniel? Would you kill us all?" As she spoke, the numberless other women in the room removed the same long, curved blades as Anna had held. There were too many of them, and if Batory gave the command, my fate would be sealed.

"What you do does not matter. The sacrifice is nearly

complete." She pulled the same long knife from inside her cloak and grabbed the rope holding Vladimir over the pit. With one swift slash she cut the rope from its mooring. Only her holding the top half kept the cross from plunging into the abyss below.

"When we are finished here, we will have immortality. And not a vain promise of such — a fantasy, a dream of another world. No, we will rule here. For all time."

Now she turned from me and held her free hand up to the sky. From deep within her came guttural cries. Words I suppose, but of an old tongue, one I doubted had ever been spoken by the mouth of man. I looked from her to Lily. There was resignation in her face, sadness too, but strangely, no fear. She looked at me with a cold determination, a commanding look that said I was to do as she wished. She mouthed one word, "Run!"

I looked from her to where Charles lay. He was moving now. Then he looked up at me and winked. I cocked my head to the side, confused. But it was then I saw the long, slender stick he held — the dynamite from the night before.

Things moved quickly. Charles had a match in his hand. I knew several things at once. This was my only hope, and if the women saw what Charles was doing, all would be lost. I also knew there would be no saving Lily. But I determined in that moment if she would die, those responsible for her demise would taste death first.

"Batory!" I cried.

She looked down at me and smiled. I raised the pistol in my right hand, aimed at her chest, and fired. The sound of the gun echoed like cannon fire throughout the chamber. Then there was silence. Batory stood her ground, a look of shock spreading over her face as quickly as the circle of crimson grew across her chest.

The next few seconds were a blur. In the corner of my eye, I saw the flickering light of the now-lit dynamite. Charles had collapsed, apparently having given his last breath for the act. Batory fell to her knees, and her grip released on the rope she held, plunging cross and Vladimir into the darkness below. Almost in unison, the other women howled with unnatural might.

I leveled my pistol again, striking down the woman who stood closest to me — Anna. Then, I fired wildly, fired until the hammer of the pistol merely clicked against the empty chambers. I looked at Lily, one last time.

"Go!" she screamed.

I should have stayed, I should have tried to save her, even if any attempt was impossible. Instead I ran, as fast as my legs could carry me, up the spiraling steps, through the secret door. As it slammed behind me, there was a rumble from below, and then the whole Earth began to shake. I ran out of the Scholomance, up to the world above, while it seemed as though the entire mountain was collapsing behind me.

What happened next is shrouded in haze. I left that fortress behind, saddling one of the horses in the stable and riding it out of the gates and down the mountain. I have told you the things I saw that night inside that chamber. But the specters that floated down around me on that ride, the howling wolf that dogged my steps, the flying beast that soared against the Beltane moon, those things I will take to my grave.

I reached the village below after sunrise. Just beyond the edge of town, my horse fell dead beneath me. I suppose I was lucky he made it that far. I walked aimlessly down the main street, my mind no longer working. The innkeeper met me.

"You must not stay here tonight," he said.

Bless that man. I might not be here without him. He put me on the first coach to Budapest with strict instructions I was to be placed on a train to Venice as soon as I arrived. He paid for all of my accommodations, a cost I would reimburse him for generously in days gone by.

In three days, I arrived in Venice. There, Lawrence nursed me back to health. I credit him this — he never asked me what happened, never inquired as to what I saw. Two weeks later, he transported me to Rome, primarily so he could tell my father without falsehood my tour was complete.

In all those days that followed, though, I never slept through the night. Never completely. I would always awake, screaming for Lily, sobbing uncontrollably. Those terrors come less frequently now. But sometimes, when the night is right and the moon is full, I find myself transported back to that place. I hear that sound, that awful sound that robbed me of my mind and nearly cost me my sanity in the years afterward.

For I have neglected one part of my story. The pit must have been deep, and Vladimir's fall long, but as I ran up the stairs, his body must have finally reached the bottom of that ungodly chasm. In the long second between when I reached the summit of those steps, but before the sound of Charles' explosion filled the air, another roar split the night, the same roar that haunts my dreams.

An unearthly cry, an otherworldly thunder, the deep and impossible howl of a beast awakening in the heart of the abyss.

Part IV

Chapter
19

Carter Weston:

The bartender threw another log on the fire, and as he did, the already burning wood cracked and spat embers into the air. They burned for a moment, lived for only an instant, before vanishing into the night. The wind blew with its greatest intensity, and the snow fell in sheets. The heart of the storm was upon us, revealing that its earlier fury had been only a preview of things to come.

Daniel sat silently now, the blood having long ago left his face and hands. He had relived the ordeal in the telling, and to my eyes, it appeared it had taken all his strength to complete it.

"It is fortunate," Captain Gray said, "that a man with your particular interests came upon us tonight. I would say," he said, holding a thick cigar he had recently lit in the air, "it was fate. Do you believe in such things?" he asked.

"Well, sir," I replied, glad he had not asked about the fantastic story that had just been told, "It would be presumptuous of me, I think, to make a judgment on such topics, at my age. While I feel as though I have seen many things, I am learning there is much more to encounter."

Captain Gray smiled, taking a long draw on his cigar. "And that is wisdom, my young companion. Wisdom, indeed. Well, my friends," he said, turning to the others. "It is late, but the storm is at its worst. I believe there is time for one more tale, one more story for our young friend."

"Yes," William said, "and even if there were no storm, I would insist he hear my words."

William looked at me, and in his eyes I saw the same steely resolve to impart some wisdom to me that had been in those of the others. I appreciated what they were doing, as much as I didn't understand why they were doing it.

"It is, indeed, fate that you have come here," William continued, "for you and I are not all that different."

I leaned forward in my chair. As the winter tempest fell upon us in its greatest fury, William transported us back into the past.

Chapter 20

William:

I was a student then, much like you, finishing a course of study in medicine of the brain. Something had always drawn me to the insane, to those creatures in human form whose minds, and sometimes souls, I fear, are lost. Of course, the best place to study such a — how shall we say it — delicate subject was the same institution that drew you, Miskatonic University. A strange place that was filled with mystery and dark secrets. Those of us in the sciences always felt ostracized, distant from Miskatonic's more esoteric pursuits. I muddled through, though I was never more than an outsider.

It was the fall of my senior year when the head of my department, Dr. Seward, called me to his estate for dinner. Dr. Seward was a leader in his field, a true visionary in the study of that greatest of mysteries: man's unfathomable mind.

"Ah, Dr. Hamilton," I remember he said as I arrived at his door. "Please, come in."

I walked into his modestly furnished home. The smell of fine fare wafted in from the kitchen where his wife was busy at work.

"Come into my office. I have something I want to discuss with you."

I followed Dr. Seward into an adjacent room, one well apportioned with the latest works in our field, many of which I had read myself in my studies. Dr. Seward poured a glass of brandy and handed it to me. He made another for himself and sat down.

"I received a letter today, one that instantly made me think of you. Tell me, William, what are your plans when you finish your studies?"

"Well sir," I said, "I had intended to find a position at an asylum. I would like to work with patients. I was never one for the University."

"Exactly as I had thought," he said, leaning forward in his seat. "A colleague of mine, Dr. Harker, is the head of the asylum the state opened a few years ago. The one up in Danvers. It appears he is interested in hiring an apprentice. I believe this represents an invaluable opportunity."

"I don't know what to say," I responded, shocked and excited by this unexpected possibility.

"A position at a place such as Danvers is not for everyone," he said, his tone suddenly turning darker. "It can weigh on a man, make him question many things. Are you a man of faith?" he asked.

"Yes sir. I would say that I am."

The doctor nodded his head several times and said, "I can tell you this. If you decide to remain in this profession, that faith will be tested. You will see things that will shake you to your very core, that will make you question whether a just God can exist. The brain," he said, pointing to his temple, "is a grand mystery. For it is what is inside we seek to understand. There are no miracles, my friend. If the people within the walls of an asylum are to ever regain their being — their souls, if you so desire — it will be as a result of our pursuits. Prayers, unless they are made to us, are unavailing."

"I take it then, you do not believe?" I asked.

I expected a quick response, as the doctor had made his lack of faith quiet clear. But instead he sat still for a moment, staring at me but not really seeing.

"No, Dr. Hamilton," he replied finally, "no, I believe there is something greater than you or me. But I have seen enough that I do not necessarily believe whatever that is must be good." Then the doctor smiled. "Enough of such talk. So I can count on you then?"

"When would they have me start?"

"Why, immediately."

"Immediately," I said, more than a little disappointed. "I don't think that will be possible. As you know, I won't graduate until the end of next term."

"Oh," he said, raising his hand as if he was physically brushing away this problem, "I can take care of that. If you want the position, then it is yours."

There was no need to think it over.

"Of course, sir. I'd be honored."

"Excellent," he replied. "You won't regret it, Dr. Hamilton."

* * *

Eight short days later, a carriage arrived in Arkham Green to convey myself and a small bag of my clothing and personal belongings to the Danvers State Insane Asylum. It was raining that afternoon, a late fall downpour. Despite my enthusiasm for what lay before me, I could feel my apprehension growing, as the latent fears and doubts within my soul seemed to gain strength with every drop of falling rain.

We drove away from Miskatonic, from the place I had spent the better part of four years, and on to an unknown future, the dawning of my career in medicine. We rode along the banks of the Miskatonic River for some time, finally crossing the unending flow and passing into the Makitan Forest. I need not tell to you what dark words are spoken of that place, of the arcane rites the students of Miskatonic claim are performed there. I averted my eyes until we were far afield of that accursed forest.

We traveled farther into the country, until the only signs of human habitation were the rock walls bordering the road and high roofs of the occasional barn. I watched the rain fall through the carriage window until finally, after what seemed like an eternity of back roads and desolate countryside, I saw it. The asylum was a city on a hill, a shining palace, sitting like the home of some medieval lord on the summit of a high mass of rock and soil. It was massive, a turreted and gabled masterpiece. But, in my mind and heart, I knew the beauty without concealed a great evil within.

The carriage began its climb up the tall hill, passing through the gates and past a sign that read, "Welcome to the Danvers State Insane Asylum." Up we climbed, the massive structure looming larger in the ever-shortening distance. Then, I saw something that, to this point in our travels, we had not encountered. A horse-drawn cart was coming down the hill. Our carriage was forced to pull to the side, as the cart itself was too large to pass. I watched as it rode by, driven by a large man in a thick rain coat. A priest sat at his side. It was the cargo, though, that caught my interest the most. In the back of the cart was a long wooden box that could only be one thing: a coffin.

Apparently the asylum cemetery lay just below where we had passed. A body would be interred that day, a life lost, with no one but the grave digger and a man of God present to acknowledge its existence. But I rapidly forgot that thought as the horses pulled again, and we climbed the last few hundred feet to the entrance of the asylum.

The road curved upward, then flattened out. Before long we entered a long driveway. It was shaded by trees on either side, trees that, despite their apparent youth, nevertheless stood tall and true over the approach to the hospital. One, in particular, was different from the rest. A tall, rugged oak. Unlike the others, it was ancient with strong, thick branches pointed down to the Earth. I admired it as we went, but before I knew it, we had exited the trees' protective cover. As the rain thundered down around us, we pulled into the semi-circular drive in front of the main entrance.

I opened the door to the carriage and stepped out into the rain, walking quickly to the awning that covered the asylum's front vestibule. My driver brought the bag in which resided all of my life's possessions. He dropped it with a thud onto the ground. I removed a coin from my waistcoat and gave it to him. He tipped his cap and turned to go. I watched the carriage pull away into the coming night, and in that moment, I was completely alone. I walked to the entrance and opened the door. My adventure had begun.

Chapter 21

I was immediately surprised by what I saw. The entranceway was larger and brighter than I had expected, with a great vaulted ceiling rising up above me. A man in a suit stood a few feet away, speaking cheerfully to a woman who was clearly a nurse. I stood in the doorway for a moment until he sensed me. He looked up from the woman, studied me for a second, and smiled.

"Dr. Hamilton, I presume," he said, striding over, thrusting out his hand to grasp mine.

"Yes, sir," I replied, "though please, call me William."

"William it is then," he said, never releasing my hand. "I am Dr. Harker. Follow me."

Dr. Harker moved quickly — this was a man who walked with a purpose — toward the grand staircase sitting at the end of the equally grand entranceway. I followed, surveying as I went. It was a beautiful room, richly apportioned as if one were entering the finest hotel. A concession to visitors, no doubt.

The hospital itself lay farther on behind a heavy door at the far end of the entranceway. That steel curtain made me doubt anything beyond would resemble this room. We walked up the stairs to a series of offices on the second floor. Dr. Harker produced a key from his pocket and opened one, gesturing inside.

I had a seat behind the doctor's desk. I couldn't help but notice the human skull sitting on the corner closest to me. As he walked to his chair, the doctor noticed my gaze.

"I see you are admiring one of my favorite trinkets," he said, gesturing toward it as he sat down. "Strange thing, skulls. If it were a human head sitting on my desk, no doubt you would have *me* committed, correct?" he said with a smile. "But it is a great tradition amongst learned men — doctors, lawyers, philosophers. Going back to the Greeks and maybe beyond, if you believe some of the more esoteric tales about the Egyptians."

"And why do you keep one, sir?" I asked.

"Oh, for the same reason they did," he replied. "To remind me, as it would remind them, of the transitory nature of life. It ebbs and flows, and, inevitably, it ends. Each of us will come to this. The only relevant question is whether we will end our days sealed in a coffin deep beneath the Earth or sitting on someone's desk."

"That's a rather bleak outlook, isn't it?" I said with a bit of nervous laughter.

The doctor simply smiled. He reached down and lifted an envelope off of his desk, opened it and removed the letter inside. He picked up his glasses and said, "Dr. Seward has given you quite the recommendation. I've known him for a very long time, and I can say without hesitation he is not one to give false praise. You should be proud."

"Well, sir," I said, slightly embarrassed, "I'm certainly honored Dr. Seward thinks so highly of me."

"Yes, yes," he replied, now putting his glasses back on the table. "And, in your academic pursuits, you show great promise. But I feel it is my duty to warn you. What you will see here, what you will hear, they cannot teach in books. What you will experience in this place," he continued, leaning back in his chair, "will test your commitment to this field.

"More than once I have seen bright young students walk through those doors just like you have and leave broken men. So I want you to always remember this: there may come a time when you know the clinical world is not for you. Leave then, before it is too late."

His words were stern, but I had expected them. Still, I couldn't help but feel a chill course through my body as he spoke. This very fear had haunted my steps since Dr. Seward had told me of this opportunity.

"I will do my best, sir."

Dr. Harker smiled again, this time a hopeful smile, though tinged with a touch of doubt. "Yes, my young friend. That is all we can have you do, isn't it?"

There was a quick knock on the door. "Ah, yes," Dr. Harker said before commanding, "Come in!"

The door opened and a man entered. He was tall, lean and fit, probably five or so years older than I. There was a haughtiness to him, but one not altogether disagreeable. Pride can be one of man's more distasteful attributes, but when you enter a situation in which you are unsure, as I was that day, it is comforting to have a confident companion.

"David," Dr. Harker said as he stood, walking around his desk and grasping the man's hand. "This is Dr. William Hamilton. He is joining us from Miskatonic University. I was hoping you could supply him with some of your knowledge. Dr. Winthrop here," he said, turning back to me, "is my chief assistant. One day when I am gone, he'll be in charge. For now, I want you to rely on him for any questions while you get yourself settled. And my door is always open," he said, holding out his hand.

"Of course, sir," I said, "and thank you again for this opportunity." He smiled again, and with that, I turned and left with Dr. Winthrop.

As the door closed behind us, Dr. Winthrop finally spoke.

"Welcome to Danvers, Dr. Hamilton. I must say, I cannot imagine what you must be thinking right now."

I laughed nervously. "No, sir," I said. "I don't really know what to think."

"Well, you will catch on soon enough, I have no doubt," he continued as we strolled down the main staircase. "Dr. Harker is an uncanny judge of character, and he clearly found you worthy. So," he continued, changing the subject, "I have many things to show you and more to tell you. And they are all of critical importance. Never forget where you are, Dr. Hamilton, and you will do fine."

"I'll do my best," I said, nodding once.

"This," Dr. Winthrop continued, sweeping his hand in front of him, "is main administration." He stopped and looked at me, then said cryptically, "All of this is ours."

"Ours?" I said as we stopped in the middle of the ornate entranceway.

Dr. Winthrop grinned. "The rest is theirs, Dr. Hamilton. This hospital was built to house five hundred patients. Five hundred. Half men, half women. We have nearly two thousand here now. Make no mistake about it, beyond this door," he said, pointing at the large portal in front of us, "they are in charge. We just do what we can."

Dr. Winthrop pulled two large keys from his pocket.

"These are master keys, Dr. Hamilton," he said, holding them up in the air. "These keys will open every door in this complex. Every one, save for Dr. Harker's office." He held one key out to me. As I put my hand on it, he said, "You guard this key with your life, Dr. Hamilton. No matter what happens, you must not lose it. Do you understand?"

"Yes, sir," I muttered.

"Good," he said, finally releasing his hold on the key. "I want you to note the warning," he continued, as he slipped the large skeleton into the lock. I heard the heavy tumblers rolling within. Dr. Winthrop pointed to a large sign placed in the center of the door. "BEWARE!" it screamed in great capital letters. "Patients will escape! Exercise Extreme Caution Upon Entering! Door Must Remain LOCKED!"

"This is the last barrier, the final checkpoint before escape. Always make sure this door is closed and locked." He swung the door open, gesturing me in before closing and locking it behind him. "These are the staff's quarters. The staff cafeteria is through the doors on the right," he said pointing to a large room in front of us. "You will take your meals there with the rest of us. Learn to like it. An unfortunate side-effect of our isolation is we have no other options. And that set of doors on the left is the staff dormitory."

"So, this area is sort of a central hub?"

"Exactly. Are you familiar with the work of Dr. Thomas Kirkbride?"

"Of course," I said, as Dr. Winthrop opened the door to the cafeteria so I could have a look.

"Well, as you know then, Dr. Kirkbride believes a patient's surroundings have an effect on his mental health. That's why they selected this site. They wanted tranquility, peacefulness, beauty. It also had an effect on the architecture of this place. I'm sure you noticed on your ride up that our little building is quite impressive."

"How could I not? It's like something out of a dream."

Dr. Winthrop chuckled. "That is an apt description. Anyway, as you noted, this is the central hub. Dr. Harker would tell you the hospital is designed on the shape of a bird. I've always thought it better resembles a bat. The administrative building is the body. That's where we are now. On either side of us are the two wings. The wing to your right as you go through the main door is where the women are housed. The wing on your left has the men."

We stepped back outside of the cafeteria. "I'll take you into the male wing now."

We walked to a large iron door adorned with the same sign I had seen earlier. Dr. Winthrop removed his key once again and slid it into a lock. I felt myself shiver as he did. I had done some work with patients while a student, but this was to be a totally different experience. Dr. Winthrop opened the door and in we went.

"Good afternoon, Jacob," he said to a white-coated man sitting at a desk near the door.

"Afternoon, doctor," he replied.

"How are our guests today?"

"Nothing unusual."

"Good. Jacob, I want you to meet our newest addition. This is Dr. William Hamilton."

The man nodded to me.

"My pleasure," I said with a smile. He didn't smile back.

"Jacob is one of our orderlies. He keeps things quiet around here."

Jacob coughed out a laugh. "We can barely hold on, doctor. There are just too many of them."

"I know, Jacob. Do the best you can."

Jacob simply frowned. I could tell this conversation had happened many times in the past, and the result was always the same. I looked around the corridor in which we stood. It was brighter than I had expected, with high windows arrayed along the walls. Patients, wearing ill-fitted white gowns, milled about, more or less oblivious to our presence. Dr. Winthrop said a few more words to Jacob, and we continued walking.

"Don't worry about Jacob," he said. "He is less than pleased with our current patient population."

"About that," I began, "you said earlier the hospital was designed to house five hundred, and yet you have four times that number. Why is that?"

"Honestly, you've put your finger on a bit of a mystery," he replied as we passed an elderly man sitting on the floor, rocking himself back and forth while muttering a bit of unintelligible gibberish. "We take all who come to us, of course, but we never could have predicted the last few years. It seems they come in greater numbers every month. I fear the situation will only grow worse. Sometimes, it's as if the whole world has gone mad."

As we walked toward another door at the far end of the corridor, Dr. Winthrop returned to his description of the hospital layout. "In this section," he said, "we house our most docile patients, the ones least likely to cause problems. But I caution you to remember that, although there is little to worry about here, these men and the women across the way are disturbed. Do not trust them."

We reached the other door, and Winthrop once again removed the key from his pocket. "Now, in the next corridor we have our less well behaved guests."

He slid the key in the lock and threw open the door. What met my eyes was something out of Dante's Inferno. There seemed to be ungodly screams and howls emanating from all around me. Directly in front of us, two orderlies were struggling to attach a strait jacket to a wild beast of a man. I knew now why the old London Royal Asylum had spawned the term Bedlam.

"The previous ward," Dr. Winthrop yelled above the noise, "houses the curables. Here are the incurables. Our job is not to fix these people. We treat them as humanely as possible, we study them to the extent they are interesting, and we try and keep them from killing themselves, other inmates, and most importantly, us. There will always be a large number of orderlies in this area, for obvious reasons."

We strode into the midst of that hellhole, the viscous, vulgar taunts, the hate-filled howls, the threats of violence and death. And, then, we reached another door. Dr. Winthrop unlocked it, pulled it open and gestured for me to enter. The next chamber was dramatically different. It was not, as the previous one, a dormitory. Instead, it was a short antechamber of sorts. Dr. Winthrop closed the door behind us and locked it. He then moved toward the other door only a short walk away. He unlocked and opened it, and, once again, waited for me to enter.

I was surprised at what I saw. Given the extra security provided for this section of the hospital and considering my previous experience, I had expected it to be somehow worse, louder, more frantic. Instead, it was eerily quiet, darker, the air thick and unmoving. There were no patients I could see here, and none of the rooms were open as they had been in the other wards.

Dr. Winthrop closed the door behind him, acknowledging two orderlies who stood guard at the entrance. He turned to me and said, "And this, my new friend, is the A wing. It is here where we house the particularly dangerous — the criminally insane, the psychotic."

"It's quieter than I would have expected," I said. Dr. Winthrop smiled.

"Surprising, isn't it? But no, the wildly mad are the howlers, and while they can be dangerous, theirs is a more animalistic rage. They are no more threatening than the beasts of the fields," he said as we continued to stroll, almost leisurely, through the darkened corridor. "Man has long conquered them, no? The truly dangerous are not men who have lost their ability to reason, but those who retain it while being thoroughly evil, those without remorse or compassion. No, my friend, it is not reason that separates us from the rest of the animals, it is our moral nature. It is these creatures — I dare not call them men — that are truly demonic."

As we walked, Dr. Winthrop enlightened me with the stories of horror each of the locked doors along the corridor represented. Most had murdered, many more than once. There were cannibals and demon worshipers and slaughterers of sons and daughters, mothers and fathers.

"Obviously we will start you off with the curables. Once you have been here a while, there will probably be some more difficult cases that spark your interest. Everyone has their own personal projects. You will find yours, no doubt.

"A few other things," he continued as we walked back into the main administration wing. "This is not a building. It is more like a town. We have multiple structures around the campus, including a pump house for water, greenhouse for food, machine shops, and extra staff dormitories. Basically everything you can imagine one might need. In other words, we are entirely self-sufficient. Particularly when the snows come in the winter.

"This place was built on this hill primarily for its aesthetic value. Unfortunately, the winter snows do not seem to appreciate our delicate sensibilities. There will be weeks at a time when the roads up the hill are blocked. Fortunately, there are underground tunnels connecting all of the buildings. If one wishes, there is no need to ever go outside in the winter. When the time comes, I will take you down there. Bit of a maze, that. There is another set of tunnels below that one, but I can't imagine why you would ever need to go there. Very dark, small, dirty."

After what seemed like quite a long time, we finally arrived at the room that was to be mine.

"Well, Dr. Hamilton . . ."

"Please, call me William."

"Yes, William. I am sure you are quite tired. Take the evening. We will reconvene in the morning."

With that, I was left to my own devices. Somewhere below, I heard a man scream.

Chapter 22

The next few weeks came and went in a blur. It was chaos, a rush of new names and people, of learning my role in the asylum and the nature of the patients within it. Late fall gave way to winter. The snows came early, as they often do in New England, though not in such quantity that we were isolated. Not yet, at least.

Dr. Winthrop turned out to be right; I did find a project, a patient whose particular neurosis fascinated me. It was Dr. Winthrop himself who brought him to my attention.

"I've someone I want you to talk to," he said, taking me aside after breakfast one day. "His name is Robert."

"Robert what?" I asked.

"Well, we don't really know. He's been in the care of the state for virtually all his life. He was left on our doorstep ten years ago."

"Left here? You mean he is a child?"

"Well, he's probably fifteen now."

Winthrop nodded, and for a moment I looked away. I had never dealt with a child before, and I wasn't sure I was ready.

"Anyway," he continued, "he's been with us for several years, and he's always been a model patient. Quiet, keeps to himself. Completely insane, of course. Lives in a world of his own creation. But, nonetheless, never a problem. Lately, however, he's gone into a sort of mania. He won't eat. He barely sleeps. The orderlies find him staring into the corner of his room, rocking back and forth and mumbling to himself. Frankly, we are not as concerned with that last bit as we are his appetite. If he won't eat," Dr. Winthrop said as he stopped and turned to me, "well, he won't last. Take a look at him?"

"Of course," I said, "as soon as I finish with some other things."

"Excellent," he replied, slapping me on the shoulder. "Let me know how it goes."

Three hours later, I entered the incurables ward to find my new patient.

"I'll take you to him," one of the orderlies offered.

"Why is he being kept here?" I asked as we walked towards his room. "I was under the impression he wasn't a danger."

"He never has been, sir. But Dr. Winthrop thought, with the sudden change in his behavior, it would be better to keep him in a more secure area." The man pulled out a large ring of keys from his pocket and slipped one in the door, opening it. "Just in case."

I stepped inside, and the orderly slammed the door behind me. As I heard the bolt slide in place, I looked at the boy sitting in the center of the room. It seemed he had been crying. But now he was simply sitting there, staring at nothing in particular, his arms crossed tightly across his chest. He rocked ever so slightly, but there was nothing about him that bespoke violence.

I stood there for a second, letting him, to the extent he was capable, come to accept my presence in his world. But it was clear he didn't notice me.

"Mr. Robert," I said, still not approaching, still afraid to invoke any latent rage that might be simmering beneath the surface. We had the ability to chain potentially violent patients to the wall, but Dr. Harker was deeply opposed to the practice, and so it was used only in the wing for the criminally insane. If Robert decided to attack me, there was nothing to stop him until the orderlies arrived. That would take at least a few minutes. He was only a child, that was true. But one who has never seen it cannot imagine the fury of a human being, bereft of his reason and mind, completely uncontrolled.

"I'm Dr. Hamilton. I'm here to help you."

Up until that point there was no indication he was aware, in any way, of my presence. But now he stopped rocking and looked up at me with a thoroughly blank look. Then, he smiled.

"You can't help me, doc," he said. "I've been here as long as I've been alive. Do you think you are the first?"

"Well, no," I said, taking a step closer, "but Dr. Winthrop told me something has changed recently. You're not sleeping or eating. We can't have that, Robert. We want you healthy."

The blank look had returned. He stared at me dumbly, as if nothing I said had penetrated his mind.

"My mother always told me, when I was little, before she brought me here," he said, looking up at me earnestly, but his voice had that unnerving sing-song chant the insane will often have, "if I shut my eyes and counted to ten, they would be gone when I opened them. And they always were, but now . . ."

His voice trailed off, and he simply shook his head. Then, he closed his eyes and started counting. "1 . . . 2 . . . 3 . . . " He counted in time, and I could feel a strange sense of anticipation building inside of me. I'm not sure what I expected to happen. "4 . . . 5 . . . 6 . . ." The air grew heavier, thicker, denser. "7 . . . 8 . . . 9." A shadow seemed to fall upon the room, a gloom, as if darkness were a thing itself rather than the mere absence of light. ". . . 10." Then, he opened his eyes.

For a moment he looked in mine, but then, his gaze shifted. It landed somewhere above me, somewhere beyond me. Then, his mouth fell open, and the blood left his face as he went as white as a New England winter. He scurried backwards across the floor, not stopping until his back slammed against the wall.

He buried his head in his hands, moaning and crying a string of unintelligible words. For a moment, and only for a moment really, I felt as if there was someone else in the room. The hairs on the back of my neck stood on end. It was ridiculous, my mind said, but I nevertheless found myself turning around to see what was behind me.

As I did, I thought I saw a flicker of movement in my peripheral vision, as if a bird had just flown across the back of the room. But it must have been nothing. We were, indeed, alone. I turned back to where Robert was cowering in the corner.

"Robert," I said calmly, "there is no one there. No one but me and you."

For a second, he stopped shaking, and the color came back into his face. He looked sternly at me and said, "You should say what you mean, doctor."

"What?" I asked, honestly confused.

Robert shook his head and said, "You say there is nothing there, but you mean you see nothing. It's not the same thing. I know you felt it, too."

I considered challenging him on this point, but decided such a move would not be productive.

"Alright, why don't you tell me what you see?"

Robert began to laugh, and soon that laugh had turned into a cackle. "You want me to tell you what I see?" he asked dismissively.

"Well, yes. I can't see it, but I would like to know what it is. Describe it to me."

It was a tried and true method for dealing with Robert's particular kind of psychosis. Make him describe what he saw, or what he thought he saw I should say, and the construct would fall apart. It was always easier to imagine a thing in one's mind than to describe it to another.

"Tell me, doctor," Robert began. All of the sudden, there was a coldness to his voice, a determination that was not common with the other patients I saw that suffered as he did. The insane, even those who were older, are all too often like children. And, like children, it is easy to grow attached to them, to feel as if you must protect them. My first impression of Robert was he would stay true to this form. But somehow, he was different. He had changed.

"How would you describe love to a man who has never known it, or fear to one who has never felt it? No, what I see, your mind is not capable of comprehending."

I admit, although I had been trained to control my feelings in situations such as this, at that moment, I was angry.

"You would be surprised what I can comprehend, Robert. Why don't you just try?"

He nodded once, and I saw some of the coldness, some of the distance, melt away. When he spoke, the fear had crept back into his voice.

"I see clearly," he began, "what you see darkly."

"What?" I asked softly. It was an answer unlike any I had ever heard. He spoke now in a whisper

"The shadow in the night," he said, raising his hand and waving it in front of his face, "that moves across the room, that you catch in the corner of your eye. But then you turn your head, and it's gone. You have seen it. All men have. You saw it earlier, just now."

"No," I lied, even though I wasn't sure why.

"Yes. You did. I saw it in your face. The wind blows. You see the trees bend at its touch, but you are blind to the force that moves them. I see the wind. I see the hand that smites."

"Can you describe it for me, what you see?"

Robert coughed out a laugh. "I told you I cannot. It is not of this world. A bending, curving line, a plane turned in on itself. It is an impossibility, a thing that cannot be. A shimmering darkness, a three-lobed, burning eye. That which is and is not, that was and will be."

"And you see this here, now?"

"No," he replied. "It is gone now."

"Does it see you?"

"No," he repeated, "it does not see me. It sleeps. They all sleep. We view this world through a glass, darkly. But when the sleeper is awakened, we will all see them, then. We will all see *him*, then. Clearly."

"Him?" I asked.

Now his voice fell to the barest of whispers. "The one who sleeps beneath the waves. That rests in the citadel of that ancient city, spoken of now only in legend and song. He walks in other realms, dances beneath the Beltane moon. His mind is vast, and he comes to me in my dreams. Horrible dreams, they are. Filled with violence and darkness. They hurt me," he said, his voice growing more feverish.

"Just relax, Robert."

"No, you don't understand," he screamed. "It's too much! His mind is too vast! The pain has become unbearable!"

"Become?"

"It wasn't always so," he continued, his voice falling back towards normal. "Before, it came only in flashes, only in moments. An image, a shadow. Then, it was gone. But now it fills me, it fills my mind and rips at my soul. He is the molder of dreams, and though he may sleep, the power of his intellect does not rest."

"That's why you don't sleep."

He didn't speak then, only nodded.

"Why does it grow? Why do you see it more now than you did before?"

Again, he was silent. I thought for an instant he wouldn't answer me, that I had gone too far or he had told me all he knew already. But he nodded again, as if agreeing to an unspoken request.

"That is not dead which can eternal lie. And with strange aeons, even death may die."

"I don't understand," I said.

He only smiled. "And that, doctor, is why you cannot help me." He put his head back against the wall, staring up at the ceiling. I knew he was done with me. I tried to ask him more questions, but he had no more answers. I left him with more mysteries than when I had first entered.

Chapter 23

"So how did it go?"

I'd barely slept the night before. I had been anticipating Dr. Winthrop's visit with much trepidation. My encounter with Robert had not gone as I had expected, and frankly I didn't know what to think. His mind was clearly broken, but I had not expected the clarity of his hallucinations, the detail with which he spoke, or the authority behind his words.

"I don't know what to make of it, Dr. Winthrop," I said as we walked down the hallway towards the cafeteria.

He arched one eyebrow. "Really? What do you mean?"

"Well, the way he spoke. It was unlike anything I have ever heard from a fifteen year old, particularly one who is mad. Does he have any education?"

"Education?" Dr. Winthrop repeated, sounding somewhere between surprise and disgust. "Some of the nurses may have taken pity on him at one point and taught him to read. Other than that, no."

"I just don't understand how he could manufacture the things he was saying."

"He is insane, William. Surely you are aware of their often remarkable ability to create some of the most amazing fantasies. Far better than the most accomplished poet could ever dream."

"I understand that, Dr. Winthrop. But I feel as though one

must have something to draw on, some well of inspiration. I just can't imagine what that could be for one so young."

"Did he explain why he wouldn't sleep?"

"Well," I began hesitantly, "it's his dreams."

"His dreams?"

"Apparently he suffers from nightmares. Pretty bad ones from the way he talks."

Winthrop coughed out a laugh. "I could be bounded in a nutshell," he quoted, "and count myself a king of infinite space, were it not that I have bad dreams."

"Yes, something like that," I said through a frown.

"Well, don't worry about it. I had Dr. Stevens mix up a sleeping draught. Given his insomnia over the last week, it should knock him out cold. He'll be better for it, too."

"I hope you're right, Dr. Winthrop. It will be interesting to see his reaction."

At that moment, the asylum alarm sounded. I saw the fear in Dr. Winthrop's eyes as he realized what was happening. No doubt he saw the same terror in my own. It was the first time I heard that alarm, and it could mean only that some disaster had befallen the asylum.

For a moment we hesitated, but then Dr. Winthrop ran down the hallway, and I followed closely behind. He seemed to leap down the stairs, his key in hand. No sooner had he burst through the main door than I was there, as well, stopping only to lock the portal behind me. The curable wing, normally such a calm and peaceful place, was a-gibber with shouts and activity. My clinical mind observed it would take weeks to repair the damage of this night.

"Dr. Winthrop! Dr. Hamilton!"

It was Jacob, the orderly. He rushed toward us from the incurable wing.

"It's in here, doctor," he said to Dr. Winthrop.

"What is?" Dr. Winthrop asked as we rushed to the next wing.

"I can't say, doctor. I ain't never seen nothing like it. It's awful. Simply awful."

Dr. Winthrop glanced at me. I tried to give him the most confident look I could, but he could see I was shaken.

I heard the howls and screams of the patients in the incurables wing even before Jacob threw open the door. Once inside, the bedlam was almost unbearable. There were several orderlies, each struggling to keep order with the patients. Jacob led us to one of the rooms, and I realized to my horror it was Robert's.

Jacob looked back at us both, as if to ensure we still wanted to go forward. When he saw our resolve remained strong, he turned the key in the door and flung it open.

For me, at that moment, time stood still. The noise, the violence, the insanity behind me, it all seemed to cease. In that moment, there was only me and the scene that lay before me.

I have heard men say there are things for which words are insufficient, scenes the human mind can barely comprehend, much less describe. I suppose I believed that, or at least I thought I did. But seeing is believing, as they say, and what I saw that night has never left me, though to this day I am incapable of properly describing it.

Robert sat on the floor, and I suppose if you didn't look at his face, you might think he was just resting. But that face, oh God that horrible face. It was white, pale, the color of death. As white as his face was his hair — hair that had been a lustrous black only a day before was now a color normally reserved for the oldest of men. It was his expression, though. His expression was the most horrible of all.

His mouth was open, but not just open. No, it was gaping, like a chasm in the middle of his face. Wider and more distorted than a human being should be capable of, as if the final horror had been so great as to tear the very ligaments that held his jaw in place. But it was the eyes that were the worst, his still-open eyes. If the very image of the final thing he saw had been captured there, it could not have better told the horror he must have known than those frozen, glassy eyes. Whatever cosmic evil he witnessed, I pray God I never know.

Dr. Winthrop threw himself violently to the side and began to vomit. I suppose I might have as well, but instead I collapsed mercifully into oblivion.

*   *   *

I sat in one of the large leather chairs in Dr. Harker's office. Dr. Winthrop was slouched down in the seat beside me. He rubbed his temples with his hands, and it was clear to me he had not yet recovered from what we experienced.

"Thank you for coming, Officer Braddock," Dr. Harker said to the officially-clad man standing by the door. "I know it is not an easy trip out here."

"There'll be no needin' to thank me," he said. "The Captain wanted me to let you know how much he appreciated your message. It's not often we are involved in incidents such as these."

"There's no need to thank me, either," Dr. Harker replied. "We would have handled this internally, of course, but I think it goes without saying we've never seen anything like this before."

"Not in all my days at least," said Dr. Anderson, the hospital's primary medical doctor.

Despite what had happened, there was comfort in that. Obviously, I had never encountered anything like what I saw in that room. I hoped I never would again.

I had woken some time earlier in the hospital infirmary. At first, I had no notion of how long I had been out. I had no dreams, and by my reckoning, it was but an instant. I learned only later I had slept for hours, long enough for Dr. Harker to send for a constable from the nearest town.

As he had said, it was an unusual move. The asylum was a city unto itself, a ship at sea, and Dr. Harker was its captain. Matters of life or death were under his command. When a patient died, the family of the deceased would be notified to the extent possible. If there were no family, the decedent would be buried on the asylum property with nothing but a small stone and a number to mark where he lay. The numbers corresponded to those names kept in a book in the asylum office. A fire destroyed the book containing the names of the deceased from the asylum's first five years. Those poor souls would forever remain unknown, unremembered, and unmourned.

Be that as it was, this circumstance was unique, and horribly so. It was a real mystery, and I knew Dr. Harker was more than a little concerned that foul play may have been involved. Dr. Anderson had been accustomed to performing only the barest of examinations over the deceased, but in this case, Dr. Harker had requested special diligence. We had come to Dr. Harker's office now to hear his report. Blame might also be cast, and as Robert's attending physician, more than a little blame was likely to fall on me.

"Do you still believe foul play was involved?" Braddock asked.

I saw Dr. Harker glance up uncertainly at Dr. Anderson. I recognized the look immediately. Doctors tend to be practical men. They see a problem and they fix it. Or they at least attempt to understand it. So the uncertainty of this case was unsettling to him. I think it may have even frightened him.

"The truth is," Dr. Harker finally said, "we aren't sure what to think."

"So, it could have been one of the other inmates?"

"Patients," Dr. Winthrop corrected, speaking for the first time.

"Yes, patients," Braddock repeated.

"It couldn't have been one of them," answered Dr. Winthrop. "I spoke to Jacob, one of our orderlies," he explained, "and he said Robert was locked in his room, just like he had been every night. No one went in, and he didn't go out."

"Could the orderly be lying?" Braddock asked. "After all, if he accidentally left the door open, he would have the most to lose."

"I've known Jacob for many years," Dr. Harker said dismissively, "and he wouldn't lie to us."

"Besides," Dr. Winthrop interrupted, "we were keeping Robert in the incurables wing for this very reason. For his . . . protection."

The last phrase seemed to slide off of Dr. Winthrop's tongue. He recognized the irony in his words but was too far along to change them. I saw Dr. Harker shift uneasily in his chair while Braddock twirled his pocket watch chain in his fingers absentmindedly.

"In any event," Dr. Winthrop continued after the uncomfortable moment had passed, "Jacob would have been only one of the orderlies in that wing last night. If that room had been opened, one of them would have noticed it."

"How did they find him?" Braddock asked while Dr. Harker pulled out a pipe and lit it.

"That's another thing," Dr. Winthrop said with a sigh. "Jacob said last night . . . well . . . the patients were strange, I guess."

"Strange? How so?"

"They were quiet."

"Quiet?"

"Yes, quiet. And, if you knew what normally goes on in the incurables ward, you would know that was unusual, indeed."

"That they were quiet last night?"

"Jacob said they were as quiet as the grave. He and the other orderlies discussed it. They thought something was wrong, so they kept a close watch. Jacob said he looked through the bars in Robert's door at least three or four times. He was asleep each time, but restless.

Tossing and turning. But then, as if on cue, as if they had planned it, every patient in the asylum started howling, screaming bloody murder. The orderlies tried to shut them up. It was as they ran up and down the ward, banging on every door, screaming and threatening, that Jacob glanced into Robert's room. It was then he saw him."

"Strange," Braddock said in the evening's least perceptive comment. Dr. Winthrop simply sank down further in his chair. In his mind, it seemed there was nothing more to say.

"Do you have anything to add, doctor?" Braddock said, turning to Dr. Anderson.

"I have many things to add, but I am not sure any of them will answer your questions."

"Please, doctor, whatever you have will be helpful, I am sure."

"I examined the body as soon as I could," Anderson began. "I served in the 28th, you know, as a doctor during the war. I was with them at Gettysburg, Chancellorsville, Antietam. I've seen a lot of men die, cut down by cannon shot and bullets, disease, and infection. I'm not proud to say there's not much that moves me now. But I've never seen anything like this. Not in war, not in peace."

"Could it have been a murder? Or maybe a suicide?"

Dr. Anderson shook his head.

"No. There are no signs of trauma, no outward signs of a struggle. There are no stab wounds, bullet holes. No indication he was strangled or suffocated. There's no poison in the blood, and no suggestion he was hit in the head or beaten to death."

"I've heard," I said, speaking for the first time, "if a man dies in his dreams, he dies in his waking life, as well."

Dr. Harker looked unblinkingly at me for a moment and then said, "With all due respect, Dr. Hamilton, of all the possible theories I have heard, that is the one I am least likely to believe."

"Well," Dr. Anderson interjected, "actually, the young doctor is not far off."

Dr. Harker chuckled. "How can you say that? We don't even know how he died."

"No, we know how he died. I was just getting to that. When I opened him up, his entire body cavity was filled with blood. It didn't take me long to see why. His heart had exploded."

"Exploded?" Dr. Harker exclaimed, sitting forward in his chair. "How is that possible?"

"Given what we know, that there was no outside intruder, that Robert was asleep but struggling each time the orderlies looked in on him — that there was no sound from the room, no screams, nothing. He must have been asleep when it happened. He had a dream, a horrible dream by the look of things. It frightened him so that his heart couldn't take it. Somehow, through some sort of extraordinary sense we don't understand, the other patients knew when it happened. That's the only explanation I have, as insane," he said with a chuckle, "as it might sound."

"Well," Braddock said, flipping closed the little book on which he had been keeping notes. "I think I have heard enough. Like I said, we appreciate your keeping us informed when something like this happens at the hospital. But it sounds to me as if there is no evidence this was anything more than a death by natural causes, even if it was caused by the victim's own unstable mind.

"It is my understanding the boy, known only as Robert, had no family to speak of, so there will be no one to ask any more questions after I leave. I'll report back to the Captain, but I would be very surprised if anything more comes of this. Now, if you will excuse me, I'll be getting back. Doctors," he said as he raised his cap.

Dr. Anderson walked out with him, leaving only Dr. Winthrop and me to answer whatever questions Dr. Harker still possessed.

"Dr. Hamilton," he began, "please understand no one blames you for what happened to poor Robert. But I must ask if you said anything or did anything that may have helped to cause this unfortunate accident."

"I can't imagine I did, sir," I replied. "It was a very simple introductory interview. He did most of the talking, explaining what he saw and why he was having trouble sleeping. Dr. Winthrop and I prescribed a sleeping draught to help him, but nothing out of the ordinary. If I had any idea something like this was going to happen . . ."

Dr. Harker raised his hand. "As I said, no one is blaming you or Dr. Winthrop. These things happen, and more often than not, when a patient dies no one bats an eye. It was only because of the . . . unusual circumstances we even went through this formality. Don't worry. There will be no inquest, no notation on either of your records. It will be as it sadly always is — as if poor Robert never existed."

I am ashamed to say it now, but there was comfort in that.

Comfort in the fact I had dodged the day's disaster without permanent damage to either my psyche or my career. But the day was not over, and even more wicked things were coming my way.

Chapter 24

I passed the remainder of the day as best I could, but it took most of my energies to keep that final image of Robert out of my mind. I finished my rounds quickly, seeing the last of my charges just as Tom, our resident handyman and jack of all trades, loaded Robert's body into the rear of his cart.

"Lucky in a way," he said as he climbed into the driver's box next to me and Father Weatherby, the priest who lived at the asylum and ministered to its doctors and residents. "Another week, and the ground would have been too hard. Frozen solid. Then, we'd have to store him somewhere in the sub-tunnels till the dirt was soft enough to make a hole. Bad fate, that."

"Yes," I said simply.

We rode out into a somewhat warm, but nevertheless winter's day. The snows had held off for the past week, and what had come before was largely melted. As I looked up at the hard gray sky, I felt this was as good a day as any for a funeral, particularly for one so young. It was only the three of us, and I suppose it would normally have been only two. Doctors didn't normally attend the funerals of their patients.

It was, I had been told, better not to grow too attached to them. Their lives tended to be violent and short, and many of them were given to dangerous tendencies. A doctor who grew too close to one of the insane was likely to let his guard down, and death could come quickly.

But Robert was different. He was a young man, a child, really. And even though I had only known him for a short time, one visit in fact, he had made an impression on me. That impression was set forever because of how he died.

We reached the hole Tom had carved, a large pile of frozen dirt sitting next to it. I took a moment to appreciate how difficult it must have been for Tom to make that hole, and despite his nonchalant attitude only a few minutes before, I think if its future resident had not been a child, the hole would have remained un-dug till spring.

Tom climbed down from the front of the cart, and I followed him. Normally, he and the Father would have served as the deceased's lone pall bearers, but today I gave the old priest a deserved break. We carried the wooden coffin to the front of the gaping wound in the earth, and with two sturdy ropes, we lowered it down into the blackness below. As Tom began to cover the coffin with hard clumps of dirt, Father Weatherby spoke.

"Lord, we commend this child to you. In your loving bosom will he find the peace he always lacked in life. There will be no weeping, no mourning in the world to come. So, too, will the visions of darkness that haunted him throughout his young days pass away into a brighter morning. His fate is the same as all men, for from dust we come, and to dust we must return. May we all do so in the grace of the Father's love. In the name of the Father, and the Son, and the Holy Spirit."

I crossed myself silently and mouthed amen. Father Weatherby closed his Bible with a thud. We stood quietly as the pile of dirt grew steadily smaller while that covering Robert's body climbed higher and higher, finally reaching the level of the ground before forming a small mound. The mound was all that was left to mark Robert's existence — that and a small stone that read "777."

I heard the rumble before I saw it, the sound of a heavy carriage being drawn quickly by several powerful horses. The three of us turned and looked as it roared around the bend. It was a police wagon, the kind with a covered and barred space in the back for carrying criminals.

There were two policemen in the driver's box. One I didn't recognize. The other was Officer Braddock. There was a third man, a well-dressed gentleman, older than I, but not by much. He had a familiar look about him, and I knew I had seen him before. But after only a few seconds, the carriage curved back around the bend and was gone.

I looked to Tom and Father Weatherby and said, "I think we

should get back." They nodded in agreement, and I added, "Quickly now," though if Tom heard me, I'm not sure he cared.

We rode the cart back up the hill towards the Asylum, but it was slow progress. As the horses plodded along, I began to grow more impatient to learn what event was transpiring above. Were the police here for someone? Or were they bringing another patient? The presence of Braddock had convinced me this had something to do with Robert's death, though I couldn't know or even imagine, really, what that connection could be.

Finally, after what seemed to be an intolerable amount of time, the cart arrived at the front door of the asylum. As I leapt from the cart down to the gravel rock below, Dr. Winthrop burst through the doors.

"There you are!" he yelled as he approached. "Dr. Harker needs you at once."

"Why? What's going on?"

"I wouldn't even know where to begin," he said. "I'll say only you should brace yourself for a shock."

Dr. Winthrop's words were as alarming as they were cryptic. We walked quickly inside and up the stairs to Dr. Harker's office. As we entered, I saw Braddock and the officer I didn't recognize. Braddock had a strange look on his face, and he simply nodded to me. The young gentleman I saw before was also standing there, while Dr. Harker was hunched behind his desk, looking as if he had aged a decade in the few hours since I had last seen him. His face was buried in his hands, and when he looked up at me, he appeared as if he were gravely ill.

"Ah, Dr. Hamilton, please sit down," he said weakly. "I am afraid we are going to need to call upon you for a most difficult assignment," he continued as I took a seat next to Dr. Winthrop. "Dr. Winthrop will supervise, of course, but it appears that most of the burden will fall upon you."

"What is this about?" I asked.

Dr. Harker just stared at me. Whatever it was, he didn't have the strength to tell me.

"Perhaps I should take over from here," the heretofore unknown policeman said. After a moment's hesitation, Dr. Harker nodded.

"Dr. Hamilton," Braddock said, "this is Inspector Davenport from Boston. He contacted me earlier today about an incident. I'll let him explain."

"Yes," Davenport said curtly. "Dr. Hamilton, are you familiar with a Dr. Atticus Seward?"

"Of course," I said with a nervous chuckle. "He was my professor at Miskatonic, and I would count him as a friend. Is he alright?" I asked, looking from Davenport to Dr. Harker. Dr. Harker simply averted his eyes.

"Physically," Davenport said, "he is fine. This gentleman here," he continued, gesturing to the man at his right, "is Professor Atley Thayerson. Professor Thayerson found Dr. Seward early this morning."

"Around two in the morning," Thayerson interjected. "I couldn't sleep. I often can't, it seems," he said, his eyes wandering with his mind. "In any event, I often take walks around the campus at night. The cold air calms the blood. I was passing by Huntington Library when I found him."

Thayerson paused for a moment, and it allowed me to ascertain where I had seen him before. He was a young professor, one that had been hired to teach at Miskatonic a few years prior to the beginning of my studies there. I did not know him well; he was a history and folklore professor, and a man of my particular interests rarely found need to engage the disciplines he taught.

"Dr. Seward . . . " Thayerson began again, though once more he couldn't find the courage to finish his thought.

"When he found Dr. Seward," Davenport interrupted, "he was covered in blood."

"Blood!" I exclaimed, nearly rising from my seat. "Was he injured?"

"It wasn't his own," Dr. Harker said, finally speaking. I let myself fall back into the chair, the consequences of his words washing over me.

"Not his own," I said, more in statement than question.

"No," Davenport continued. "Not his own. He was covered in it from head to toe, and whoever it came from has most assuredly shuffled off this mortal coil."

"But this doesn't make any sense," I said. "Dr. Seward wouldn't hurt anyone. He is one of the nicest men I've ever known. Surely, he offered some explanation for what happened."

"He hasn't said a word," Davenport replied. "Other than to say he would only speak to you."

"Me?" I replied, completely befuddled. "Why me?"

"How can we know?" Davenport responded. "He would give us no answers. Frankly, given the circumstances, we would probably have brought him here anyway. But we are most interested to find out the whereabouts of Professor Thacker."

"Professor Thacker?" I asked. It was yet another name in this morbid play about which I knew nothing.

"Professor Thacker," Thayerson said, "is a colleague of mine. He is an expert in ancient, near-Eastern languages. A genius, but not one with whom I would expect Dr. Seward to have an acquaintance."

"Then, what does he have to do with this?" I asked, still not comprehending the totality of the situation.

"We believe," Davenport answered, "it was his blood."

"His blood?"

"Professor Thacker left his house late last night. When he did, he told his wife he was meeting with Dr. Seward. He hasn't been seen since."

"But what do you want me to do? I'm a doctor. I know nothing about being a detective."

"We understand that, Dr. Hamilton. But Dr. Seward is quite mad. Find out what you can. We have every expectation Professor Thacker is dead, but we would like to recover his body if possible. It will make the legal proceedings, which surely must follow this incident, much easier."

"I'll do what I can," I said, looking around the room. "But understand Dr. Seward was more than a teacher to me. He was a mentor, an expert in his field, and a brilliant man, as well. If you expect me to somehow trick him into giving away information, it won't work. No matter what game we play with Dr. Seward, he will always run the show."

"I'm afraid the young doctor is right," Dr. Harker said. "I've known Atticus all my life. He will give us nothing he doesn't want to give us."

"Understood," Davenport replied. "Just do your best, Dr. Hamilton. We will leave Dr. Seward in your care for as long as I can manage. We will delay the investigation to the extent we can, but at some point Seward will have to stand trial, if for no other purpose than to confine him to your care for the rest of his days. Good luck, gentlemen," Davenport said as he placed his hat upon his head. "Wire me if you learn anything."

A moment later, Davenport, Braddock, and Thayerson were gone.

"I'm sorry, Dr. Harker," I said timidly. I knew Dr. Seward was his oldest friend, and Dr. Seward had often spoken lovingly of him in our meetings together.

"It goes without saying," Dr. Harker said without acknowledging my comment, "we have a difficult situation on our hands, gentlemen."

"Yes, it does. A strange one, too," I replied. "None of this makes sense; from a man like Dr. Seward committing murder, to this Professor Thayerson and his story of how he found him. And now bringing him here? It just doesn't add up."

"No," Dr. Harker said, "it doesn't. But all we can do is attempt to discern what did occur. As you are no doubt aware, Dr. Seward had many friends in Boston. This whole incident is an embarrassment to them and Miskatonic University. If Dr. Seward were anyone else, he would be sitting in a jail cell right now. No, it's not just about finding out the truth. They want an excuse, a way to cover this up. But that's not what we are going to do. Dr. Hamilton, I want answers. I want to know how we came to this."

"But, why me, sir? Why not you?"

Dr. Harker frowned. "I do not believe Dr. Seward is a murderer. But he is deeply involved in this. He will no doubt attempt to gain an advantage over you, to use your friendship and admiration of him to his advantage. As you so accurately told the detective, Dr. Seward has the edge."

I looked from Dr. Harker to Dr. Winthrop, but there were no more words of advice. This challenge was my own, and I would face it alone.

Chapter 25

Darkness had long fallen on Danvers Asylum, but I knew no matter my misgivings, I could not put off the inevitable. I made my way to the west wing where the male patients were held.

The incurables ward was particularly chaotic, and I wondered if they somehow sensed the tension among the doctors, or if Robert's bizarre death still resonated with them. But when the door to the incurables ward closed behind me, the heavy silence of the criminally insane was upon me.

I remember thinking, back on that first day when I arrived, it was peaceful. How things had changed in the fleeting months that had passed. Now it chilled my blood. Dr. Seward was in the last room at the end of the hall. As I walked down the hallway, I tried to avoid looking into the cells — and they were cells — that housed some of the most deranged men in New England.

But it was impossible to avoid them all. Justice Mastis had his face pressed up against the bars of his door. Mastis was an abomination. In a former life, he had been a puppeteer, and I suppose in his own way, he brought joy to an untold number of children. But something evil had stirred within him, and Mastis snapped. He killed his wife, but killing her had not been enough. After he chopped up her body, he gutted her. They found him sitting on the floor, his hand shoved up her stomach cavity, fingers working the mouth and jaw of her corpse.

The constable who stumbled upon that scene shot him on sight. It was unfortunate for all that he lived, but he kept mostly to himself. He spoke only to the puppet he had created out of a pillow case and some buttons from his clothes. He called the puppet by the same name as his dead wife.

In the cell next to Mastis was the Butcher of Bedford. I grew up in Massachusetts, and I remembered his story from my youth. He was famous, from Newbury to Bridgewater, Boston to Springfield, for his pork sausage. People would come from every town and village, from neighboring states and foreign lands, just to try it.

There was a secret ingredient some said, something that separated his wurst from all others. Then somebody noticed Bedford was a town without a problem that plagues modern man. There were no vagrants, no poor, no wandering homeless. I don't know how they found out, how they discovered the secret, but one day they stumbled upon where Bedford's downtrodden had gone. My mother would sometimes say how glad she was she had never purchased any sausage from the Butcher. I remembered better.

It was that type of man who inhabited this place — the most vile, the most disturbed. The darkest of man's imaginings can never match the reality of the depths of his depravity. In some places, one may see the human race's finest character, its greatest heights. Not here. I stood in front of the door to Dr. Seward's cell. This was the man I had called friend and had admired; the man in whose image I would have mirrored my life.

"Alright, Jacob," I said quietly. "I'll go inside. Please don't disturb us unless I call you. Dr. Seward was very specific in his instructions. I am to go in alone, and frankly I am not sure you should even have come this far." I turned and looked over my shoulder at the door behind, and in that moment I was glad Jacob was there. "But the danger is real," I finally said, "and I would not venture inside alone."

Jacob nodded once to show he understood. He slid the key into the cell door and pulled it open. I stepped inside and heard it slam behind me. The feeling of oppression was instant. The room was dark, and the fear I felt made it darker. But it wasn't so dark that I could not see the man I had known in a radically different world, one that seemed very far away at that moment.

"William!" he said brightly. He smiled, and the blood caked on his face cracked like gruesome paint on a deranged clown. "I would get up, William, but as you can see, I am a little indisposed." He gently shook the chains that held him. They jingled lightly, like the bells on Fortunato's cap.

"They chained you?"

"It would appear so," Dr. Seward replied matter-of-factly.

He sat, held back by the chains, looking so pitiful that, for an instant, I almost forgot why he was there, why I was there. But then I looked at his tattered clothing, stained crimson in blood that was not his own, and I recovered my poise. I decided to make a gesture to further ensure his trust.

"Jacob!" I called. I saw Dr. Seward stiffen. He wanted us to be alone, and a little bit of the friendliness he had shown to this point faded. I heard the key slide in the cell lock, and Jacob stepped inside.

"Yes, doctor? Is something wrong?"

"Jacob, I want you to unchain Dr. Seward."

"But sir, Inspector Davenport was very clear Dr. Seward was not to go without restraints."

"Jacob, I have no doubt in his domain, Inspector Davenport's word holds sway. But this is not his domain, and Dr. Seward is my patient. Unchain him. If I need you, I will call."

Jacob hesitated for a second, but my gaze was stern. Finally, he nodded. He walked over to where the doctor sat, unchaining him gingerly. Though Jacob was prepared for violence, Dr. Seward made no aggressive move. Jacob backed up to where I stood, never taking his eyes off of Seward.

"That will be all, Jacob. You can leave us now."

"Are you sure, doctor?"

"Yes, Jacob. I am sure."

"Right, sir," he said, stepping towards the door.

"And, Jacob," I turned and said, "after I leave, please ensure the doctor has a bath. He is not a prisoner here."

"Not yet, at least," the doctor said with a smile as he rubbed his now unencumbered wrists. Jacob and I both turned to look at him. For another moment we hesitated then Jacob jammed the key into the lock and stepped outside. I had a feeling he didn't go far.

"That was very kind of you, William."

"Dr. Seward," I said, stepping forward, "I want you to know I am terribly sorry about all this, but I am sure you understand . . ."

"Oh, I'm well aware," he said quickly, in an almost manic style to which I was not accustomed. "They think me quite mad, yes?"

"Yes," I replied, drawing out the word. "Dr. Seward, are you aware of your situation?"

"Of course!" he replied brightly. "When a man is sick, you take him to the doctor. You are a doctor of the mind, and apparently my mind is not quite what it used to be."

"Dr. Seward," I continued, ignoring his last comments, "we are very concerned about Dr. Thacker. Dr. Thacker is a friend of yours, right? I am sure you want nothing ill to befall him."

"Oh, no harm will come to Dr. Thacker."

"He is alright, then?" I asked, a sudden feeling of hope in my heart. It was quickly dashed.

"It's hard to harm the dead. No, I wager whatever suffering Dr. Thacker may have endured in his final moments is now over."

Dr. Seward laughed. It chilled me, that laugh. I had heard it before, but never from a man who was sane.

"Dr. Seward," I said solemnly, "I need to know what happened last night. I need to know what happened to Dr. Thacker."

We stared at each other. Dr. Seward's eyes narrowed, and I had the sinking suspicion everything that had transpired was merely a part of an act, the first part of a play Dr. Seward had written.

"Are you familiar," he said without the mania that had crept into his voice before, as if I was sitting back in his office at Miskatonic, "with the history of this place?"

"I am not."

"This asylum was supposed to have been in Boston, you know?" he asked in the manner of one relaying some interesting, but trivial, fact to a friend. "Near the old hospital that closed down. I was one of the men charged with designing this place. We determined a rural location would be more appropriate. And so we built it here."

"Well, that is very interesting, Dr. Seward, but . . ."

"I am not finished, Dr. Hamilton," he said sternly. I fell silent, cursing myself for allowing him to take control.

"We picked this hill, this out-of-the-way outcropping. A beautiful place. We wondered how it remained deserted, wondered about the abandoned structures overlooking the village below."

"Danvers?"

Dr. Seward chuckled. "Yes, Danvers. That's what they call it now. But two hundred years ago it went by a different name. Two hundred years ago, it was known as Salem. Yes," he said, seeing my mouth drop in surprise, "witch-haunted Salem. There is a tree on this hill. I am sure you saw it when you arrived. A great Oak tree, tall and strong, with branches that point straight down to Hell. It was from that tree they hanged the first of the witches, before it became clear a more permanent fixture was required." Seward waited for a response, but I gave him none. He smiled. "But that's not all. Do you know the name John Hawthorne?"

"Of course," I said. I doubt there was a man or woman alive within a hundred miles of Boston who had not heard that accursed name.

"Then, you know what he did? The great jurist? The high inquisitor of Salem? He who kindled the flames of the Burning Time? He who stood like a great, pharisaical god, the zealous fire raging in his eyes as the innocents were hanged before him? Where you stand now was once his house. Yes," he said, seeing the chill roll through me, "that great devil of a man called this his home. It is no wonder it was judged cursed by those around it."

I listened as Dr. Seward spoke. His words were fevered now, coming fast and hard. He was stern, too, lucid and logical. But it was the passion in his voice that scared me.

"What do you know of Giles Corey?" Seward asked. I simply shook my head. Nothing would have been my only answer.

"Ah, the state of education these days," he said dryly. "Giles Corey was charged by John Hawthorne with witchcraft. He was adjudged guilty, of course, by all the learned men of Salem, John Hawthorne being only the most zealous amongst them.

"But Giles Corey knew his innocence, in the face of the certainty of those who accused him. And, despite the efforts of his erstwhile friends and neighbors to convince him of his guilt, he refused to confess. So the great and just John Hawthorne ordered he be pressed, right here on this hill, perhaps where you stand tonight, so he might come to recognize the truth of the charges against him.

"While Hawthorne stood watch, stone weights were placed upon Corey, one after another, slowly crushing the life out of him. 'Confess your crimes, Giles Corey,' Hawthorne was said to say, 'and you will be free.' Do you know what Corey said, William Hamilton? What his final words were?"

He looked at me expectantly, but I said nothing.

"'More weight.' And so they killed him, Dr. Hamilton. Crushed him to death. But it can never be said that Giles Corey confessed to a crime he didn't commit. We would all do well to follow that example."

Dr. Seward looked up to me, and I could tell by his face he was done for the night.

"I'll have Jacob make arrangements for a bath. Tomorrow then, Dr. Seward?"

"Dr. Hamilton, I can honestly say I'm not going anywhere. Tomorrow it is. And Dr. Hamilton," he said as I turned to go, "will you bring me a Bible? Surely even the insane are permitted that?"

"Of course," I said with my hand on the handle of the cell door, "I will have one brought right down."

I gave Jacob his instructions and then walked back to my room. I was exhausted from the events of the day, and Dr. Seward's words had only added to my confusion. If Dr. Seward were innocent, as was certainly implied by his Giles Corey ramblings, then why not say so? But I admit I gave it little thought then. I was certain this was but the beginning of a long and twisted journey.

Chapter 26

"So he admits that Thacker is dead?"

The next morning, I sat across from Dr. Harker with Dr. Winthrop at my side. I had given them a report of the conversation. We had remained in silence for a while, but finally Dr. Harker spoke.

"Yes, he was quite unequivocal in that."

"But you didn't press him on how he died? Who killed him? How he came to be covered in Thacker's blood?" Dr. Winthrop asked impatiently. I could tell by how he reacted to my story that he did not approve of my methods.

"No, Dr. Winthrop. I didn't think a direct approach would have accomplished anything."

"No doubt you were right there," Dr. Harker interjected. I could sense Dr. Winthrop deflate beside me. "Dr. Seward is no fool, and you will need to maintain that nimble mind if you are to navigate this mystery. Tell me, Dr. Hamilton, do you believe Dr. Seward is insane?"

Now I hesitated.

"That is what I thought."

"It's not that he isn't insane," I said quickly, "but it is impossible for me to tell for sure at this point. He certainly seemed as though he was, when I first encountered him. He was jittery, manic. Then he changed in an instant. He was stern, like he always was in class. But throughout it all, I felt as though he was attempting to convince me of his innocence, without ever saying so explicitly."

Dr. Harker nodded thoughtfully. "Well, we know for certain," he said, "if he is insane, he wasn't always thus. There is nothing organic there, nothing inherent. I have known Dr. Seward since we were boys at Harvard, and if he is mad now, then it is a recent development."

"I asked Dr. Anderson to take a look at him. He says there are no signs of physical injury. If his mind is broken, it is from the inside, not out."

"Dr. Hamilton, I think you should get back to your patient. I will wait to inform our friends from the police about Dr. Thacker. If he is dead, the delay can do him no harm."

* * *

Sometime later, I found myself back in Dr. Seward's cell. The transformation was dramatic. He had bathed and changed from his soiled clothes into a hospital robe. He was wearing his reading glasses, and I noticed he was perusing the copy of the Bible I had sent down with Jacob.

"Hello, doctor," I said as cheerfully as I could. He looked up from the leather-bound volume and smiled.

"Ah, William. I was looking forward to this visit. I was reading something I wanted to share with you."

"I was surprised at your request, doctor. I seem to remember you are not a man of faith."

Dr. Seward cocked his head to the side and squinted at me. "Now, Dr. Hamilton, if we are to have these little chats, I can't have you misquoting me. I remember our discussion quite well on the night you took this position. Strange how things like this work out." Dr. Seward's eyes seemed to glaze over, and I wondered if I had lost him. Then, just as suddenly, they cleared. "But no," he said, jerking his gaze back to me, "I never said I was not a man of faith. Not a man of your faith, perhaps, but I have faith. I believe."

"Why the Bible, then?"

"Ah, you fall into the same trap as the skeptic, Dr. Hamilton. There are few things I am in a position to promise, but this I can say without doubt. In nothing will you find all truth. No faith, no science, no creed can give you that. But I would wager there is no faith, no superstition, no legend, in which you will not find at least *some* truth. And, in this book," he said, holding up the Bible, "there is much to be learned."

"On that we can agree, doctor."

"In any event," he said, "I was reading something earlier I wanted to share with you. I find a particular chapter of Revelation to be simply fascinating. Let me read it to you. 'And the Dragon stood upon the sand of the sea. And I saw a beast rise up out of the sea, having seven heads and ten horns, and upon his horns ten crowns, and upon his heads the name of blasphemy. And the beast which I saw was like unto a leopard, and his feet were as the feet of a bear, and his mouth as the mouth of a lion: and the dragon gave him his power, and his seat, and great authority. If any man have an ear, let him hear.'" He closed the book with a thud. "Now, what do you think about that?"

I shrugged my shoulders. "I can't say I have much of an opinion." I tried to seem as uninterested as possible. The more Dr. Seward talked, the more I could grow to understand what was going on in his mind.

"No opinion?" he said. His voice was shocked, but a little too much so. I doubted he was buying my ruse, but for now he was playing along. "So," he continued, in the tone of a teacher, "you don't believe in the beast?"

"It's an allegory, doctor. Like the flood."

"Ah yes!" he exclaimed. "How interesting you bring that up." He flipped back through the Book towards the beginning. "Shall I read some more?" he asked. I simply nodded. "Let's see," he said, turning a couple pages quickly. "Here we are. 'There were giants in the Earth in those days; and also after that, when the sons of God came in unto the daughters of men, and they bore children to the daughters of men, the same mighty men which were of old, men of renown. And God saw that the wickedness of man was great in the earth, and that every imagination of the thoughts of his heart was only evil continually.'" Once again he closed the Book and looked up at me. "And what is that, my young friend. Mere legend? Myth?"

"Doctor," I said, "surely you don't take such a tale as the literal truth?"

"Of course not," he replied. "But as I said before, in all myth is truth. And do we not see, in the myths of all civilizations, this belief, this feeling, that the gods have lived amongst us? That they have walked on the Earth? That they have ruled it? And at some point were overthrown? From the ancient sands of Egypt to garden-girdled Babylon. From the schools of Greece to the most high and palmy state of Rome, all speak of the same legend, the same faith."

"I guess I don't follow."

"Have you not noticed," he asked, "the ancients all speak of a common foe? Of an enemy, so great, so powerful, that none can stand against it? Plato, in his wisdom, told us of Atlantis, that great island kingdom, which ruled the world with its knowledge and power. The Orientals know of a transpacific empire, so mighty it spanned the globe in its influence.

"The seven Rishi cities of India. Their ancient texts speak of a war, a battle in which great flying machines engaged one another, with weapons so powerful that a single bolt could destroy an entire city. Are we so arrogant, so proud, that we think it is all myth, all legend? But let us consider," he said, taking a step towards me, "what if, what if there is but a kernel of truth in those legends? What would it mean? I believe it would signify," he said, when it became evident that I wouldn't answer, "there was something greater than ourselves, something that had ruled this world before we did."

"But say there was some great civilization before us," I said, "while interesting, of course, what impact would that have beyond the academic?"

But though I tried to play the uninterested party, I couldn't help but notice a shadow seemed to fall across the room as he spoke, a darkness that obscured all but Seward's face. It was as if we were standing in the midst of a great void, we two the only beings in the whole world.

"Yes," he said, rubbing his chin thoughtfully, "I suppose that would be true, were it not for the universal promise that those great powers would return. The sons of God came to Earth," he said, looking at me, his eyes now burning brightly, "and then they were destroyed by the flood. They were separated, as the first book of the Bible says, divided by God between the land and the sea, between the light and the dark. This story is universal.

"Atlantis sank beneath the oceans, the cities of Lemur fell beneath the waves, the seven Rishi cities gave way to the sea. But it is said they all shall rise again. As we have just seen, Revelation speaks of one foe in particular, a great lord of the depths. If he is to rise from the deep, then it stands to reason he lies there now, waiting, sleeping."

"Dr. Seward," I said, interrupting, "this is all very interesting, but I cannot see as how it is relevant to what happened to Dr. Thacker."

Dr. Seward stared at me, rooted in place in the center of his cell. The minutes seemed to stretch to hours. But he simply stood there, his eyes seeing me but also looking within himself, as if he was considering something.

"I never meant to bring you into this," he said finally, a look of sadness falling across his face. But the look was quickly gone.

Whatever afflicted Seward, it gave him the ability to drift from emotional extremes in but the blink of an eye. His face stiffened again, and he continued.

"But what if I were to tell you the stories were all true, at least in part? What if I were to say there was a faith, older than the Sphinx of Egypt, more ancient than the ziggurats of Phoenicia, a nameless cult, an unknown fear? Practiced throughout the world, including your own Miskatonic? Particularly that arcane place?"

"Are you an adherent of that faith?"

"Me?" he asked with faux innocence. "And here I thought we were talking about Dr. Thacker." There was a gleam in his eye, and I knew I had stumbled upon some truth.

"Dr. Thacker was a cultist?"

"Dr. Thacker," he said, "was deeply involved in one of Miskatonic's more secretive societies."

"You stumbled upon this?" I asked, now taking a step forward.

"I discovered it, yes," Dr. Seward said, making a step to the left. We were now circling each other, staring into each other's eyes.

"And?"

"And the beast will not rise alone. The dragon must summon him."

"Was Thacker the dragon?"

Dr. Seward laughed. "No, Thacker was a fool. I followed him, once I knew what he was doing, when I knew what he sought to accomplish. The beast sleeps now, but he waits to be awakened. There are some of us who have taken it upon ourselves to ensure that never happens."

"So you are a crusader?"

"Ha!" he coughed. "Nothing so bold. Simply a watcher."

"What did you see?"

Dr. Seward smiled. "Actually, I think I have said enough for now. Perhaps you will join me tomorrow. I think by then you will know more."

"More?" I asked. "How will I know more if you do not share it with me?"

Dr. Seward's smile never broke. "Have faith," he said.

"One last thing, doctor. This beast, does it have a name?"

Dr. Seward stared at me, the corners of his mouth twitching into a wide smile. As they did, whatever mask he had put before me fell away, and I knew he was, indeed, mad.

"Oh, yes," he said, in the voice of another, "he has many names: Leviathan, Kracken, Dagon. But only one is his own, one I will not utter here, one which was not made for the mouth of man."

Then, his smile faded, and the mask was replaced.

"Go now, doctor. You need your rest, and I fear tomorrow may be the most tiring day of them all."

So I did. There was no point in arguing with him anyway. I had learned much about Dr. Seward's particular brand of insanity. It was only a matter of time until Dr. Thacker's fate was revealed in its entirety. But I could not know there was yet another twist to come.

Chapter 27

I awoke the next morning to a banging on my door. I dressed quickly and found Dr. Winthrop waiting outside.

"There has been a development," he said mysteriously. "Dr. Harker needs you at once."

I found Dr. Harker in his office. Braddock was there as well. I could tell instantly something was wrong. Dr. Harker was stoic, but Braddock was a pale white.

"What's happened?" I asked.

"It would appear," Dr. Harker finally said after a pause, "there is more to Dr. Seward's saga than the disappearance of Dr. Thacker. There is also a girl missing," he continued. "Sara Quincy, the daughter of one of Boston's more eminent families. I knew her grandfather at the University. She vanished two nights ago, the same night Dr. Seward was discovered."

"But what does this have to do with him?"

"Nothing, we thought," Braddock answered. "But we have been able to piece together the hours following her disappearance, and we have tracked her to Miskatonic."

"Miskatonic?" I stammered.

"Whatever Dr. Seward was doing that night," Dr. Harker stated solemnly, "it was dark, indeed. We can no longer hide this. The death of a Miskatonic professor at the hands of another was bad enough, but now there is a child involved."

"Inspector Davenport is on his way," Braddock continued. "With the distance and the turn in the weather, I wager it will take him a few hours to arrive. I thought out of courtesy to the hospital, I would let you know."

"We appreciate that very much," Dr. Harker offered. Braddock nodded once, and I knew that was enough for him.

Harker turned to me. "Go once more," he said, "and see what you can learn from Dr. Seward. I am afraid the time for game playing is over. We need to know what Seward knows, and now. A child's life depends on it."

I said nothing, but instead turned on my heels and veritably ran from Dr. Harker's office. I don't know if it was the life of the girl or my anger at being deceived, but I had determined I would get the truth from Dr. Seward, one way or another. When I reached his door, I jammed my key into the lock and threw it open. I could see the shock on Dr. Seward's face.

"Why didn't you tell me about the girl?" I bellowed.

"The girl?" he said, looking truly confused. "What girl?"

"The girl! The girl!" I shrieked. An outsider would have wondered who was the doctor and who the patient.

"Dr. Hamilton," he said, "William, slow down. I don't know what you are talking about."

"That night," I said, now pacing the room, "that night Dr. Thacker disappeared. A girl from Boston was taken. The police have traced her to you and your little cult. But somehow you failed to mention that. Mark my word on this, doctor," I spat, pointing at him with one finger, "the police are coming for you now, and when they do, you can expect a harsher brand of questioning than anything you've heard from me."

"Oh, William," he said calmly, closing the Bible I had given him in his lap, "I'm so sorry. I didn't know. Ask me anything, and I will tell you. No more games."

"No more games?" I repeated.

"You have my word," he swore.

"What happened that night?"

"It's as I said. I learned that Dr. Thacker was a member of a most ancient faith, a cult as you call it, though I would not use so vulgar a term. It is a religion if there ever was one, and a faith that has truth at its heart."

"And how did you come to know of this faith?"

"A man does not stay long at Miskatonic without hearing of it, or whispered words to that effect, at least. You heard them, even if your ears didn't let you listen at the time."

It was true. There had always been rumors about Miskatonic, about the ancient ruins that lay beneath many of its buildings. Where they had come from, none knew. Certainly not the indigenous peoples. But few asked too many questions, and I had come to believe the rumors were nothing more than myth.

"In any event," he continued, "I learned Dr. Thacker was a member of this society. I knew of its evil, and I had determined to follow Thacker in order to ascertain his intentions. There are others that know of the order, many who fight against it."

"Two nights ago, what made you follow him, then?"

"It was the night of Samhein, an ancient holy day, little more than a children's festival now. But in the elder days, it held the bitterest significance."

"So, you followed him," I said, still pacing. "And where did he go?"

"Huntington Library."

"The library?"

"Yes, he slipped inside, and he met several others there, each hooded and cloaked. Their faces were obscured to me."

"Then what?"

"There is nothing else, William, nothing more that I can tell."

"Doctor," I said sharply, growing frustrated, "you were found covered in blood. Someone else's blood. Thacker's blood. You must remember what happened."

"It's all a blur, then," he continued, but the way he looked off to the side, the way his eyes glazed, I was suddenly afraid perhaps this event was truly too much for his mind to handle. For an instant, I considered stopping for fear I might snap his mind and send him into a catatonic state. Instead, I grabbed him by the shoulders and shook him as violently as I could.

"Think, damn it!" I commanded. "What did you see?"

Dr. Seward began to shake. His eyes rolled into the back of his head. But as suddenly as it began, it stopped. He looked at me, but there was something about him that told me he was no longer truly with me. When he spoke, it was a voice that was not his, but one that sounded familiar nonetheless. "Choose truth, not passion. A winding staircase. Seek the light, not the darkness."

Now I simply held him still, staring at him. Gibberish. Rubbish. I pushed him away, my disgust evident.

"The sleeper must not waken," he stammered. And in a flash, I had a compulsion. To this day I don't know why I said it. Perhaps it was that his voice reminded me of another. But in no event would I have expected his reaction.

"That is not dead which can eternal lie," I quoted. "And with strange aeons even death may die."

Dr. Seward's body went rigid. Then he slowly turned, his face a mask of shock, but even through that mask I could see a simmering rage bubbling up beneath. His eyes changed again, and somehow I knew it was Dr. Seward who looked upon me at that moment.

"What did you say?" he barely whispered.

"What's the matter, doctor? Perhaps I understand more than you think."

Then, shock.

"Who told you that!" he screamed, leaping across the room and grabbing me about the neck. I felt my body flung backwards, slamming painfully into the iron door. "Who told you that!" he repeated, smashing my head into the concrete floor. The world started to go black, but everywhere there were tiny flashes, little explosions of light. As suddenly as it started, I felt Dr. Seward thrown off of me. I was pulled outside and the door slammed again. I was sitting in the hall, Jacob kneeling down beside me.

"Good Lord, doctor. It's a damn good thing I came when I did."

"Jacob," I said, patting him on the shoulder, "yes, yes it was."

He lifted me to my feet. "Would you like the infirmary then, doctor?

"No, no," I said, my mind still not working. "Just take me to my room. I'll be fine."

He led me upstairs, but it wasn't until he closed the door of my room behind him that I had a moment to consider what had just happened. I had sent Jacob on to Dr. Harker. I had learned little from my encounter with Dr. Seward, but I hoped what I had would be helpful to the police.

My head felt like it had been split in two, and I couldn't quite wrap my mind around the violence that had just been inflicted upon me. Dr. Seward was not elderly, but he wasn't young either, and the strength he had shown was otherworldly. There was something to that arcane couplet Robert had quoted to me, what now seemed like ages ago. Ages. But it had only been two days.

Then the clouds cleared. Two days, the very same night Dr. Seward had spoken of. The very same night Dr. Seward had been discovered, covered in the blood of a dead colleague. Like an explosion splits the night with a suddenness to match its force, it all came together for me.

Dr. Seward had tried to tell me, tried to explain. A beast, long dormant, long asleep. Robert had spoken of them, floating just beyond man's consciousness, images of gods past. The legends, the myths, the secret whisperings of nameless cults and ancient faiths. No, not legends, not images, but real beings so astronomical in their scope that even their dreams, their non-corporeal wanderings, were capable of killing a man.

It had all come to Mistaktonic, and in some dread cavern, men had sought to awaken those gods from their timeless sleep. If Robert had seen the same phantoms that haunted Dr. Seward, then that could mean only one thing. Robert wasn't insane at all.

I leapt from my desk where I sat and rushed to the door. I needed to speak to Dr. Seward again, no matter what his state, no matter what threat he might be to me in his madness, the origin of which I now knew. I grabbed the handle and pulled. But the door didn't budge. It was locked. Apparently, Jacob had locked it when he left me behind.

I reached into my right pants pocket, then my left. Empty. I looked around the room, confused. But then a cold shudder began to creep through me. I grabbed the sides of my trousers, as if that would make my key, the key that opened every door in the building, the key I had in my possession before I entered Seward's cell, the key I had not needed since Jacob walked me to my room, suddenly appear. But it was no use. I banged on my door. I screamed, I yelled. I began to think no one would hear me, that I might be locked in my own room all night. Suddenly I heard a key jiggling frantically in the lock. The door flew open, revealing a very concerned looking Dr. Winthrop.

"What the Devil is going on?" he asked.

Before I could answer, I burst past him and into the hallway. As he ran behind me, I replied, "Seward!"

"What of him!"

"He has stolen my key!"

For a moment Dr. Winthrop stopped, but it was clear I had no time to discuss it. We ran down the stairs to the main door. I waited for Dr. Winthrop behind me. He hurriedly unlocked the door and opened it. Jacob's seat was empty. There were no orderlies to be seen.

"Where is Jacob?" I asked as we rushed down the corridor.

"He should be here. Someone had to stay behind."

"Behind?"

"We had a problem in the female ward," he said as he unlocked yet another door. "It was complete bedlam. The lot of them started howling and screaming. Attacking each other and the staff. We had to pull the orderlies from the men's ward."

The same cold chill began to spread through me once again. "What about the men?" I asked.

"Luckily," Dr. Winthrop said, as he prepared to unlock the door leading to the ward for the criminally insane, "they were particularly quiet today." He jerked open the door, but neither of us moved. Dr. Winthrop inhaled sharply. "What foul creature . . . " he finally muttered. But there could be only one answer, only one person who could have left Jacob there on the hallway floor, his throat torn out as if by some wild beast. But it was no beast. The cell door at the end of the hall stood open. Dr. Seward had escaped.

Without a word, I ran to the wall and pulled the rope that triggered the mechanical alarm.

"He tricked me," I said bitterly.

"What do we do now?" Dr. Winthrop asked, as if I was the one who had been at the hospital for years.

"What do we have in the way of weapons?"

"There is a locker in Dr. Harker's office." Dr. Winthrop went white. "Could Seward have made his way there?"

"Unlikely," I said. "Too well traveled, and his door is the only one in the building that key won't open."

"Seward might not know that."

"I wouldn't wager on Seward being unaware of anything," I said as several orderlies came running towards us.

"Are you all right, sirs?" one I knew as Franklin asked.

I spoke quickly. "Seward has escaped. He killed Jacob. We have to search the hospital immediately. Inspector Davenport will be here tonight. When he arrives, have him and his men report to Dr. Harker at once."

"There's a blizzard, William." Dr. Winthrop said. I looked up at a window high upon the wall of the asylum. Even though it was dark outside, I could see the swirling snow beating against the glass. I had been so disoriented by Dr. Seward's earlier attack that I hadn't even noticed.

"Alright. Well, let's hope Davenport is dedicated. If he doesn't arrive, we will handle the situation as best we can. But this makes it all the more important that we find Seward now. If he escapes into the forest, we will never track him in this snow." I turned back to Franklin and said, "I want you and your men to search the cafeteria, the dormitories, and all the exits. Search the grounds outside those exits, as well. If Seward is in the building, we will find him. If he has left through one of the exits, the snow should reveal his tracks for now."

"What will you do, sir?"

"Dr. Winthrop and I will take the tunnels. Good luck."

Franklin nodded once and began to give orders to his troops.

"The tunnels?" Dr. Winthrop asked uncertainly as we rushed up to Dr. Harker's office.

"I think that's the path Seward will take. The tunnels go to the surrounding buildings. Make it there, and he can escape more easily. And the sub-tunnels run out all the way to the edge of the forest."

I knocked on Dr. Harker's locked office door. Though I expected it, we were still both relieved when he opened it.

"Problem, boys?" he asked without any real concern.

I looked at Dr. Winthrop and quickly explained. Fear crept into Dr. Harker's eyes, and when he dropped the papers he had been holding, I was afraid he might faint.

"Find him, William. Before he goes too far and does more harm."

"We will need the guns, Dr. Harker."

I could tell he wanted to object, but despite his friendship with Dr. Seward, he could no longer protect him. Finally, he simply nodded, reaching into his desk and handing me the key. I pulled out two pistols, giving one to Dr. Winthrop and taking the other. As we left, Dr. Harker grabbed my arm.

"Try and take him alive, William. If it is at all possible."
I nodded once, and the hunt began.

Chapter 28

Dr. Winthrop and I headed into the maintenance area where the entrance to the tunnels was located. We opened the heavy iron door that marked the opening to the main tunnels, and I followed Dr. Winthrop to the portal beyond which allowed access to the sub-tunnels. It was small and fairly innocuous. I wasn't sure I could have found it without his help.

"Be careful down there. It's much narrower than here. The tunnels follow the pipes that bring water up from the aquifer to the various parts of the building. There are many, and it's easy to get lost. Just follow the path to the right until you come to a three-tunnel fork. Take the left tunnel, and then your first right. That tunnel should lead you straight out to the forest. Once you are out, you'll be a little disoriented, but it shouldn't be hard to find your way back up to the main entrance. If you don't find Seward, meet me there. If you do, fire a shot."

Dr. Winthrop offered me his hand. While we had worked closely together during my stay at the asylum, I never felt as though there was any love lost between us. But now, in that instant at least, I could see concern in his eyes. I took his hand, shook it once, and nodded. Dr. Winthrop turned away and began his search. I slipped through the small opening in the wall and did the same.

The main tunnel system was often used by the staff and was rather well kept. The same could not be said for the sub-tunnels. They existed primarily to provide access to the web of water-bearing pipes, a technological miracle of sorts, which supplied fresh water to every wing of the building. The air was thick with dust, and though I tried to avoid them, spider webs stuck to my face and clothes. My lantern provided only the barest of light.

I stood for a minute at the entrance, wondering if it was worth it to advance. I knew Dr. Winthrop thought our efforts futile. I could barely find the entrance to the sub-tunnels. Dr. Seward, who to my knowledge had never been to the asylum before becoming a patient there, would have never stumbled upon them. But I wasn't worried about his stumblings. It is difficult to describe what I thought then, what I assumed he was capable of. Deep within my bones, I knew he had passed here before I had, even if there was no evidence within of his coming or going.

I walked down the right corridor. As I walked, my footfalls echoed down the length of the tunnels and beyond. In that claustrophobic space it was as if each were a cannon shot, a boom, boom, boom, announcing my presence to whatever waited beyond. It was then my mind began to betray me. I began to hear and see things that couldn't be.

First I heard the sound of footsteps just behind my own. I initially thought it an echo, but this was different. It seemed to have its own reverberation. I began to feel as if something were following me. Three or four times I turned quickly, hoping to catch a glimpse of my pursuer. Each time, nothing. Just the soft swirl of dust and silence.

I continued down the path until I reached the split. I took the leftmost tunnel as Dr. Winthrop had commanded. Now I was deep under the heart of the asylum, but I might as well have been at the bottom of the Earth. I kept my hands steady in an effort to maintain my calm. I was particularly careful with the hand holding the lantern before me, its solitary light the only reminder I had not fallen into some Stygian Hell.

Just beyond me, at the edge of my sight, something had disturbed the dust; I stopped. It wasn't falling softly, but rather rushing in tight spirals as if something had passed through its veil. The swirls grew faster, and they seemed to breathe, in and out, in and out, as if they were collecting themselves in a mass. Before my eyes, the figure of a man appeared. A large man, almost too big for the tunnels. I stood staring at him, or it, the featureless outline, the faceless image in a dark cloud. It didn't move, and I shuddered as I realized I could no longer trust my own sight.

Just as quickly as I convinced myself this was truly nothing but dust, the image lurched to the left and into a tunnel running off of mine. I began to run after it, sure now I had caught an image of Dr. Seward fleeing. I sped down the tunnel, forgetting where I was and where I was going. The swirling haze moved just beyond my reach, left, then right, then right again, until I had taken so many turns I couldn't distinguish the last from the first.

I stopped. The dust simply floated now, floated like it had before, floated like it no doubt had been all along. My mind had played me the fool, and in my mad rush to catch the phantom always just beyond my grasp, I had fallen hopelessly lost. I stood there, clenching my lantern, listening to the silence, wondering what to do next. Then it happened, a moment that haunts me to this day, that I still relive every night in my dreams.

For the briefest moment the fragile flame flickered, and then it was gone. The blackest night I had ever experienced fell on me in an instant. I was plunged into the abyss, and though I didn't move, I felt as if I were falling into black insanity. In that instant the fear was so real, the panic so palpable, that my mind bent toward breaking. I wanted to run screaming into the tunneled darkness, searching for light.

Suddenly, in the instant in which the cold hand of madness clutched me, I heard a voice. Not from without, but within. A child's voice, one I had heard before. It said one word: "Hold."

In that moment, as if I had been physically pulled back from the brink of some dark chasm, I did hold. Onto myself, onto my sense of control, my discipline. I stood stock still, determined I could unravel this problem. The voice came then, not the one of the child, not the one that had given comfort. The voice of another, the one whose eyes needed no light to see in the darkness.

"Hello, Dr. Hamilton."

The hairs stood up on the back of my neck, the blood within my veins stopped cold like water frozen to ice. It was a high voice, a haughty voice, bloodless and cruel. But it was Dr. Seward's, I had no doubt about that. It was beneath me, above me, to my right and my left, below and beyond. It was a whisper in my ear, as if he were standing right behind me.

It also roared like thunder up and down the halls. Whether it was the acoustics of that place or something more, something less natural and more sinister, I did not know. But it gave me no bearing on where he was.

"So good of you to join me tonight. I was afraid I might be forced to slip away without ever saying goodbye."

I took a small step backwards, letting my back hit against the wall. If he were here, at least he wouldn't get the jump on me from behind. I held the lantern in my left hand — though unlit, it could still be a weapon — and pulled the pistol from beneath my waistcoat with my right.

"Oh, Dr. Hamilton," the voice said dryly, "surely you wouldn't shoot your old mentor, your old friend."

"I hope it doesn't come to that," I said, somehow unsurprised that despite the coal black gloom Dr. Seward could see my every move. "But that is your choice. You lied to me, Dr. Seward. You lied the whole time."

"Ah, William," the voice boomed and whispered at the same time, "I am sorry you think that. In fact, I told you very few lies. Your ears have heard more truth than most men in a lifetime."

"Then, tell me more truths, doctor," I yelled, determined to keep him talking in the hope that something would reveal his location, that he would betray himself, that I would have one clean shot. "You killed Thacker, didn't you? And the girl, too?"

"I told you before, William, I am no murderer. Neither died at my hands. Well, I suppose one might quibble about the girl. But Thacker, he fell to one far mightier than I. You already know of him, of his kind."

"I know only what you have told me," I spat back, "and I believe none of it."

Dr. Seward cackled, and as he did, his laughter rolled back and forth through the tunnels, changed its pitch and its tone, seemed to flow up and down, stronger, then lighter, over and against itself, as if it were a hundred men laughing instead of one.

"Now who lies, Dr. Hamilton? No, my friend, it is not only I who has spoken to you of those giants, those sons of the gods just beyond man's sight, lurking in our collective subconscious. There was another. A boy."

"Robert . . ." I whispered almost unconsciously.

"Yes, Robert."

"But how can you know about him?"

"Because I have seen him, William, just as I see you now. A pity, really. All your knowledge, all your training and expertise, and you, like everyone else, thought him mad. But he was not mad. Or was he?

"I suppose it depends on the definition. Imagine what it must have been like, William, to see what others cannot? A blind man sees nothing. He lives in a world of darkness. They say in the kingdom of the blind, the one-eyed man is king. But they are wrong. The one-eyed man is a madman. Mentally insane, criminally deranged.

"Imagine it, telling those without sight what you witness every day of your life? Could they come to any other conclusion than you have lost your mind? No, better to say in the kingdom of the mad, it is the sane man that is condemned, for he sees what the others cannot.

"That was Robert, Dr. Hamilton. It was not madness that gave him the third eye, the burning vision that sees them. Their minds so strong that even in their dreams, they walk the Earth. A blessing, a curse. Better to see than to be seen. For while seeing them may bring true madness, being seen will bring only death. The petrifying gaze of Medusa, the death-darting eye of the Cockatrice, the dreadful sight of the Basilisk, the stone-cold stare of the Regulus. There is truth in myth, my friend. Around you they walk even now, floating before your blind eyes. They are the flash in the corner of your vision, the shadow moving where no one walks, the feeling of a presence when you are completely alone, the whisperer in the darkness. That which is, and was, and will be again."

I stood like a statue, listening as Dr. Seward spoke, as he wove his tale of Robert's horror. I shuddered to think what it must have been like, to live in a place such as this, to see with your own eyes such horrors but to have none believe you. I suppose such is the life of every man we call insane. Everyone's world makes sense to themselves, even if outsiders cannot see the creatures that float and dance in the darkness. But Dr. Seward had fallen silent now, and I knew that to not engage him would be to lose him.

"Despite the awfulness of the things you describe, you sought to raise them nonetheless?"

"It is useless to resist," he answered. "They are coming. As surely as you and I live, they will return. The ancient cities will rise from beneath the waves, and he that has slept these long ages of men will awaken. You will be destroyed, Dr. Hamilton. We merely sought the same thing as the Christian and the Jew and the Mohammedan — eternal life. But not some mere promise of it, a lie wrapped in swaddling clothes. No, immortality on Earth and rule over those that remain."

"And for that you killed Thacker?"

Dr. Seward sighed, and when he did it was like a wind blowing through the tunnel.

"I told you, I didn't kill Thacker. The same thing that took your young friend killed him. We weren't ready for the ceremony."

"Weren't ready?" I asked. I didn't care about his babbling, not really, but I still couldn't place his voice, and I feared with each passing moment he might leave.

"You wouldn't understand. There are books of wisdom far more ancient than your Bible, written by hands that aren't always human. We had one in our possession, an ancient tome, the name of which would mean nothing to you, but would stop the hearts of those who fear it. The *Necronomicon*, its blood-inked pages filled with arcane knowledge beyond the understanding of even the wisest men. We believed it was enough, that with it alone we could wake the sleeper. As Thacker was ripped limb from limb by the same one who killed your Robert, I knew we were wrong." Dr. Seward paused. Before I could ask another question, he said, "But I have tarried too long. I must depart, for I still have much to accomplish. Farewell, my old friend."

"Seward!" I yelled. "Show yourself!"

My voice echoed down the corridor, but only silence answered. My heart started to race within me as hope fled and despair filled the void. But then I saw a glow in the darkness. At first, I knew my mind had broken, that such was not possible. But it was there nonetheless, floating in the dust, calling me. I took a step towards it, and it floated away. Another cautious step, and then another. Each time it fled ever so slightly, though never increasing the distance. I began running, following the glow through corridor after corridor, turn after turn, until finally the glow no longer moved away. Instead it had become the literal light at the end of the tunnel — I had found the exit.

I rushed out into the swirling night, the falling dust replaced by torrents of snow. Despite the snow, the light of the full moon seemed to illuminate the whole field. Not more than a hundred feet away, I saw Dr. Seward running towards the cover of the forest.

"Seward!" I yelled, my voice echoing off the ice like the roar of some wild beast. Dr. Seward stopped dead in his tracks, hesitating for a long moment in mid-stride. Then he straightened himself, pausing at his full height, finally turning on his heel.

"Surprising," he said simply, with an evil grin I had never before seen on that face.

I leveled my gun at his chest.

"We go back now. Inspector Davenport will be here shortly to take you to Boston. You can lead him to that poor girl's body."

The grin turned to a smirk.

"You've read this book before, I think. I'm not going back."

I pulled back the hammer on the revolver. I didn't say a word. There was no need. The gun said enough.

"You can't kill me, Dr. Hamilton."

I pulled the trigger. The explosion echoed off of the ice and snow. The bullet caught Dr. Seward in his right shoulder, just as I had intended. Dr. Seward grabbed his arm, the smile gone, and looked at me with shock. But it was a feigned surprise. Soon, the smile returned, followed by a cackling laugh. He raised his hand to me. There was no blood. No blood on his shoulder either.

I let the gun fall to my side as I stared at the impossibility. Dr. Seward laughed on, his voice growing higher, his howl more deranged. But then the laugh caught somewhere deep within his throat. The smile remained locked on his face, but he wasn't looking at me anymore. I had seen this look before, seen eyes locked just over my shoulder, seen the face fall into shock.

But this time was different. This time I could feel the presence behind me, see its breath crystallize in the cold air around me. But it was the sound that chilled me more than the winter's wind, the guttural growl and the swish of whip-like tentacles that seemed to strike the air beside me. I didn't look behind, but I could see them in my peripheral vision, impossible extensions of that which should not be.

I watched Seward change before my eyes, as his mouth began to quiver, his body to shake. Then the amazing, the impossible, the unfathomable. Dr. Seward's hair, black as ravens' feathers despite his age, turned white before my very eyes. The color seemed to drain away, starting from the tips and traveling to the scalp. His mouth fell open, twisting, stretching, breaking in a silent scream.

I don't know what happened after that. The mind can only take so much. My last memory is falling into a dark and welcome void.

They found me like that, Dr. Winthrop and Inspector Davenport, Braddock and Dr. Harker. I was lying in the snow, Dr. Seward's body not ten feet from mine. I told them what I saw. They didn't believe me. And how could they when a bullet hole was all that remained where the back of Dr. Seward's skull should have been?

I left the asylum then, left and came here to Anchorhead. I took up an apprenticeship with the local doctor and replaced him when he died. I'm fairly happy now, and I do not often regret leaving my chosen profession behind. But I never forget some truths. That what we see is not all there is, and that just beyond my vision float beings as unbelievably powerful as they are filled with a burning hatred of mankind. And sometimes, when the light is right — or should I say the darkness — if I turn quickly enough, I catch a glimpse of a thing that cannot be . . . that should not be . . . but that is, nevertheless.

Part V

Chapter 29

Carter Weston:

The tavern was quiet now, save for the clatter of the bartender as he gathered abandoned plates and beer steins. The wind no longer howled, the snow having stopped about the time it started in William's story.

"Gentlemen," Captain Gray said, "I believe we may have worn out our welcome."

The other three nodded. Indeed, we were the tavern's only remaining denizens. Gray rose from his chair and walked over to the bar. He spoke with the burly man behind it for a moment, and to my great surprise the man bellowed a raucous laugh. Gray handed him something — a large bill or two no doubt — and walked back to where we still sat. The other three rose to meet him. Since it looked as though the night was ended, I stood as well.

Gray shook the men's hands, whispering a few words to each. One by one, they turned to go. Jack simply nodded, while Daniel took my hand briefly. Only William spoke.

"Good luck, my friend," he said. "But never forget what lurks in the shadows."

Then he, too, was gone, leaving only myself and Gray behind.

"Well, Mr. Weston, it appears we are alone."

~ 185 ~

Gray had that twinkle in his eye, that half smile that told me the night was not quite over.

"I would like you to stay at my estate tonight, Mr. Weston. What do you say?"

"Well, I don't know," I replied, surprised at his suggestion, "I've already been to the Inn, and I . . ."

Gray raised his hand. "I sent my man to gather your things two hours ago. They are already in the guest room in my home. I also paid your bill at the Inn, with a little extra for any trouble the lady of the house may have endured."

I chuckled. "I see you are a man who gets what he wants."

"Eh, I may have retired, but the captain of a ship never truly leaves the helm," he said, slapping me on the back as we walked towards the door. "And a ship at sea is one of the last truly despotic places on Earth. The captain is king. One gets used to command."

He opened the door and I stepped outside. The night was still, dead. People speak of the calm before the storm, but more truly remarkable is the calm after a blizzard. No birds sang, no dogs barked. Silence has a sound, and I heard it that night. A low constant murmur, a hum, like the rolling of the sea, but without the breakers.

There was the glow, too, the subtle phosphorescence of freshly fallen snow, as it seems to collect every ray of light, every flicker of a candle, every twinkling of a star. Collect it, intensify it, and release it back into the darkness.

That was the world I walked into, one of perpetual silence and light. It looked as if a great white blanket had fallen across that little town. A white sheet, the imperfect shape of the buildings and trees it covered, broken only by the footsteps of those who had gone before. We walked in silence, a silence shattered when a large, black carriage rolled out from a side street, stopping in front of us. The driver climbed down from his perch and pulled the door open. He gestured inside without a word. I looked at the Captain.

"Please," he said with a sweep of his hand, "you first."

I climbed into the black cavern beyond and found a very well-apportioned cabin inside. It was clear to me the Captain had prospered during his travels. He climbed in behind me, sitting with his back to the driver. The clouds had thinned somewhat, and the light from the full moon beamed in through the carriage window and onto my face. But the Captain sat in shadow and darkness.

Suddenly there was a burst of light as he struck a match, dropping the flaming end into the bowl of a pipe he held. As he drew quick, short breaths, the pipe flamed until finally it smoldered on its own. The captain shook out the match with a quick flick of his hand. Now, he was in darkness again, his face revealed only for the briefest of moments when he drew the smoke into his lungs. I felt the jerk of the horses, and we began our difficult journey through the snow-bound streets.

"So, my young friend," he said after we had traveled only a short distance, "what really brings you to our little town?"

I hesitated. Though I did my best to sell the story of a journey related to my academic pursuits, I had always sensed, despite his seeming acceptance, the Captain had never fully believed that lie.

"What do you mean?" I replied, though I felt foolish as soon as the words left my mouth.

"I've heard of a lot of things, but heading out in the midst of a blizzard to collect old wives' tales, that's a new one."

I considered whether to simply tell the Captain my mission at that moment. I felt a trust in him, though I wasn't sure why, and rationally I could give no objective reason to support that view. It was my rational mind that won out in the end. He sat shrouded in darkness, and I gave him no reply.

"But," he said finally and to my relief, "it is really not my concern why you are here, though I do consider it my good fortune that I found you. And yours too, I suppose. Given the purpose of your visit."

There was the sting of sarcasm in that last sentence.

"The four of us rarely meet, lest it be in thunder, lightning , or in rain. And tonight, snow." The captain laughed lightly, but he wasn't silent for long. "Fate, I suppose, we were there as you arrived. And our good luck that I read you immediately as a man seeking company, even if you were not aware of that quest at the time. No doubt you were worried on your train down from Arkham, that you would spend many days, even weeks, searching for the thing you seek. Yet you found it quite by accident on your very first night here."

It was eerie, the way he spoke, and more unnerving how accurate his words were, though he knew nothing of my real purpose and that in fact, the object of that quest was no closer than when I'd arrived. Though I hoped to enlist the Captain in my mission at some point, I did not know how many days would pass before that moment would come.

"I wonder, now you have heard all three, what did you think of my old friends' stories? I am interested only because it is those stories that tie us, four different men, together. And for your academic analysis, of course," he threw in casually at the end. The captain was clearly enjoying my failed ruse.

As the carriage rocked along, now traveling higher, I thought carefully about the Captain's question. Other than during the telling of each tale, I had not considered their content in much depth. The stories had come quickly, one after another, each different, each unique, and each compelling enough that my mind did not wander to the tales already told.

"Well," I began, "obviously each man suffered greatly in his story, and I would wager each was deeply affected by the events he witnessed."

"Some would call them broken men," the Captain interjected. "But I would not be so cold, so cruel, or so quick to judge. Those slanderers would be wrong, too. What one can say for sure is each man lost his innocence, his youth, in those days that passed so long ago. One can never truly know when he steps outside his door whether today will be a day that passes without consequence, or if it will be one that changes everything.

"Each man made a choice: Jack to take his first expedition outside the care of his father; Daniel to travel to Europe and then seek adventure in the East; William to launch his career at Danvers. Each of those choices was as innocuous as it was justified. Jack had traveled the western woods his entire life. He knew them, if not as well as his father, well enough. If he was to be his own man, he would need to leave his father's sheltering arms and step out on his own. Daniel sought adventure and an experience to warm the cold nights of boredom that no doubt would have followed as a lawyer in Boston or any other town. William was simply grabbing hold of an opportunity that could not be refused.

"Each of them suffered for those choices, but each also overcame. How many men, if they had seen what Jack saw, endured what he endured, would have dedicated the remainder of their lives to traveling those mysterious and uncharted woods? How many would have simply rested in the comforting bosom of their wealthy father for the remainder of their lives if they saw the things Daniel saw in that hellish monastery? And William, my God, most men would have been inmates in the very asylum in which they worked. But no, he went on and has done quite well for himself. Each made a choice, and each has lived with that choice. I wonder, what choice did you make today?"

I felt a chill, and not from the cold air, when the Captain turned the conversation to me. That I could not see his face made it all the worse. So I chose the easiest path, the path most would choose in such a moment. I avoided the question.

"It makes me wonder, too, how did you end up with these men? You spoke of their stories, but I have yet to hear your tale. And from what I have seen, it seems as though whatever befell them, you have managed to avoid?"

There was a chuckle in the darkness. "Ah yes, it is true, you do not know my story. All in good time. If you are to understand and appreciate mine, you must first truly know theirs. Tell me what else struck you of what you heard tonight."

"The most obvious thing," I said after another moment's thought, "was the uncanny consistency in each. Though I found some aspects to be truly remarkable, to the point of obvious hallucination, the underlying core, this notion of a creeping fear just beyond the boundaries of our civilization, one as ancient as it is malicious, was constant."

"But you, of course, do not believe in such a faith, or such a fear?"

"You are beginning to sound like Dr. Seward now," I answered with a chuckle. Captain Gray did not laugh. And if I could have penetrated that darkness, I was sure I would have seen he didn't smile either. But when he inhaled sharply on his pipe, the glow from the flaming embers revealed a sly smirk.

"Yes," he said, exhaling a thick cloud of smoke, "Seward saw enough that faith was not required. Faith comes by hearing, and you have heard. But you do not believe?"

"Do I believe your three friends spoke the truth tonight? Absolutely. But what underlies it, I have a more difficult time believing."

"And yet did you not come here this night, driven by something akin to what they have claimed?"

"Perhaps," I said simply.

"Ah, yes. Perhaps."

The captain fell silent then, puffing slowly on his pipe, watching me from behind the veil of darkness. Though his eyes were cloaked, I could feel them studying me. I looked away, out the window into the night beyond. We were climbing a hill now. I could see, built on its crest, a mansion. It sat perched on a cliff. The roaring sea was below, like something out of a dream. Yes, the Captain had prospered indeed. The carriage pulled around a fountain, silent and frozen now, to a large entrance of thick double doors. With a jerk, the carriage door was open.

The captain exited first, and I followed. We strode together into the ornate foyer.

"Andrew will take you to your room," he said, gesturing to a man waiting within. "I will be in my study. Please, make yourself comfortable and join me when you can."

He turned and walked into a large study off to the side which, in my brief view, seemed to be filled with books. I followed Andrew up the stairs to my rather spacious room. A large bed filled the center, and the paintings on the wall were all scenes of the sea. I walked to the imposing window that made up most of the far end. The ocean was beyond, stretching out forever, or so it seemed. I watched the waves smash against the cliff, and wondered what kind of man would choose to brave those waters. With that thought, I left my room and walked down to the Captain's study.

As I opened the heavy oaken doors — everything in that house was sturdy, as if built to withstand the fury of the ocean beyond — I realized my earlier view was but a glimpse of the totality of what the Captain had humbly referred to as a "study."

The room itself was massive, a personal library really, with shelves of books rising all the way to the edge of the high-vaulted ceiling. There was a movable ladder that could be maneuvered to any part of the room necessary to recover the desired volume. The floor was wooden, but etched into those boards was the image of a great compass. The captain stood in front of a large desk centered squarely over a giant E. Behind him was a massive window, stretching from wall to wall and floor to ceiling. Behind it, once again, was the sea.

The weather had broken and the clouds with it. A mighty full moon held sway over the tides, filling the upper right hand quadrant of the window at the same time. The captain poured a dark liquid from a decanter into two large glasses. He was as generous as that mysterious liquid was no doubt strong.

As I walked across the room, I glanced with unmasked curiosity at the books the Captain loved. It seemed to my eye they were on a myriad of topics: history, navigation, philosophy, geography. The wisdom of the ages in one room. But it was those more ancient tomes — and judging by their location in a locked cabinet next to the Captain's desk, more valuable, too — that most drew my eye.

Arcane, tenebrous books of Delphic wisdom. The fabled *Grand Grimoire* and John Dee's *Sworn Book of Honorius*. There was the *Clavis*

Salomonis leaning on a copy of *Liber de Diabole,* and many more books I didn't recognize. But their grizzled covers and discolored pages spoke of their age and how they had been well-used. It was a collection any library, particularly the one at Miskatonic, would have found irresistible.

Something else stunned me the most, stopped me half way across that floor in the center of that great carven compass. Something else that caused me to drop my jaw in shock and look hastily up to the man who was staring with an expectant grin spreading wide across his face.

Sitting on the corner of the Captain's desk was a book I had only heard of, in whispered words and tales, in the very stories to which I had been privy that night, in fact. But there it sat, sturdy leather binding and clasp, with two words burned into the center of the cover: *El Azif.* But that was not the name by which it was known, the name that howled on the winds, that shook strong men in their beds in the darkest hours of the night. No, this was the *Necronomicon.*

"That book," Captain Gray said, pointing down at that forbidden work, "cost me as much as I paid to build this house."

I veritably leapt from where I stood to the desk, sitting quickly down in a chair. I spread my hands over that ancient leather before catching myself. "May I?" I asked, everything within me yearning to unlock its secrets.

"Of course," Gray said with a smile, sitting the glass of what I assumed was brandy in front of me before stepping around to the chair behind the desk. I unclasped the lock and began to gently turn the withered pages.

"This is one of the Latin translations of Olaus Wormius, of course. No blood, I'm afraid."

It was true. Faded black ink met my eye rather than the deep brown said to stain the original copy, the copy held deep within the vaults of the Huntington Library at Miskatonic. Few were permitted access to that rare and priceless treasure, and mine was a treat I wondered if even Thayerson had experienced.

For a moment, I shuddered as I thought back to William's story, of the mention of my mentor. Thayerson must have been only a young man then. How strange he should play a double role in the events of that night.

"What do you think?" Captain Gray said, shattering my thoughts.

"There are hardly words," I said, looking down at some indecipherable diagram. I was amazed then, as I am amazed now, at its sophistication. The theories of non-Euclidean geometry were in their mere infancy in those days, and yet what I held before me, written when the plains of Giza were yet empty, contained illustrations which even the most enlightened and progressive mathematician would have found remarkable. I have come to understand the truth about that dread tome, that it contains secrets about our world and the spaces between space that we even now can hardly fathom.

"The *Necronomicon*," the Captain said as he drank deep from his glass, "is as infamous as it is elusive. Many speak of it, but few have held it as you now do, and even fewer can understand its mysteries. It is not, as many believe, a book of magic. In fact, it is more akin to a journal, one kept by a man who traveled this Earth in search of the darkest and most Hellish of truths, truths that transcend our world, stretching out into a world beyond."

"Alhazred."

"Yes. Abdul Alhazred, who has been called mad not only by his contemporaries, but also by many modern scholars. But I do not believe he was mad. I think he simply saw things the world was not ready to acknowledge. I fear, however, we will all come to acknowledge them soon."

"Why do you say that?" I said, as I closed the cover on the book once again.

The captain leaned forward. He looked at me, arching one eyebrow as he did.

"I always knew," he said, "you would come."

"Me?"

"Perhaps not you," he said, leaning back in his chair, "but certainly one like you. The stories you heard tonight were, in my mind, linked by a common truth. They speak to the uniqueness, to the auspicious nature of this age. I believe that the Rising will soon begin, or that at least, men will seek to bring it about."

"The Rising?"

"When they who were before will be again. When they will pass through the Gate binding this world to the worlds beyond the eye. That book speaks of it," he said, pointing to the *Necronomicon*, "along with others. Yes, the Rising, when he who ruled this world before he was cast down into darkness will rise from his slumber beneath the waves, and walk the Earth again."

"But what has this to do with me?"

The captain stared into my eyes for a long moment, and something about his gaze cast a pall of fear over my heart. In one swift motion he reached beneath his desk and slammed a parcel in front of me. It was wrapped in a tattered cloth and bound by simple twine.

"Open it," he commanded, "and find what you seek."

Neither of us moved. He looked at me, his eyes filled with expectation, but tinged with fear as well, I thought. I looked down at the package in front of me. Then, I reached forward and pulled on the thin piece of twine. It gave way with hardly any effort. I unwrapped the cloth and revealed yet another book, but this one was unlike any of the others that filled that library.

The cover was made of a material that was entirely unfamiliar to me. It was red, dark crimson really, and flecked with what appeared to be gold. These golden flakes seemed to shimmer, though whether by the pale moonlight or on their own accord I could not tell. The paper was not stained, not torn or tattered as the pages of the *Necronomicon* had been.

"Open it," he commanded again.

I obliged, flipping back the cover. It creaked under my hands, as if it had never been opened before. To my surprise, the words were in English. *"The Inferno of the Witch"* it read, as plainly as if it had been written before me that moment.

"That is why you came, is it not?" Captain Gray said as he applied a match to his pipe.

"Something like this," I said, dropping all pretense, "but this cannot be the book. I am looking for a much older work, far older than even your copy of the *Necronomicon*."

"Oh yes?" he said, holding the still flaming match in one hand, but putting the pipe down. "Oh well, no use for that, then."

In an instant, before I could even think to stop him, the Captain flung what remained of his glass of brandy onto the book before me. Then, with a flick of his wrist, he threw the match after it. I watched it spin through the air, still lit, before landing on the open pages before me. There was a pause, a moment before the fall, as there always is. And then, a great whoosh! The book erupted into flames. I was stunned by this act, the severity of it, the suddenness. That it was not the book I sought was clear, but to burn it! It was like burning a person. I looked up at the Captain in mixed shock and disgust. He merely smiled, puffing away at his pipe.

"Look at it."

I looked down. And then I saw what he meant. The fire burned, but it did not consume, not beyond the brandy anyway. A strange blue flame danced across the page, kissing the gold lettering, but never scarring it. The flame died as its sole source of fuel petered away. When it was gone the Book remained, as untouched as if nothing had happened.

"My friend, this is the Book you seek."

I sat stunned, dumbfounded. I was a youth then, and through all the stories, the tales, the eye-witness accounts, I had held fast to my skepticism, one built on arrogance and ignorance in equal parts. But what my own eyes had seen, I could not deny.

"But how?" I said dumbly.

Captain Gray laughed.

"It goes without saying this is no ordinary book. It is indestructible, incorruptible, eternal. Turn the pages. You will see they are all in English. I suspect you expected a Latin copy? Well, first of all, this is no copy. And you expected Latin because the last person to write about that book was Fabius Lupercus, a Roman.

"You've heard the common trope, no doubt, that we cannot know the truth of the Bible because it has been translated, and in translation comes change? For my part, I have long held that a God who can create this world can ensure the fidelity of His work. But the Devil — and the author of this fell work is he, I can assure you of that — he was cleverer still. The Book will work its evil, no matter its master. The man who holds it will see it written in his own tongue. Fabius Lupercus read it in Latin. Perhaps it was Greek before that. German after. Who can say?"

"What tongue was it written in?"

"Ah, the question of questions. None your eyes have ever seen, I wager. Nor any man's. I have studied the history of that book these past thirty years. It is the reason for this library, the cause of what some might call my obsession with the occult. From these books I have traced some of its history."

With that, his story began.

Chapter
30

Captain Jonathan Gray:

How long has the Book been? Always, as best I can tell. Words, my young friend. Words are all the power in the Universe. It was by words God created the Earth, the heavens and Hell. Is it any surprise that a book be the most powerful force in the world?

The Book is first mentioned in an ancient Egyptian text known simply as the Nile Scroll. Its author is unknown. Its date is more than five thousand years before our own time. It speaks of an ancient sea people who came to Egypt, a desert land filled with nomads and migrating tribes, seeking only to scrape out a living in a destitute plain. The leader of the race from the sea was Menes, whose name means, "The Keeper of the Book." Even the Book itself, in a time when men chiseled words into stone or brushed them onto papyrus scrolls, must have been a source of wonder to all who saw it.

They say the Book gave Menes the power to command the Nile itself, to raise and lower it as his needs would be. To give the fertile waters of life to his followers, and to deny them to those who resisted. Few did. Menes united the land of Egypt, from the mouth of the Nile to the first cataract. They called him by a new name: Pharaoh. A mighty civilization rose, and for two thousand years, the power of the Book gave the Pharaohs command of the world.

Then a man named Joseph came to that land, and with him, he brought his family. A great nation grew, a cancer, a foreign people whose strength increased with every passing year. There rose a Pharaoh who did not know Joseph. He enslaved Joseph's people, but their God heard their cries, and a prince of Egypt led them to freedom.

They say when Ramesses released the Israelites, the Egyptians gave unto them their treasures so they, and their God, would leave that land forever. The greatest of those treasures? This Book. When Ramesses learned the great Book was lost, he followed Moses to the shores of the Red Sea. He found the people of Israel on the other shore, having passed through the midst of the waters.

The armies of Pharaoh pursued, through a valley whose walls were not rock but rather the churning depths. On the other side, Moses held in one hand his staff. And in the other? Need I tell you? Is it any surprise the sea consumed the Egyptians? Then the sons of Moses became the people of the Book.

The land of Canaan trembled before their arms, and the Book went before them. For several hundred years, the Book disappeared from the sight of the people. It was placed in a golden chest crowned with cherubim, its companion two slabs of stone with nothing written upon them but ten simple sentences.

But the Israelites grew corrupt, as all great people do. The golden ark that held the Book was lost, passing from one empire to another. It was a relic to most, and its import was forgotten. That is, until Alexander the Great found the work and, intrigued by its peculiar nature, sent it to his old teacher and friend.

Aristotle never mentions the Book in his voluminous writings, and in truth, we only know he possessed it through the journal of Fabius Lupercus. The Book fell to the Romans upon the conquest of Athens, and Fabius, a former student at the Academy and Tribune in the Seventh Legion of Lucius Cornelius Sulla, was on hand when the city fell. He returned the Book to Rome. It remained a treasure of the Republic, passing to Julius Caesar and his descendants beyond.

We cannot know how or when it was used, but we do know the armies of Rome swept the world. Unfortunately, the history of the Book falls silent then, lost to antiquity. Despite my studies, what paths it may have taken and into whose possession it might have passed before I found it, we cannot know. Or should I say, before it fell to the man from whose dead hands it came to me.

* * *

It was thirty years ago, the maiden voyage of my ship, the Kadath, and my first as a captain. Her keel was laid out in Newburyport, and she was manned by a crew of hard New Englanders. They say a man who makes his living by the sea is naturally superstitious, but it's not so. They've simply seen more than those whose feet have never left solid ground. But that voyage would have shaken even the hardiest soul.

We were carrying a cargo of cotton shipped by rail up to Boston and bound for London. It was a journey I had made many times, but never as the captain of the ship. We had only been at sea for a week when the storm hit. That morning, I knew we had much to fear. As the sun rose in the heavens, the sky was blood dark, the reddest I had ever seen.

"Furl the sails, Mr. Drake," I remember telling my First Mate. There was no doubt in my mind we were in for a fight.

The storm came quickly. It started with a gentle breeze, one that curled through your hair and kissed your cheeks. It was almost pleasant. In fact, it was pleasant, like a whisper in your ear by a beautiful girl. She speaks to you, caresses you, lulls you into a sense of security, a sense of hope. Then the dark clouds come, the thunder, the lightning . The wind is no longer a whisper, but a howl. No longer a caress, but a slap. That was what fell upon us that night.

Few men have seen those horrors. Few men have felt thirty-foot waves smash against and over their ship, rocking it so far to the side I wondered if we would founder then and there. Few have felt their stomachs climb into their throats as the bow seems to point straight down to Hell itself, sliding like an avalanche down a mountain of water. We felt it that day.

I remember one man, Will Flat. His father had been a friend of mine, a crewman on a ship I had served on during the war. He had fallen to disease a year before that voyage. I was there when he died. He told me to take care of his son, so I had taken him with me. It was his first trip.

I saw him the moment before it happened. He was standing near the railing. Too near, I remember thinking. A wave hit us. How many had come before it? How many after? I cannot say. But it was that wave I remember the most. Will was standing at the rail. Then, the water receded, and he was gone.

I ran down to the deck. One of the men had already thrown a line to where Will struggled against the drag of the water, pulling against the invisible hand — one I had felt a decade before — that seems to reach up from the depths to yank you down to whatever lies beneath. He grabbed the rope, and for a moment my heart swelled with hope. Then another wave crashed over us, and he was no more. The rope floated alone in the water. Nothing of Will remained.

What followed happened in an instant. There was no time for sorrow. I had spent enough years on the sea to know that. But it wasn't any order from me that brought my men out of their shock. No, it was something else, something that turned them from sadness to fear in an instant.

Drake saw it first.

There had been a crackle of lightning, followed heavy on by a clanging thunder. "Heavenly Jesus," I heard Drake say. I would have thought he was speaking of poor Will or of the fury of the storm still raging around us. But there was something in his voice. A tremor. I turned to him, but his eyes were on the heavens. When I saw it, I feared even Jesus couldn't save us.

It was a ship, a two masted brigantine. A cargo ship. Blue hull with a golden railing. It was at full sail, a fool thing in that storm. Its bearing was upon us, directly on us, and in that gale it could make no move, no turn that would avoid us. I stood there as if turned to stone and my men with me.

We watched as death approached, watched as it sliced through the waves. No, not through them, but over them, as if its sheer speed were so great it no longer touched the water. It was in that moment I noticed something else — a peculiar glow — as if the very wooden beams holding the ship together reflected the now constant lightning.

At the last possible instant, the ship turned. An impossible turn, as if the raging seas gave no resistance. That insane vessel was now abreast. I scanned its decks in the brief seconds in which it passed us. If there was a crew, I didn't see them. Not a man moved on that deck.

My eyes went to the wheel. A man stood there. I had spent enough years at sea to know the look of command that bespeaks a captain. This was the master of that ship. He was tall, six feet by the look of him. He wore a sailor's great coat — blue with large brass buttons. He was clean-shaven but for a large tuft of hair on his chin.

He didn't look at me, not 'til the last second, and in his eyes I saw a mixture of defiance, determination and hate. Then he looked away, spinning the wheel with the ferocity necessary to maintain some semblance of control over that hurtling beast. The ship passed. Written in great golden letters on its stern were two words — *Lydia Lenore*. Lightning struck, and thunder boomed through the sky, shaking the timber beneath my feet. When the flash had passed and the rumble subsided, the ship was gone.

I held fast, locked by fear and amazement to where I stood.

"The Dutchman!" Drake yelled, falling to his knees. "The Dutchman!" someone else cried as the murmurs of fear and desperation began to spread like the plague through the crew. I was losing them, and in my own terror, I hadn't the heart to bring them back. We would probably have foundered then, a crewless ship with no captain, tossed about in a maelstrom.

In all my days at sea before and since, I have never seen anything I would call an omen. But in that night, we had two.

There was a hissing, buzzing sound — I remember that distinctly. Then, an explosion of blue light. I looked up, and the masts were on fire. But not a fire that consumed, not a fire that burned. It ran up and down the mast like a dog chasing game. The yardarms were tipped with it, a pulsating flame that seemed to ebb and flow as the sea.

"'Tis St. Elmo's Fire," Drake cried.

In that cry I heard a different feeling, one of hope and determination. Without a word from me, the men leapt into work. We fought back against the storm, against the sea. It was a battle that raged all night, but by the third hour of the day, we won. The sea quieted, as if Jonah had been tossed into the mouth of the ocean. We were exhausted, all. I relieved my men of their duties; we were safe for now. Sleep came quickly. It was dreamless and void of the fury of the sea.

* * *

When I woke the next morning, I felt, in my heart, a rising sense of panic. Have you ever awoken in a place not your home, and for the briefest moment forgotten where you are or how you got there? That was what I felt that day. I sat bolt upright in my bed. Nothing moved, and that was the problem. A ship *is* movement. But not that morning. I sat still, as if rooted firmly upon the ground.

A few moments later I emerged from my cabin. The men stood about, as still as the ship they were on. I looked out at the waters. It was a sea of glass: flat, even, unmoving. No breeze blew. The sails were limp. No wind stirred their folds. But it was the complete silence that moved me the most, even as the ship did not. The waves did not lap against the boat. The mainsail did not snap taut. The rigging did not clank against the wooden masts. We were, as the poet has said, "As idle as a painted ship, upon a painted ocean."

I stood riveted, for how long I cannot now say.

"Captain," Drake said, the merest tremble in his voice, "may I speak with you."

"Of course," I said absentmindedly, still not believing my own eyes.

"Privately, sir?"

Finally, I awoke from my stupor. "Ye-es," I stuttered, and then "Yes," more firmly. "I feel we have much to discuss."

We stepped into my stateroom, Drake carrying a rolled-up chart in his hand. He placed it on a table, unrolling it without a word.

"Every night I've taken our bearings," he said. "As you can see, nothing unusual."

I looked down at the map. There were small circles penciled in at regular intervals, starting at Boston and heading to the middle of the Atlantic.

"This was our location before the storm, according to the last bearing I took."

He pointed to the last circle on the chart, sitting precisely where it should be. Then, he straightened himself and put his hands behind his back, waiting for me to make the inevitable conclusion. I stared at that circle for five minutes, my mind turning over that almost perfectly round marking and what it meant for our current predicament. Finally, I understood.

"This can't be right, Drake." I said quietly. "It can't be right."

"I know, sir. But I've been at sea all my life. Each night was clear before the storm. It's no difficult thing to chart a course, and I would wager my life each of those positions is correct."

He spoke the truth. I knew even as I could not believe what the chart was telling me.

"I know, Drake. I'd wager my life on your readings, as well."

"But you are right, sir. They can't be right. I've seen something like this," he said, pointing towards the door, "only one other time. Twenty years ago. We were carrying cargo to Brazil. We had just crossed the equator when we hit the doldrums. For four days the wind didn't blow. I hoped I would never see the likes of it again."

"Drake," I said quietly, "according to your last chart position, we were three thousand miles from the doldrums when the storm hit. Three thousand miles. We can't have been blown that far off course."

"And I have never heard of anything like this at our present latitude," he said, finishing my thoughts.

I looked down at the chart again and nodded.

"But if these positions are wrong, it wouldn't just mean you charted them incorrectly. It would also mean I sailed us three thousand miles south when I meant to take us north and east. While I am prepared to admit possible mistakes, I doubt even a man on his first voyage could make such an error."

Now, both of us were silent. I looked down at the chart again, tracing that northeasterly path I had traveled dozens, no, a hundred times.

"Tonight, take a new reading. Then we will know one way or another."

For a moment, Drake said nothing. I looked up at him and saw true fear in his eyes. Without speaking, I asked the question. He answered.

"There's more, sir."

"More?"

"More."

"Worse?"

"Worse."

We looked at each other, and he continued.

"I took another reading. Last night. After you and the rest of the men turned in. I wanted to know how far the storm had blown us off course."

Of course he had. It was why he had been the one man I wouldn't have set sail without.

"We aren't in the doldrums, are we?"

"No sir, we are not."

"Drake," I said as evenly as I could, "where are we?"

"I have no idea. Sir."

* * *

As the sun dipped in the western sky, or what I assumed was still the western sky, Drake and I stood on the deck, watching the complete absence of motion. I had released the men earlier to their own devices. Ordinarily a ship is constant energy, constant movement. Yelled commands and controlled confusion. Not that day. Nothing changed, and thus there was nothing to change.

But I had another reason, a darker reason, for wanting the men occupied in pursuits other than those involving the ship. If what Drake said was true, and I had no reason to doubt it was, what we were about to see would have driven them to madness and mutiny.

The sun was gone now, and the gloaming was upon us. Darkness comes quickly on the sea, and so it came that evening. It was a warm night, but as the stars began to peek out from the blackness, I felt a cold chill ripple up my spine, and a shiver answered it. Men speak of the void that is night, of its darkness, of its impenetrable blackness. At sea, alone and far from any artificial glow, it is all the worse. But there is peace in the familiar, and no matter how dark or frightening it may be, it is nothing compared to the unknown.

I have sailed to every port of call in every half-civilized nation on this Earth, but never before and never since have I seen anything like that. The sun was long gone on to its next appointment, but the sky remained a dark crimson mixed with an inky purple. But it wasn't empty. It seemed to move, to quiver and roll, to pulsate and change. The colors would shift, sometimes to an almost pinkish hue, then a dark violet or even a gentle lavender, then back to a glowing crimson. Yes, that was it. The sky glowed, as if it was a thing rather than the absence thereof, a glowing, moving, colored thing. There were still stars. But they were unlike any I had ever seen before. Gone were the familiar, the comforting, shimmering diamonds I had come to know and love. Can you imagine it? To a man of the sea, the stars are worth more than their beauty. Far more. They are guideposts, our ball of twine in an endless, undulating labyrinth of water. But Polaris was gone. Betelgeuse, vanished. No more Big Dipper. Orion had fled. The Great Bear was slain.

But there were stars. Oh yes, there were stars. Just not the pin-points of light I had come to expect. No, these were great orbs of fire. Some shone clear and bright as the sun, and yet their light gave no illumination. Others seemed to pulsate, beating like the heart of some great beast. Still others seemed to dance together, twirling in great pinwheels as we watched. More would fade in and out, like the beam of a light house turning out of view, only to return a few seconds later. As I watched them, I had the feeling I was staring up through the sea to the sky, rather than sitting upon its surface. But one thing could not be denied — there was nowhere on Earth with that sky. Nowhere.

"Drake," I whispered, never taking my eyes off that ungodly vision. "Drake, are we dead?"

"I don't know, sir," he answered solemnly. "But if we are, this is most assuredly Hell."

Chapter

31

I did not sleep that night, not really. How could you with that looming monstrosity above, when the very sky over your head was an enemy? The sun had only begun to stream through the windows of my cabin when there was a banging on my door. It was Drake. He didn't have to say anything. The ship sitting on the horizon said it all.

"How long has she been there?" I asked, stepping out onto the foredeck.

"I don't know, sir, but she was there when the sun rose. She hasn't moved since, unsurprisingly."

It was yet another day of perfect stillness. I spied the ship through my glass. It was a two-masted brig. It was at full sail. Or at least it was rigged that way. With no wind, the sails made for an almost comic scene, hanging as impotently as ours.

"There's been not a breeze, Captain. I don't know where she came from or how she got here."

There was something familiar with the ship, something that seemed to beckon to me. I scanned the decks. Nothing stirred.

"Should we hail her, sir?"

I closed my glass and said, "Try, Drake. But given I don't see anyone on deck, I don't know how much luck you will have."

Drake nodded sharply and then turned, barking orders to the men who stood gawking. Within moments, one of the mates was signaling with semaphore flags. I watched for some response, but there was nothing.

The men were worried, I knew. The ship was an ill omen to some and a mystery to others. They knew well not a whisper of wind had blown for a full day and night. The ship had no stack, and it was clear it wasn't steam powered. It had appeared out of nowhere, somehow drawing within sight-range without any obvious source of power.

"Drake, come into my cabin for a second."

Once the door was closed behind him and we were well out of the hearing of my men, I asked him what he thought.

"Well, sir, I don't like it, but I can't say it surprises me any more than anything else we've seen to this point."

"No," I said, crossing my arms across my chest, "but I don't think we can just leave that ship out there."

"What do you mean to do, sir?" Drake asked, though I could see in his eyes he understood precisely what I intended.

"We can't know how long we will be here," I said. "I fear the men will notice the night sky eventually, no matter how we try to keep it from them. We can't have that ship sitting at the edge of the horizon, unknown and unresponsive. Besides, they need something to occupy them."

"You mean to explore it then?"

"I do."

"I don't like it, Captain. Everything is wrong here, and I do not think we should leave the ship."

"I don't either. Which is why you are staying here." I raised my hand as Drake began his inevitable protest. "There's no point. I can't send you in my place, and I can't bring you with me. I'll take Phillips, Jackson, and Stone."

Drake nodded. He knew debate was pointless. For my part, I felt rejuvenated. After twenty-four hours of sitting on our hands, now it was time for action. I could see in the men's eyes the same fire. The weapon's locker was opened, the yawl was prepared. Before I stepped into the boat, I turned to Drake.

"I would tell you not to leave without us, but it appears that is not going to be a problem."

"I would tell you," Drake said with a smile, "if the wind picks up, we'll be gone before you feel the breeze." Then, his smile faded. "Be careful, Jonathan. Whatever happened on that ship is unholy."

I nodded once and stepped into the boat. I immediately felt strange. The water was just as silent and unmoving as before. The boat didn't rock, except in response to our own movements. The waves did not lap against its side. Stone pulled the oars back, and his mighty stroke moved us away from the ship, but not as far as it should have. I looked down into that Stygian water. It was thick somehow. Viscous. Like oil, but not. It seemed to cling to Stone's oars. I looked at the other men in the boat. These were my bravest, my strongest. But now I could see the fear in their eyes. All except Stone. His temperament matched his name.

We pushed through the sludge, the thick, mucus tide. Slowly, the ship on the horizon grew larger, while the haven of our own fell farther and farther behind. Closer we drew, and with every stroke of the oars, I felt my heart sink. Soon, it could not be denied. I turned back and looked at Stone. His eyes remained hard, but there was a quiver there, a tremble. He knew the same thing as I, and it had shaken even him.

* * *

It was a brig, alright. Two-masted. A cargo ship. Blue hull with a gold railing. We pulled the yawl up to its side. For once, and only once, I was glad for the flat, unmoving water. A rope ladder lay hung over the edge of the ship. Stone handed me a pistol. I put one hand on the ladder and yanked it three times. It held fast, so I pulled myself up and over the railing onto the deck. The other three followed.

You are expecting, no doubt, that I will tell you the horrors I saw on deck, that I will speak of carnage and bloodshed, of death and destruction. If I had such to tell, you would know it now. But what I saw that day was all the more horrible.

The deck was pristine. It looked as if it had been cleaned that very day. The sails were perfectly set, the rigging expertly tied. But nothing moved. We stood still, listening to the silence.

"Jackson, Phillips, the crew's mess. Stone, check the cargo. Meet back here with what you find."

The men disappeared, Jackson and Phillips through a door on the far end, Stone into the depths of the ship. Meanwhile, I waited. A graveyard isn't that quiet. There the breeze rustles the trees, the birds sing, a dog barks. Not on that ship. I felt the heaviness of silence, the weight of absence. My mind began to wander, and as it did, the images it created grew progressively worse, more morbid.

I wondered if I would hear a scream from below, see Stone emerge half eaten, face ripped off, chased by some heretofore unknown and unseen monstrosity. But there was nothing. I turned, looking back at the Captain's cabin. It was then I saw the name of the ship, exactly as I had expected, printed in gold lettering: *Lydia Lenore.*

All three men returned exactly as they had left, except Phillips carried what appeared to be a cup of tea. His hand was shaking.

"The mess was empty, sir, empty of the crew that is. A meal had been set. Dinner by the look of it. It was half eaten. It was still warm, sir," he said, his voice cracking.

"That's not possible," I replied without thinking. That's when Phillips held up the cup. I took it. Hot to the touch. I felt myself sway where I was standing, but the sound of the cup smashing against the deck snapped me back to my senses.

"Are you alright, Captain?" Stone asked.

I looked at him dumbly. "What of the cargo?"

"Intact, sir. No damage I can see, and nothing missing. Whatever happened here, it wasn't about the cargo." I nodded. I would only learn later Stone was wrong.

"What's more," he continued, "the ship's yawl is still on board. A ship this size wouldn't have more than one."

"So, they didn't leave?" I said.

"Not on their own, they didn't."

"There's nothing for us here," I said. "We'll check the Captain's cabin and head back."

We walked quickly to the cabin. None of us wanted to stay any longer than necessary. I grabbed the handle. The door didn't move. I gave it a shove. Nothing.

"Let me, Captain," Stone said. He heaved the small axe he carried down at the door's latch. The wood splintered, and the latch broke. Then, with a push of his hand, the door was open. Light streamed inside.

"Sweet Jesus!"

Stone stumbled backwards. Were it not for the sheer shock, I probably would have fallen to the floor. There was nothing particularly strange about the room. Like the rest of the ship, nothing was out of order, nothing was where it shouldn't be. It was so normal, in fact, that across a great wooden desk sat the captain.

I could tell, even though he was sitting, he was tall, six feet by the look of him. He wore a sailor's great coat — blue with large brass buttons. He was clean-shaven but for a large tuft of hair on his chin. His eyes were open, and in them I saw a mixture of defiance, determination, and hate. But there was also fear there. Great, unanswered fear. For what must have seemed an eternity to my men I stared across that short distance at him. Stared until I realized, although he looked as if he might speak to us at any moment, he was dead. Undeniably dead. Irretrievably dead.

I took a step inside. One step, a cautious step. Then another. Moving more slowly than I ever had across such a space, I stepped sideways around the desk. Almost to my surprise, the captain's eyes didn't follow me. I looked down at him. His skin was still pink, and I had a feeling that if I touched him, he would still be warm too. And then something overcame me, and I couldn't help but reach my hand out to his. His hand was warm, but it was something else, as well. Slimy, oily. Coated in something.

I almost ran at that point. But my eyes were drawn to the object in front of him. It was his log, sitting open. The pen was still in his hand. Beneath his other hand was a leather tome, the same dark crimson book you see before you today. And then, for the first time in a long time, I heard something.

It started out as a whisper. Not one, but many. A chorus. A song. It was a tongue I didn't know, but I understood it, nonetheless.

"Take the Book. Seize it and make it your own."

So I did. I don't know why I listened. In truth, I couldn't resist. I pulled out the leather bag I had carried from our ship. I removed the Book carefully from the captain's grasp. His hand seemed to cling to it, even in death. I also took the captain's log. I walked gingerly from the room, but I never turned my back on the captain. His eyes seemed to follow me, and it was with great relief that I stepped back into the sunlight.

"Let's go," I said.

* * *

As we walked to the side of the ship, I had the sinking feeling the yawl would be gone, but it was there just as we left it. We climbed in one at a time, with Stone taking his position at the oars. With every stroke, we were moving by small steps closer and closer to safety. Stone was a strong man, and he always put all of his effort into whatever job he had been given, but I could see he was giving it something extra now.

I sat there, trying my best to keep my eyes on the *Kadath* in the distance. As a light breeze blew through my hair, I found my eyes drawn back to the ghost ship behind. In fact, it must have taken at least three stokes of the oars before I noticed that breeze, the breeze that had been absent for the past two days, the breeze that now began to blow with more purpose. I looked up at Stone. He had stopped rowing, a dazed look on his face. But only for a moment.

Now he pulled ferociously, as the breeze turned into a wind and the wind into a gale. The clouds came from nowhere, filling the sky with black mountains. The waves crashed over the side of the little yawl, but we never were in danger of swamping. A strange thing, as the waves were as violent as I had seen in any storm. Drake, bless his soul, had lowered anchor and furled the sail while we were away, apparently due to some preternatural sense that the wind was coming. Blessed was that moment when my feet were once again on the relatively solid foundation of the ship. Drake was waiting.

"Looks like you made it back just in time," he said. "Find anything worth finding?"

"Nothing. A dead captain and untouched cargo," I yelled over the now howling wind.

"What of the crew?"

"Gone. I brought back a couple books. One of them is the captain's log. Perhaps we can learn something from that."

At that instant, Drake went as white as a winter squall.

"Mary, Mother of God," he said, crossing himself. "She's coming around."

I spun on my feet and stared back across the now rolling sea. Sure enough, the ship was turning.

"The wind must have caught her just right," I stuttered. But I didn't really believe it. For a moment we both stood there, staring, the men doing the same. Then something snapped, and I was back.

"Raise the anchor," I commanded. "Stone, unfurl the sail! To the wheel, Drake! Bring us round to port side!"

The men forgot what they saw. There was the organized chaos

and controlled confusion that better becomes a ship, with men running here and there, yelling and cursing at each other. The wind was ferocious, and it was dangerous to go to full sail at that moment, but the ship bearing down upon us had to be avoided. I ran and took the wheel from Drake.

"She's turning to match us, sir!" he yelled above the wind and now the rain. I looked at that ship, growing larger every second. Sure enough, she had turned into us and was, once again, on a collision course. I spun the wheel hard in my hand until it stuck, the rudder full to starboard. The ship jumped to the side, turning hard against the waves and the wind. Once again, the ship matched us. It was now close enough I could see it fully. Nothing had changed on the deck, nothing except the wheel which now was attended.

The captain stood there, as impossible as it was. Though every fiber of my rational mind screamed out "No!" my brain could not deny what my eyes saw. He stood astride the wheel like the Colossus of Rhodes, his hair matted down around his face, his great coat caught up in the wind, streaming behind him like the cape of some Hell-spawned warlock. His eyes were alight with the Devil's passion, his mouth open in a roaring cackle.

The ship was upon us. In a moment, it would split us in half. But then it happened. The ropes that held the rigging began to snap. The wooden masts cracked. There was a horrible roar as the ship broke in half. Then, not five feet from us, the middle of the ship exploded. The bowsprit jutted up straight into the sky, like a finger pointing up to God. Both sides of the now split-in-half ship sank, straight down, as an iron drops into the sea. The last thing I saw of that cursed ship was the captain, his dead eyes filled with anger and hate as he slipped below the surface of the deep.

In an instant, the clouds cleared and the sun shone again. The wind no longer howled, the sea no longer roared back in response. The wind that blew was a good wind, the kind you prayed for on sea trips. I looked at Drake and his eyes reflected the thought in mine. We never spoke of it again.

* * *

The next morning, Drake brought me his map. He spread it out on the table and said, "We were in the doldrums for a day and a half with another half day of good wind. This was our last position before the storm. This is our position now." He pointed at a freshly drawn circle on the map. It was precisely the distance one would expect to travel in two days.

Chapter 32

Carter Weston:

The Captain sat across from me, his cigar burning a fiery circle into the night. He picked up the bottle of brandy and refilled my glass.

"I read the Captain's journal," he said. "I won't trouble you with its details but I will say this, I always knew you would come. And I promised myself on that day, I would give you this book." He pointed down at the crimson tome before him. "Even though, in my sailing days, I never left port without it."

"You kept the Book with you?" I said, somewhat surprised. The Captain chuckled.

"That Book made my fortune. It built this house. I never lost a ship. Never was late. In fact, I always made the best possible time. That Book, my friend, will never be destroyed. It can't be. And the one thing I knew for sure was no ship of mine would ever run into trouble as long as it was with me."

"Then why give it to me?"

The Captain's eyes went dark, his smile faded.

"The Book seeks its owner. It calls you now. Don't you hear it?"

In the moment of silence that followed, my blood slowed. I shuddered. There was a tinkling, and the air grew denser. A humming buzz. Then words. Words of an unknown tongue. And then I heard them. I felt them in my bones. I imbibed them, breathed them in and let them fill me up. They all said one thing, "Take what is yours!"

"The Book is filled with contradictions. It is as ancient as days, but it appears to the reader to be newly printed. The work is entirely evil, but the man who seeks the Book, even though he does so for power and to do diabolical deeds," the Captain whispered, "will not find it. The Book takes its own path. Which is why it is strange you came here to find it, and now it is yours. But maybe not so strange. Alas, only you know your purpose."

He pushed the Book to me.

"The Book is yours. But remember this, my friend. This gift I give is also a curse. The Book is yours only as long as it wants to be yours. It will seek another. When it does, you must make a choice. To give, or to keep. You will make that choice for your own reasons, but know whatever path you choose will be the damnation of someone. Whether you or all of mankind, only time will tell."

With that, he snuffed out what remained of his cigar.

"I take my leave of you now. You may stay here as long as you like, but I have purchased a ticket for you on tomorrow's ten o'clock train. When you wake, I shall be gone. May the God you serve bless you and keep you."

I took his hand and then watched as he strode out of the door. For a moment I was alone, but I didn't feel it. There was another there, as well. It sat on the Captain's desk, bound in crimson skin.

Part VI

Chapter

33

I awoke the next morning to the sun beaming through the great window on the eastern side of the bedroom. I looked over to find my bags were gone — packed already no doubt — and a fresh change of clothes was lying across a table. While the Captain had invited me to stay, it was evident my welcome was worn out.

When I reached the foyer, my bags were waiting for me. So was Andrew.

"Captain Gray sends his regrets, but he had business in town. The carriage will take you to the train. Also, the Captain left you this."

He handed me a small leather book, held closed by a matching leather tie. There was a note, as well. As I climbed into the carriage that was to take me to the train station, I removed the stationary from its envelope. Inked upon it in strong, looping handwriting was written,

Mr. Weston,

No doubt Andrew has delivered my regrets for not seeing you off properly. In any event, I apologize. I leave you with this book and some words of advice. The leather book is, as will become readily apparent, the captain's log *from the Lydia Lenore.*

   In it, you will no doubt see much you do not understand — charting, nautical terms, the daily flotsam and jetsam of the master of a ship. But a captain's log is much more than that. It is also a journal, the official history of a ship's journey. I suggest you read it, taking the lessons you will need now that you are the master of the Book.

   One last thing. When the darkness is at its worst, when it creeps upon you like a hunter in the night, remember — it will always fear the light.

   'Til the winds blow us together again.

   Jonathan Gray

I returned the letter to its envelope, placing both in my jacket pocket. I took the little leather book in my hands and undid the binding. It creaked as it opened, the old and tattered paper threatening to disintegrate in my hands. I read the first page. Printed in highly stylized calligraphy were the words, "Captain's Log." Written below that was a name, Benjamin Butler. But before I could read any more, the carriage had arrived at the station.

Ten minutes later, I was seated in my cabin. The train was not to embark for another hour, but rather than mull about the station, I determined my time was better spent learning what secrets were held in the log I now possessed. I opened it. Much of it was nautical information I will omit here. But in the rest was quite a tale, and I felt myself transported back thirty years to the beginning of a journey that was doomed before it even had a start.

March 15, 1867

Today, we hoisted anchor in Cherbourg, a cargo of French wine and cheeses destined for Venice. The men are in good spirits, and this voyage should be both fairly short and reasonably easy. The men are anxious to return to New York, and I, for one, join them in their desires. I posted a letter to Sarah before we set off. No doubt we may arrive before it does. But I miss her so, and I feel closer to her in the writing. Her absence weighs upon me, and though I love the sea, I find each voyage to be more difficult than the last. Perhaps one day, I shall finally secure our future and retire to her arms.

March 17, 1867

This morning we passed through the Strait of Gibraltar, that narrow ribbon of water dividing Christendom from the Muslim hordes of Africa. Whenever I see that peak, that magnificent rock rising from the dark blue sea against an equally cerulean sky, like a pyramid built by God Himself, I think of Sarah. How she dreams of joining me at sea! But I would never put her in danger, so I paint a picture for her with my words. Now that we are safely in the Great Sea, the voyage to Venice should be quick and uneventful.

March 20, 1867

We have arrived in Venice. The unloading went smoothly and a good price was had for the cargo. Many of my men have never seen the canalled jewel of the Mediterranean. Our cargo of silk and spices will not be prepared for transport for another three days, and as such, I have released my sailors to the pleasures of the city. I pray God I have not erred. For my part, I intend to spend these days visiting the great churches that seem to rise from the golden waters. Ah, if only Sarah were with me.

March 21, 1867

Today was most unusual. I spent the morning in the Piazza San Marco visiting the magnificent basilica built therein. Afterward, I let the day slip away, wandering the canals of this unique polis, letting them take me where they would. There was a little cafe on an inner canal I stopped at for a sandwich and a glass of Prosecco. There was a man there, a middle-aged gentleman. He had the most interesting cane. It caught my view immediately. I have spent my life at sea, and I must admit, in another setting, it would have greatly disturbed me. It was a magnificent beast, one I doubt has ever truly plied the depths of the ocean. Only, perhaps, in the darkest dreams of man.

There was a time when the unknown mists beyond man's knowing were marked, "There be dragons." It was of this beast they spoke. The Leviathan. The Kracken. A tentacled thing, but with the face of a man. No, not a man. Something worse. An angel and demon in one. Whence he found such a thing, I do not know. It was only after staring at that staff for an unknown span of time that I glanced up to see the man was looking at me as well. He rose from his seat and walked to where I reclined.

"May I join you, sir?" he asked. He was an Englishman, and I gestured to the seat beside me. "Enjoying the afternoon, are we?"

The man was perfectly pleasant, and I knew there was no reason for my rising sense of misgiving. But there was something about him, and no matter how I tried, I could not strip the image of that cane from my mind.

"So," he began, and I knew now to the point we would go. "You are a sea captain, correct?"

"I am," I said.

"Ah, the sea. A very dangerous place to work. Any man who makes it his life must be very brave."

"It is a profession like any other. There are dangers, but no more than those of many other jobs."

"Please, Captain . . . ?"

"Butler."

"Ah, yes. Butler." He spun his cane in his hand and looked up at me under hooded eyes. "Captain Butler, I have a proposal for you."

"Well, sir, I am afraid I will have to refuse it. My men and I are scheduled to leave this city in two days."

"It will take no longer than a night, Captain Butler. And for your services, I am prepared to pay fifteen thousand pounds sterling."

The man's eyes showed he reveled in the silence that followed and the look that no doubt spread across my face. It was an absurd amount.

"I don't know what you are driving at," I finally replied. "But whatever it is cannot be legitimate."

He chuckled lightly. "It is perfectly legitimate, Captain Butler. It is illegal, that is true, but only for reasons of this city's peculiar superstitions. The same superstitions that prevent me from procuring assistance from any of the local boat captains. I had determined I would need approach a foreigner, and when I saw your ship dock, I knew you were my man."

"What exactly are you proposing?" I asked, intrigued by the offer, if not the details.

"There is an island off the grand canal. It is small, innocuous. Nothing one would notice if he were unawares. It is but a dot on local maps — those maps that still include it, I should say — bearing not even an appellation. But the island has a name and a history. It was known, when it was known, as Povaglia. The people here have another name for it — Isola Della Morte, the Island of Death. Not particularly original, but accurate nevertheless."

"I suppose that is why no one will accept your offer."

"That," he said smugly, "and the island's past. The place earned its name. A wealthy merchant once owned Povaglia. He was a cruel man, an evil tyrant who tortured his servants and abused the people of this city. But he was a Cornaro, Adolfo Cornaro, a black noble of Venice. His uncle was Doge, and though he had no use for his nephew, he nevertheless tolerated his excesses. At some point, Cornaro acquired a unique artifact, one of great antiquity and inestimable value."

"No doubt the same treasure you now seek."

"Correct," the man replied, though I sensed annoyance in his voice at the interruption. "They say the artifact had a peculiar effect on Cornaro. That he came to value it above all other things. Art, gold, jewels. Even more base pleasures like food or drink or women.

"One day, a peasant woman came to his home. A gypsy, likely, one who didn't know of Cornaro's cruelty. But she knew enough, more than she likely should have. She told him his treasure was not his own, that it remained in his possession only for a season, and then it must pass to another. She warned him ruin would come to him if he denied the artifact its destiny.

"Cornaro, never a patient man, was particularly and violently enraged at what he gauged the foolish ramblings of an old crone. He had her thrown from his house. Then he beat her until her face was broken and her body bloodied. The dogs did the rest.

"The stories do not say how long passed between the woman's visit and when Cornaro made his choice. But surely the artifact desired to leave Cornaro, and he refused it that wish. A shadow fell over Venice. A darkness came from the east. It floated on ships. It hovered about the tradesmen that come and go from this place. It scurried about in the night, creeping from one house to the next. Soon it unleashed its full fury on the city. The Plague had returned to Europe, and Venice was to be its doorway.

"There was no reason to blame Cornaro, but people somehow knew the fault lay with him. The preternatural sixth sense can't be explained. The Doge protected Cornaro from the rage of his people. That is, until his own wife fell to the Black Death. It was only their shared blood that prevented him from killing Cornaro then, but he chose a different fate.

"Do you know what they did with plague victims in those days? There were too many to bury. Far too many. So they dug a deep hole, a pit, and they tossed the bodies inside, whether the victim was fully dead or not. There was no such deep earth on Venice to cover the unnumbered dead, and so the Doge made the entire island of Povaglia a plague pit. Cornaro had brought the Plague, and now he would receive its victims as his eternal guests."

The man leaned back in his chair, his story apparently finished. "What happened to him?" I asked.

"No one knows. No one ever returned from that cursed place. It has become an infamia, a no-man's-land. The plague eventually subsided, but what became of the artifact is a mystery. I believe it remains on that island, and I want you to retrieve it for me."

"And for my trouble, you will pay fifteen thousand pounds sterling?"

"Fifteen thousand for the artifact. A thousand for your troubles, whether you find anything or not."

I looked blankly at the man, but in truth, I had barely contained my rising excitement since he had first mentioned the fifteen thousand pounds. It was a magnificent sum, enough to ensure I would never need to leave my Sarah behind again.

"I'll do it," I said finally, "but I want to see the money and have it kept by a reliable third party first."

The man smiled. "Of course, Captain," he said, extending his hand. Then, when I took it, "I have full faith both of us will look back on this day with the greatest of joy."

March 22, 1867

The Book is mine. It shall go with me all my days, and none shall take it from me. We are in the Great Sea now. I ordered my men to sail with the tide. Our cargo was not complete, but no matter. I bear a far greater treasure than any I have ever beheld. That English bastard was a fool. Fifteen thousand pounds? A pittance. No, there is nothing in this world more valuable to me than this wonderful gift.

We arrived on the island shortly after midnight. Thick clouds and a moonless night covered our approach. We moved inland in darkness, only lighting our torches when we were sure we would not be seen from the city. The island was a ruin. It was clear to me no man had trod the paths we walked in years, if not decades. The streets were overgrown, the buildings covered in vines and vegetation, returning to the earth from whence they came.

We came to Cornaro's villa. It was no great feat to find it. It sat on a small rise in the midst of the island, its proud walls and ornate construction a testament to what had been. There was a massive well in its center, a great hole in the earth, a circle of darkness. Tovar, one of my crewmen, threw his torch into the midst of that blackness. It did not fall as far as I had expected. It landed, not in the water, but in the midst of a great shimmering whiteness. It took me a moment to see that these were bones, the only mortal remains of an untold number who had spent their last moments here.

We advanced onward to the house. We found the front doors broken down, forced inwards, it seemed to me, by some great force. We walked into that great marble monstrosity. There were untold treasures there, most corrupted by time and the elements, but many still as beautiful and valuable as they had been when that place was more than a mausoleum. I did not condemn my men when they took what they found; whoever had once lived there had long forsaken that place.

We walked past the great stairwell to a pair of double doors in the rear of the mansion. It was obvious to us all this was the place we sought. A monstrous sight greeted our eyes. It was a mass of skeletons, piled upon one another in front of the door, as if in their last moments they had sought nothing more than entrance to the room beyond. My men set to work in the gruesome task of removing them, one by one, until finally the path was cleared to the doors.

To no one's surprise, they did not open, but we were more

prepared than the poor souls who had once assaulted that place. With axes we went to work, hacking away at the wooden barrier until finally it collapsed in a cloud of thick and overpowering dust.

When the dust cleared, my torch illuminated a great dining room. Sitting at the end of a long table, 'neath an elegant and, no doubt, immeasurably valuable chandelier, was yet another skeleton. This one was different. His moth-eaten and half-rotted clothing was that of a noble. This could be none other than the Cornaro of which I had heard. The Englishman had been vague about the artifact I sought, but I knew I would find it here, with him.

I walked toward his remains, and as I did, I thought I heard a whisper, nay, a chorus of whispers. I did not stop. Rather, I felt myself drawn inexorably toward him. The whispers grew into words, and then they were not words, but a song. A song calling to me, calling my name, telling me to come to them. As my torch settled over that long-dissolved corpse, I saw beneath his bony hand a gold-speckled book. And then I knew.

It was the Book that sang, that called to me, that told me it was mine, that I should take it and make it my own. Its song was beautiful, intoxicating, illuminating. I grasped the Book. Even though its former owner was long dead, it felt as though he resisted me. No matter, the Book is mine now, and I shall never relinquish it.

March 25, 1867

The Book no longer sings. It no longer speaks to me, no longer calls my name, or serenades me in words I do not know but yet understand. I feel alone now, empty. The Book remains, but I feel I have offended it somehow, as if I have turned it against me. The words ended on the morning the ship left Venice. I was certain they would return, but the ship is three days out, and nothing.

Tovar disappeared today. His fate is unknown. No man saw him go overboard, and we have been in calm seas. The men murmur among themselves. They believe he has been taken. It is no matter to me. Tovar can be replaced. But I must hear the song again.

March 26, 1867

The Book never leaves my side. I read it, though I do not understand the import of its words. No matter my passion, my dedication, the silence remains. Four more men were gone at first light. Their beds were empty. It was as if they simply woke up and walked off the ship. There was no struggle, no sign of violence. They were just gone. McCormick came to my stateroom today, at the men's request. They believe the Book is to blame, that it must be destroyed. Fools. I value none of their lives above the Book, and I would gladly sacrifice any of them — or all of them — to keep it safe.

Later

I have locked myself in my stateroom. What is left of the men are outside, pounding away at the doors. They cannot hold long. It began at supper. The food had been prepared, and the men were eating. The air was heavy, the men nervous. I do not know what inspired McCormick. Perhaps it was my rebuff earlier or the presence of the Book beneath my hand. But in the midst of the meal he stood and pointed to me.

"We are cursed by that thing!" he screamed among vile slanders and hateful mutterings. "It must be cast overboard, as Jonah was of old. Only then will this evil leave us!"

It was then it happened. I smiled as it did, as it took him, as I saw the fear and the realization spread across his face. His body went rigid, his arms out to his side like Christ on His cross. One of the men shrieked as he was lifted bodily into the air, hovering some three feet above the deck. I stood, taking the Book in my hands. In the confusion, they did not even notice I had gone. The last thing I saw before the door closed behind me was McCormick's body blinking out of existence.

There is a commotion outside, but one different than before. The men are no longer pounding at the door. Now they are screaming, but their screams seem to grow quieter with every passing second.

They are silent now, as silent as this book before me. I fancy they are all gone, that whatever has preyed upon the others has taken them, as well. But I am not alone. No, there is something beyond. Not the door, but my vision, beyond what I can see clearly. It is here now. It is with me. I can feel its cold hands — no, not hands — but something else, closing around me. But the Book is mine. I will not forsake it! I will not abandon it, not for any man, not for anything! It is mine. It is mine! It is

* * *

Captain Benjamin Butler's journal ended there, in a scraggly black line that staggered down like a lightning bolt that crashes to the ground with a great fury, but then is extinguished. Thus his mortal days came to an end, but he never — not in life, at least — surrendered the Book. I looked over to the leather bag beside me, the bag in which the Book now rested. From it, as clear as the voice of a lover, I heard a song.

Chapter 34

The train moved quickly through the New England countryside, splitting with iron legs a world buried in snow. It was a beautiful day, sun-filled with clear skies. As the car rocked beneath me, I tried to distract myself from the low hum of *that thing* by watching the children play in the great white wilderness beyond.

I laughed to myself, a dark, humorless laugh. I had traveled north in shadow and snow, but now, in the stark sunlight, on a rare but glorious January day, I felt a fear and apprehension that replaced the excitement and anticipation of only a day previous. Every second, every heart beat, was as the footsteps of doom.

The Book sat beside me, not quietly (were it so!), and I felt its weight hang around my neck, like the famed albatross of old. I felt repulsed by it, overborne by it. I could not fathom what had happened to the cursed captain of the *Lydia Lenore*, how the Book had come to own him to the point he would sacrifice anything to prevent its loss. I fully understood why Captain Gray was so quick to turn it over to me. The Book was truly dualistic — a gift to some, a curse to others.

The train arrived at the station on time, at precisely the stroke of noon. I disembarked. No one else did. I stood alone on the platform. The sun shone down from directly above me, but it was a cold light that gave no heat. I walked across the station, the only sound that of my own footsteps. The silence of the snow was thick and unbending. A single carriage sat at the end of the street. I handed the man a couple of coins, and climbed inside.

As we rode through the city, I could sense the hand of fate upon me. Miskatonic University sat on a hill across the river, hovering like a thunderhead on the horizon. I wished for its approach more than ever, wanting nothing more than to relieve myself of the weight on my heart.

The carriage dropped me at Arkham Green. I took my bags and carried them to my room. As I entered, I saw a letter sitting on my writing desk. In the arching hand I knew well was written my name. I opened it and read:

Mr. Weston,

Whenever you return from your errand, please visit me with news of your journey. I shall be in my office at precisely five o'clock daily. May it be by the time you read this note, your journey — and your mission — will have reached a successful conclusion.

Dr. Atley Thayerson

I looked up at the large clock in the corner of the room. At that moment, it tolled one o'clock. Four hours. I felt almost desperate. A visit to Thayerson's office proved fruitless. The door was locked, and the darkness within confirmed it was empty. As I walked back to my room, I felt a creeping fear that even at five o'clock, I would still find it so, as empty of life and as utterly silent as a tomb. Thayerson would never assume I would return so quickly, and it was quite possible his daily vigil would not yet have begun. I banished that thought from my mind, but though I tried, I could find no diversion to pass the hours. Instead, I sat at my desk, staring up wearily at the hands of the clock. Doubtless, no four hours, lest it was spent at the hands of the Inquisitor himself, has ever passed so slowly.

I would say I sat in silence, but such would be a lie. I did not speak, and the quiet of the fallen snow held sway beyond my door. Beside me, muffled though it might have been, that dark miracle continued. The low hum, the mysterious words in tongues unknown and unfathomed, played on. The clock struck four. Like something out of a fairy story, with every tick of the clock, the hand seemed to move more slowly, until I feared it might stop altogether.

At half past the hour, something changed. The singing grew louder, the voice more insistent. I knew then. Somehow I knew. I jumped from my chair and grabbed the leather bag. I veritably ran across Arkham Green. The song of the Book seemed to crescendo to some unholy climax.

A light was on in Thayerson's office. I rapped on the door, more insistently perhaps than I had intended. There was a gruff command to enter from within. I opened the door and stepped across the threshold.

Thayerson looked up at me, and in his familiar face I saw surprise. His gaze went from mine down to the leather bag in my hand. Then something unexpected happened. The music — the Book's song, once so persistent, once so siren-loud I thought it might drive the sanity from my mind, that Devil's chorus — ceased. At least, it ceased for me. Thayerson's eyes told a different story.

"Mr. Weston," he all but whispered, "you have done well. Come!" he commanded, motioning to me.

I stepped forward, placing the leather bag on the desk. He watched as I undid the leather tongs, as the bag fell open, revealing the shimmering gold and crimson that lay beneath. Thayerson reached forward. But then, as if stopped by some invisible force, he looked up at me.

"Take it," I said simply.

So he did, reaching down and clasping the Book in both hands, pulling it towards him as delicately as one might a child.

"You have done very well," he repeated. Then, his countenance changed. "Were you followed?" he asked, almost acquisitively.

"No," I replied. "I had no trouble at all."

"How did you find it so quickly?"

"It was in the possession of a man who no longer wanted it. He gave it freely."

"Yes, as all living men must," Thayerson said. His answer revealed much.

"This will be the University's greatest treasure," he said, rubbing his hand across the cerise cover. "Not even the *Necronomicon* is more precious."

I noted it, then, as it struck me as strange, the name of that other accursed tome crossed the threshold of his lips without the hesitation and fear that had marked its transit heretofore.

"You will be well rewarded for this, Mr. Weston," he said, finally looking up at me. "Well rewarded indeed. I apologize I cannot spend more time with you today and hear more of your travels. Perhaps tomorrow. I had not intended your rapid return and made other arrangements. In fact," he said, confirming my earlier suspicions, "I only stopped by the office for the briefest of moments. It is fortunate . . ." Then, he let the phrase drop. He and I both knew fortune had nothing to do with it.

"Yes, sir," I said, pushing the moment of discomfort away. "Tomorrow, then." I turned to go, but as I did, I stopped at the door. I turned back to Thayerson and said, "One thing, sir. Something unrelated."

"Yes?" Thayerson replied with a hint of annoyance, looking up from the Book at me.

"The rumored incident here at Miskatonic. The one that supposedly happened several years ago with the dead professor. The one who was murdered by his colleague."

"Yes?" Thayerson repeated blankly. "What of it?"

"Were you here then?"

"No," Thayerson answered without hesitation. "That was a few years before I arrived."

"Ah. Alright then," I said haltingly. "'Til tomorrow, professor."

Thayerson said nothing else. His eyes went back down to the Book before him. I stood in the doorway for a second, watching him. It was clear I was not wanted. I left him behind, the song that had once haunted my mind now echoing in his ears.

Chapter 35

As I walked back across the Green, the twilight that had fallen over Arkham matched the darkness in my heart. The Book was gone, but I did not feel the relief I had expected. Instead, I felt empty, as a woman must who, when heavy with child, miscarries. I pulled my chair to a spot dangerously close to the fire in my hearth. But I still felt a cold that, while not physical, nevertheless racked my body with chills.

I must have sat there for hours, thinking on the events of the last two days, wondering what import they might yet have, and perhaps most importantly, questioning the intentions of the man who had brought me to this place — Dr. Atley Thayerson.

He had misled me; this was clear. I considered at first perhaps William was mistaken. Maybe it was some other Miskatonic professor who had come into his life all those years ago. Or perhaps William, who I had known for no more than a few passing hours, had intended to deliberately lead me astray. Neither explanation stood up to scrutiny.

Thayerson was not the kind of name William would have accidentally uttered, and he could have no knowledge of my background. He simply had no ability to construct such a lie. But for reasons I could not grasp — or perhaps, reasons I did not wish to accept — Thayerson refused to acknowledge his participation in one of the school's darkest hours. I hoped it was simply embarrassment that led him to so act, but I feared it was something more. So, I decided on a course of action.

It was for this reason I found myself at the door of Henry Armitage. My sharp rapping on the painted oaken panels was quickly answered.

"Carter!" he exclaimed, thrusting the hand not holding a glass of brandy out towards me. I shook it quickly.

"We need to talk," I said, stepping past him into his room.

"Of course," he replied, closing the door behind me. "I suppose you have completed your task for Thayerson, then?"

"It's about that," I said. I sat down in a chair in front of Henry's fire. I was still painfully cold, and the short walk to his room had done me no favors. I found my eyes glancing around at Henry's peculiar decorations, an eclectic combination of primitive folk art and religious relics. "What do you know of the *Incendium Maleficarum*?" I finally asked. Henry blanched instantaneously.

"W-e-ll," he stuttered. "*The Witch's Fire*, you ask? Why, that is quite a book. I am surprised it interests one such as yourself. It's been lost for, oh . . . two thousand years?"

"What if I were to tell you it has been found?"

Henry's eyes narrowed and filled with suspicion. He turned his head and looked askance at me. "I would say you are wrong. Such a find would be so spectacular I am sure I would have heard about it."

"I held it in my hands not three hours ago."

Henry leapt to his feet.

"Do not say such things loosely, Carter Weston. You do not know of what you speak."

I stood, as well, matching Henry's conviction with my own. "It is a book, bound in crimson skin, written in gold. It does not age, does not corrupt. It cannot be destroyed, not at least by any power on this Earth."

Henry's mouth dropped. For a long moment he did not speak. Then he whispered, "My dear God, Carter. What have you done?"

I related my story to him. Not all of it, but enough that he would understand. The talk with Thayerson, the trip to Anchorhead, meeting the Captain and his friends. Acquiring the Book and bringing it back to Arkham. How it sang, and how that singing stopped when I handed the Book over to Thayerson. How he lied to me about his involvement with Dr. Seward. Henry listened intently, and as he did, his face began to reveal a discordant combination of fear and determination.

As I finished my discourse, Henry sat down in a large chair behind him. He put his hands together like a penitent at prayer. He sat there in that pose for what seemed, at the time, to be halfway to eternity. Then, finally, but only as I felt my mind on the verge of breaking from this unexpected delay, he lifted his eyes to me and said,

Below the thunders of the upper deep;
Far, far beneath in the abysmal sea,
His ancient, dreamless, uninvaded sleep
The Kraken sleepeth: faintest sunlights flee.

There hath he lain for ages, and will lie
Battening upon huge seaworms in his sleep,
Until the latter fire shall heat the deep;
Then once by man and angels to be seen,
In roaring he shall rise and on the surface die.

"Tennyson," I said simply.

"Tennyson," Henry replied. "Though, he could not have known what ancient and eldritch knowledge stirred him when he wrote those words, he spoke truly nevertheless." Now, he stood. "Thayerson will seek to wake the sleeper, Carter. He will seek to bring him forth from below the waves, to rise in power and might, and to rule this world as he and his once did. Others have tried before. Many have. Men who sought power or immortality or who were simply too stupid and vain to know the forces with which they dealt.

"But Thayerson has something they lacked. He possesses the *Incendium Maleficarum* and the dread *Necronomicon*. With them both, he may yet plunge this world into a second darkness from which it shall never emerge."

"Can he be stopped?" I asked, more calmly than I might have expected. After all I had seen and heard, this came as no surprise to me.

"Perhaps," Henry said. "But he must be found and quickly. You say you gave the Book to him three hours ago?"

"Yes."

Henry sighed. "Then all hope is lost. He could be anywhere, and he is no doubt well along in his plan. The moon is full tonight, and the tides are right. He could be performing the ritual even as we speak."

"No," I replied. "No, I think I know where he is. Or at least, I think I know how to find him. Come quickly, my friend. The night is dark, but there may yet be the dawn."

I saw a spark of the old flame that burned within Henry return to his eyes. He smirked at me. "Yes," he said, and then louder, "Yes! I was never one to lose hope before the game is finished."

"Get your cloak," I commanded. "Where better to find a book than a library?"

Not a minute later, we were out the door, flying quickly to Huntington Library. Henry was correct. The ritual had been tried before. And if I was right, Thayerson would be precisely where he had been thirty years past. This time, though he may have tools he once lacked, there were also those determined to oppose him.

Chapter 36

We stepped into the darkness, the sky as clear as it had been that day, but with a bright full moon serving as a poor imitation of the sun. Its fragile light was enough to guide our steps to a place we had been countless times before.

Huntington Library stood like a monolith in the distance, a great cyclopean monstrosity of learning. There had been rumors, of course. Like all of witch-haunted Arkham it seemed, Huntington had a history. It had been the first permanent building in that ancient town. It was constructed in 1640, only four years after the founding of Harvard, and a full decade before Miskatonic University came into being.

Legend had it the people of Arkham had found something on that little mound above the river. Something ancient and arcane, something built of mighty stone blocks, the working of which was far beyond the skills of the native Wampanoag, something that covered a great, but ruined, staircase that ran into the center of the Earth itself. It was a bizarre legend, an impossible tale. But it didn't end with that great vestibule.

On December 21, 1639, during the darkest and longest night of the winter, three great ships sailed into the mouth of the Miskatonic River. The people of Arkham awoke to the sound of chisels and hammers, of stone cutting and construction. The men who labored on the hill were unknown to them, clad in strange raiment, faces hooded and cloaked. But fear was greater than the people of Arkham's curiosity. For the four months that followed, the men continued their work, from the rising of the sun until it disappeared behind the western Berkshires.

Each night, the people of Arkham cowered behind their flimsy wooden doors, terrified of what lurked beyond. But it was the Beltane Eve, the night of Walpurgis, that the old men of Arkham still speak of in whispered words and phrases. They say the hills burned with an unnatural glow that night, that satanic psalms floated down to the town below, as creatures of darkness danced and gibbered in the moonlight.

When the sun rose on the first day of May 1640, the men were gone. What they left behind was a great edifice of stone.

Three days passed. When the workers did not reappear, it was determined a contingent of the town's men should go up and investigate the structure that had been left behind. It was led by Isaac Huntington. It was no great distance from the edge of the town to the hill above, but the men advanced slowly. When they reached the palace of granite, only Huntington was willing to enter.

For half an hour the men waited outside, many of them growing increasingly certain Huntington would never return. But he did. There was nothing inside, he reported. Nothing but several great open spaces, and some steps leading down to a vault below. In the vault were four murals. These four murals represented the four great societies of antiquity — Egypt, Babylon, Greece, and Rome. They were exquisitely constructed, and some say at night, if the air is right, they each glow in the candlelight. But the ancient staircase, the one that the people of Arkham had always feared, was nowhere to be seen.

I had never seen the murals. They were off limits to students, as was much of Huntington Library. It was a place filled with legend and mystery, and if we were to find Thayerson anywhere, I wagered it would be there. I hoped it as well, for if I was wrong, then all truly was lost.

Arkham Green was deserted. The library sat silently and, to all appearances, empty before us. For a moment my heart sunk, but when I pulled on the door, it opened. I looked at Henry.

"At this hour, it should be locked."

I simply nodded. We stepped inside. The moonlight streamed in through the great glass windows that had been installed by the travelers from across the seas all those years ago. We supplemented that illumination with lanterns of our own.

The entrance to the vault was in the rear of the building. I had come to that place prepared to take whatever actions were necessary to gain entrance to the crypt below, but I soon found there would be no need for violence. The great wooden doors sat open. Whatever Thayerson intended, he had no concerns he would be followed or discovered.

As we descended the steps within, the chamber below came into view. Before me on the north wall, shimmering in the light of my lantern, was the Egyptian mural. I had seen something like this before in the great and mysterious Egyptian Book of the Dead.

In the center of the image sat a scale. On one side, Anubis, the jackal-headed god of the dead, held the hand of a deceased pharaoh. On the other side was Thoth, the god of judgment, whose ibis eyes were locked on the scale before him. In the balance was the heart of the king and the feather of the truth. If the heart is heavy with sin and evil, so says the wisdom of the pyramids, then the Devourer of the Dead — part crocodile, part leopard, part hippopotamus — would swallow the king whole. But if the king were true, if he were found worthy, then he would receive from Anubis the contents of his other hand — the Ankh, the Egyptian cross, the key of life, as symbolic of eternal salvation to the Egyptians as the cross of Christ still is to us.

"What now?" Henry asked. I could hear the despondency in his voice. "If he's not here, Carter, where could he be?"

"He's here."

I took a step forward and looked closely at the image before me. There had been something playing in the back of my mind, something I knew would lead me to Thayerson. In that moment, it became clear. It was something I had heard only the night before.

"Choose truth, not passion. A winding staircase. Seek the light, not the darkness."

Even in the gloom, I could see the look of confusion spread across Henry's face. But then some clarity.

"A riddle?" he asked.

"A key," I replied.

I rubbed my hand along the mural. It was as flat and smooth as a stone long polished by the river. A part of me felt foolish, but another bit of the previous night's tales popped into my mind. I put my hand on the feather and pushed. To my surprise and yet expectation, it moved, disappearing into the wall behind. A small door at the base of the scale popped open. Henry grinned. I found myself doing the same. Even in this most dire of moments, I felt my heart leap as some of the excitement of my boyhood forced its way in.

The passage was small, and we were both forced to crawl on our knees to gain entrance. It opened into a cylindrical room. The curved walls surrounded the spiral stone staircase of legend, one that appeared to go down into the Earth itself. I glanced at Henry, but there was really no question as to what we should do next. And so we began our descent. Down and around, as the marble walls of the stairwell turned into chiseled rock. The rock was rough-hewn and ancient, as if it had been cut a thousand years before. We followed it farther and farther, so far down I wondered if we might walk into the very fires of Hell. My wonderings were soon proven baseless, however, as a turn of the stairs revealed their bottom.

We were now in a small room. On either side was a passageway. Their entrances were exactly the same, with no indication of which path was true.

"Choose the light, not the darkness," Henry mumbled.

I had thought it an empty statement, a truism with no significance. But now I was not so sure. I was no Mason, but I knew their temples were built on an east-west line. The west was shunned, for in the west darkness dwelt. But the east was the source of the light, the seat of God.

"So we should go east, towards the sun."

"But which way is east?"

I looked up the stairwell whence we came. Despite our turnings, I knew the rock wall that had birthed it faced north.

"This way," I said. Henry gave me a skeptical look. I admit in that moment I was not entirely sure of my choice, but there could be no other decision. We took what I hoped was the eastern corridor.

We stepped into a great cavern, its vaulted ceiling reaching up and beyond our vision. A downward sloping ramp of stone stretched out before us, the puny light from our lanterns barely piercing the darkness beyond. It was either walk back up the stairs or continue into the unknown. The latter was our only option. Down we went. The slope was gentle, down enough we knew we were descending, but not so steep as to make descent uncomfortable. The gloom was thick, and the air with it. I felt as though we were pressing through water more than air, and every step was more difficult to take than the last.

That sensation began to change, and so did the light. It started with a few shimmering spots on the ground, but it was only when the entire floor began to glow that I realized we had stumbled upon a dramatic shift in the cavern bottom. No more simple rough-cut stone, but rather a smooth surface, paved in a thick, semi-translucent material. It was as if somehow the entire path was nothing more or less than the single facet of a tremendous diamond. But even that does not fully capture the peculiar properties of that crystalline expanse. It seemed to absorb the very beam from our lanterns. Absorb it, amplify it, and exude it in far greater strength, until all but the most distant height of the cavern was filled with light. Then, we were no longer looking at the floor.

It was Henry who saw it first. He clutched my shoulder sharply, and when I looked at his face, I knew had he not done so, he may have fallen to the floor in terror. As I followed his gaze upward, I wondered if he overestimated my own strength.

They were forms in the rock, carved stone emerging from the wall of the cavern. But they were so much more. There, in high relief, stood the massive gods of an ancient age. These were not the crude images of the Egyptians, the Aztecs, or even the Greeks or Romans. No manufactured deities with animal appendages clumsily attached to the human form were they.

No, these were truly monsters, creatures with an inherent believability of form, despite the impossibility of their amalgamation of prehistoric wings, hellish tentacles and claws, and dragon-like teeth. So precise were the carvings, so neat the lines and the curves, so bright the eyes and sharp the points, that had I seen them in shadow and not the reflected light of the stone pathway, I would have fled in terror.

We continued walking downward, our eyes scanning the pantheon of whatever race carved this temple from the solid rock. Then, the ceiling in front of us dropped low, and there, facing us, was the most horrific figure of all. He stood on legs like a man, though his feet were better suited to the oceans and the seas than the land. So, too, were the thick, cable-like tentacles that fanned out in every direction from his body, each seeming to wriggle and writhe in the light from below, each threatening to reach out and take us at any moment.

His muscular, claw-fisted arms were draped in wing-like appendages, though whether they were meant to traverse the air or the sea or some heretofore unknown aether, I could not say. But it was his face that terrified, his cruel and lidless eyes, ever-watching, his gaping maw ready to devour. And then Henry, for the first time in my presence, and no doubt for the first time in ageless eons in that place, uttered the name of he who sleeps beneath the sea.

"Cthulhu."

For a long moment we stood and stared at that great beast from a world where black stars shone down darkness on an ageless sea. He, the oldest of the Old Ones, who had come to this Earth to rule mankind with his minions. I had known for some time it was he who had stalked the shadows and dark recesses of the legends and tales to which I had become privy in past days, but it was my undying hope I would never look upon that image. Now it was only my prayer I would never see the demon in the flesh.

"What is that?" Henry said, pointing to tiny carved specks at the feet of the god, so small in comparison that one would hardly notice their presence. It was something in the way they seemed bent over on themselves that confirmed my initial fear.

"Those are people, Henry."

I saw the doubt in his eyes, but then those eyes could deny no longer. I pulled Henry's arm, and though his gaze never broke from the figure above, we made our way underneath into the tunnel beyond.

The cavern was left behind now, replaced by a narrow but still descending tunnel. A strange smell began to waft up towards us, not strange to us, but certainly to that place. It was the salt-spray scent of the sea. As the descent continued, I began to question my bearings. Though we seemed to have traveled down an untold distance, the unmistakable roar of ocean waves reverberated down the tunnel from only a short distance beyond. The tunnel cut off sharply, opening up into yet another chamber. This one was much different than the one behind.

The cyclopean images from before were gone, but the walls were not bare. Rather than the images of gods of old, they were covered in deep set runes, the words and symbols of a language long dead and, if my expertise has shown me anything over these many years, not of this Earth.

But the cavern was not complete. Opposite of us, where there should have been a wall, was a great opening, as if a gaping mouth, drawing in the sea beyond. Waves crashed against the cavern's edge, sending jets of water up and into the expanse. These streams of water ran down and into the center of the cavern, pooling around the feet of Dr. Atley Thayerson. Or what used to be Atley Thayerson. What stood there, then, was no longer a man.

The cavern was empty, save for a great stone altar in its center, flanked by two burning torches. A small skeleton lay on the rocky floor. The fate of Sara Quincy was no longer a mystery. The flickering light of the torches cast dancing shadows down on the body that had replaced hers. Even in the weak light, I knew his face, that of a murderer condemned to death not a month before.

How Thayerson had acquired him would remain a mystery, but it was clear he had learned the lesson that pure blood was of no use in the doing of evil. And blood there was. Spilling off the altar and dripping from the curved blade Theyerson still clutched in his hands.

For his part, Thayerson stood cloaked in a garment that matched the crimson skin of one of the books before him. The *Incendium Maleficarum* and the *Necronomicon* were both open, together, no doubt, for the first time in a millennium. His face was a snarl, and his eyes were filled with a hate that was not of this world. Henry spoke first.

"God, Thayerson, what have you done?"

The thing, dressed in Thayerson's skin, stood at the edge of the altar, glaring at us.

"Your god does not hear you. But I do."

Henry continued, "Give us the book, Thayerson!" The words were stronger than his heart, bolstered by the pistol he had removed from his jacket.

"I don't think he is Thayerson. Not anymore, at least."

As if in grim confirmation, the thing began to cackle.

"You fools," he said. "Thayerson is dead. As you two soon shall be. The Book is mine. It always has been, as it always will be."

"Who are you?" I asked boldly.

"Yog-Sothoth is the Gate. The Book is the Key. Soon it shall open, and from its mouth shall pour the true rulers of this world. The waters will boil. The moon will turn to blood. The forests shall burn, and the Sun shall turn as black as the skies of Gehennasa-ru. Then will this world become as it was — a paradise for us, a hell for you."

"Are you Yog-Sothoth?" I asked.

"Yog-Sothoth? Yes, that is my name. But we have many names. For we are Legion."

"Legion?" Henry stammered.

"When the gate is opened and the Lord of the Seas has risen, our true form shall be seen by all. But not by you, for now you will die."

At that moment, I pulled from my coat the two wooden staves I had brought with me. Crossing them in front of me, I hoped Jack's story had been as true as I now believed. It was only for an instant, but in that instant, fear was in the beast's eyes. He covered it quickly, with a burning hatred that had grown within his trapped being for tens of millennia.

"Do you truly believe your emblems, your sigils of a broken God, can stop he who bends time, he who sleeps beneath the waves 'til death itself has perished, he who walks between the folds of space itself? No. For now, I shall spare you. But only so you can taste the bitter death that awaits!"

With that, he turned and flung himself into the thunderous ocean below. Henry and I ran to the edge, but there was only blackness beyond. Where he had gone with the Book was a mystery, but he had left the *Necronomicon* behind. Whatever purpose it had served was finished.

"That was quick thinking," a familiar voice said from behind.

We spun on our heels, Henry still holding the pistol in his hand. To my shock, it was Captain Gray.

"I was a fool to give you the Book, Carter. I know that now. It was a moment of weakness I won't soon repeat. I hoped I could arrive in time to prevent him from performing the ritual. Or at least stop you from trying anything foolish. In both, I see I failed."

"Captain Gray!" I exclaimed, pushing Henry's pistol down with my hand. "Why are you here?"

The Captain chuckled. "Boy, have you learned nothing? There is fate in all this. For the last thirty years, I and those of my order have prepared for this day. The Rising has begun. But, although the night may be dark, it is not too late to bring back the light."

"To stop the Rising?" I said.

"I have sent word to Newburyport. The *Kadath* will sail again. We will go together. I know where Thayerson, or should I say the thing he has become, is going."

"How can you know that?" Henry asked.

"Because there's only one place he would go. To R'lyeh, the great city of the Old Ones. It rises even as we speak. That was the ritual performed tonight, that and the bringing forth of Yog-Sothoth. But there is one ritual yet remaining. Cthulhu still sleeps, his slumber uninterrupted. The rite must be said there, before his cyclopean tomb. Only then shall the work of evil be complete. If we can make it to the island before Yog-Sothoth, we can stop this where it stands."

"And if we don't?" Henry asked.

Captain Gray's countenance grew dark, his mouth set, his eyes clear. "In that event, all is not yet lost. But the price to save this world will have grown much steeper and much dearer, indeed."

"Why do we wait?" I said.

"That's the spirit, young man," Gray said with a smile. "There is a reason fate chose you for this burden. The *Kadath* will arrive tomorrow in Arkham Harbor. We sail at dawn. From there we head south. Get sleep if you can. The journey will be long, and we will not rest again until it is completed."

With that we left that place of death, that den of evil, behind. Our journey up the winding stairs was arduous, but even upon returning to my room, I could not sleep. The purpose of my life had been revealed to me, as it seldom is to man. My only fear was I had not the strength to see it through.

Chapter 37

To say I awoke early the next morning would be to misstate fact. In truth, I did not sleep. I lay in my bed, my mind racing across the events of the past few days. My rational mind rebelled, pleaded, cajoled, attempted to convince that all that came before was a hallucination, a feverish concoction of too much wine and too many dark tales.

But it was of no effect. I had seen these things come to pass with my own eyes. And if we could not stop the evil which now danced in the darkness somewhere beyond the gates of Miskatonic University, then truly I was living in the last days. Of man, at least.

When the first rays of the sun finally did peek through, I arose to find Henry sitting in the parlor, dressed and ready.

"Slept well, I see."

"Like a rock," he replied with a wry smile.

We gathered our things; we had packed lightly. As I closed the door behind me, I wondered if I would ever see that place again.

We made our way quickly to Arkham harbor, the sun's disk having barely cleared the horizon when we arrived. The *Kadath* stood at anchor, Captain Gray leaning against the railing on her deck. He met us as we climbed aboard.

"Gentlemen, our journey begins soon. You remember my crew?"

With a wave he gestured to the three men behind him. William was the first to take my hand.

"I had hoped we would not meet again," he said, "but it would appear Arkham is as witch-haunted as ever."

"It would appear so."

Daniel and Jack were there, as well, and it felt good, even though I had met them only briefly, to see them again.

"We will be traveling light," Captain Gray said, "and I expect each of you, even you and Mr. Armitage here, to carry their weight. Mr. Weston, if I could speak to you for a second."

I followed Captain Gray into his study. He walked to his desk and picked up a sheet of paper.

"I spoke to the harbor master earlier this morning. Thayerson, or what he has become, will soon possess untold powers. But not yet. His needs are not unlike our own."

"He needs a ship," I said.

"Precisely. And only one ship left last night. Not surprising, as the tide was at its height, and no sane sailor would have tried the passage at that time. But this ship did, and by some unholy miracle, it sailed against the tide to open sea. I thought you would be interested in the vessel's name."

He pushed the piece of paper towards me. I picked it up. I looked from it to the Captain.

"It seems fate has a sense of humor."

As impossible as it would seem, the ship's name was unmistakably familiar.

"The *Lydia Lenore*?" I said.

"It would appear so."

"But you said she foundered?"

"She did. But apparently whoever christened this ship did so unawares. She was launched not three months ago. Thayerson chose well. She's the fastest ship on the seas. Truth told, I do not know if we can overtake her. That's why each man will have to do his part, sailor or not. We will travel with a skeleton crew. Our supplies will be few. We need all the speed we can muster."

Time was not our ally, and I did not keep the Captain with idle chatter. In fact, the men had already sprung to work. Henry and I helped as best we could, but in truth, we were more of a liability than an asset. Before long, Henry had retired to his cabin, studying several works of arcane knowledge he had brought with him in lieu of his clothes. I stayed on the deck, watching the sea and the land as it slipped past our ship. Arkham harbor faded into the distance, the steeple of Christ's Church was the last memento of mankind to slip away. I had never known the sea, but I took to it immediately. Henry was less enthusiastic, and it wasn't long before a sickness had overtaken him.

The ship sailed south as quickly as the winds would take us. In my naiveté, I suppose I had expected this would be a short voyage, a dash to some island just beyond Cape Cod. I had been wrong.

"Our voyage will take us down the coastal seaboard, through the Caribbean and beyond the Equator. We will make the passage of the Horn, God willing. It is to the Pacific that our prey has flown."

It was to be a voyage of weeks, not days. If the whispered words of the more experienced men were any indication, the great Cape might end our journey before it even reached its destination.

"The seas are filled with evil there, they are."

Phineas Drake was his father's son, and when that man — a sailor the Captain spoke as highly of as any man could — passed to the other side, Phineas had taken his place. The other sailors kept to themselves, speaking to us only rarely and only when necessary. They sensed a foreboding about us, and no man is more apt to surrender to the crushing hand of superstition than a seaman. But Drake feared little, if he feared at all.

"It is a narrow river of water, crunched between the ice of Antarctica and the rocks of the Andes. There is no peace there, only a roiling cauldron of ice water so cold it will kill you faster than we could drag you out. If we could find you in the swells, that is."

It was a ghastly image, and one that no doubt would have terrified us all, were it not for the horror we had already faced. An icy death somehow sounded peaceful.

* * *

"We shall put in anchor at Charleston."

Gray pointed at a spot on the map he had spread on his desk.

"Why not New York, Captain?" Drake asked. "She's closer, and we are running mighty low on supplies."

It was true. We had left the port of Arkham as soon as the tide would allow, and though the men had worked as quickly and efficiently as they could, we had been forced to ration.

"Call it a hunch, Mr. Drake. The *Lydia Lenore* left in even more of a mad dash than we. Their supplies may have been more, they may have been less than our own. I believe they will press as far as they can, just as they pressed against the high tide. To go farther than Charleston, though, would be the ruin of them. Thayerson may not be human, but his crew still is, and they need food and drink as much as we do."

"You plan on making our stand there, then?"

The Captain furrowed his brow and pursed his lips.

"No, not quite, Mr. Drake. I do not believe we will catch them so easily. I am more interested in what the harbor master has to say about their coming. Intelligence is crucial in this endeavor."

"Then, Charleston it is, sir. I will mark our heading."

As Drake left, I asked Captain Gray, "What sort of intelligence do you hope to gather?"

Gray threw his compass on his desk and walked around to where I stood. "Primarily," he said, "how far ahead they presently are, what sort of speed they are making. They left port approximately eight hours before us. Not so much we can't overtake them, though their ship is faster. I have a feeling, however, perhaps they are not making as good a time as others might."

"What do you mean?" I asked. Gray held up his hand.

"Let us see what we find in Charleston."

With that, I knew the conversation was at an end. Whatever mystery Charleston held would have to wait to be revealed.

* * *

Three days later, we arrived in Charleston harbor.

"The air is foul," Drake whispered as he peered out into the landing. I had never been to Charleston, but I could not imagine the scene that lay before me was anything but unnatural. Not a soul stirred on the docks. A mist seemed to rise from the depths, covering all it touched in its icy grip. As it crept up the side of the ship, I found myself raising my hands from the railing, lest the mist's skeletal fingers drain the very life from my body.

"Mr. Drake," the Captain said, "Mr. Weston and I will go ashore. Once we have determined the harbor is safe, we quickly procure supplies — enough to take us to the Caribbean, but not so much we can do so without hardship. Remember, speed is the key."

"But Captain, I don't think . . ."

The Captain held up his hand to stop him. It was a habit of his, a man used to command who knew the thoughts of his subordinates before they did.

"Mr. Drake, you are fully capable of sailing the ship. Should anything happen, my three compatriots and Mr. Armitage here will direct your path."

Drake frowned. He was not pleased, but neither did he argue.

Only a few minutes later, we were in a yawl, the Captain moving us closer to the harbor with every stroke of his powerful arms. He had lost little vitality with age.

"Do you believe," I asked quietly, "the others can stop Thayerson if something should happen to us?"

That thoughtful look I had now come to expect returned to the Captain's face.

"If I thought," he began, "anything would happen to us, I never would have left the ship. Believing in fate has its benefits. We are not scheduled to die here today," he said with a wink.

As I looked toward that desolate harbor, the only sound meeting my ears being the inky-black waves lapping against our oars, I wondered at his faith. We pulled our boat up to the jetty, and Captain Gray pulled me up onto solid ground. Any other time, I probably would have remarked on the strange feeling of solidity after days of rocking ocean, but my mind was elsewhere.

If you haven't heard it, you cannot comprehend the roar of the silence, the overpowering thunder of the absence of sound. I heard it that day. There is madness there, and it was with a touch of relief the bitter soundlessness was finally broken by our own footsteps. Captain Gray reached into his coat and pulled out a pistol. I wondered for a moment if that bit about fate had been solely for my benefit. I doubted anything we would meet feared the bullet.

The harbor was as we had thought — deserted. The master's office was empty, the only movement was of the door as it swung lazily on its hinges.

"Where did they all go?"

Gray frowned. "At least there can be no doubt. Thayerson was here, and he has left his mark."

It was then we heard the creak of a door opening. Gray spun on his heel, pointing his pistol in the direction of the sound. An old man with scared eyes threw up his hands.

"Don't shoot!" he begged.

Gray lowered his pistol. "I'm sorry, sir, but we thought the harbor deserted."

"No need. With what passed through this place, I can understand going armed."

I stepped forward. "Can you tell us where everyone has gone?"

"They fled after the coming of those . . . things. I know not how else to describe them. The men will return soon, no doubt, for the evil has finally deserted us."

The Captain excused himself and walked quickly to the dock. He fired a single shot into the air, the preordained signal it was safe to come ashore. He, then, returned to where we stood.

"Tell us," the Captain commanded.

The man looked from him to me for a moment. With a gesture he bid us join him in the room beyond. It was a tavern, and after pouring three drinks, one to fortify himself in the telling and the others to give us strength in the listening, he began to speak.

* * *

"It fell upon us not seven hours before you arrived. There were signs of its coming. I heard them before I saw them, the terrified screeching, the almost demonic squeals. When I looked out my window, the sky was hidden. At first, I didn't know what my eyes beheld. Great, white, undulating masses of clouds. But no, not clouds — birds. Every bird in the sea and sky it seemed. And I knew whatever they fled was coming for us.

"When the great white ship arrived, it seemed to float on a thick icy mist. That unnatural fog rolled forward, and as it reached the shore, I saw men who would curse the Devil and steal his drink cross themselves.

"They came in three boats. Their captain stood at the front of the first boat, hooded and cloaked in the black shroud of the reaper himself. I never saw his face. When the boats pulled up to the dock, he exited with his men, but he went no farther than the end of the pier. I was thankful for that, although not for long. His men, if men they were, were horrible enough. They did not walk. Rather they stumbled and shambled their way through the harbor. Their eyes were empty, as if there was no soul there, no thought. I have seen things in my days at sea, things in the night-darkened islands of the *mare carrib*, that made me doubt whether there could be a good God beyond the clouds. Men turned to slaves, to mindless beasts. The Haitians have a word for it — zombie. That was what I saw again this day. Men turned to monsters.

"Most of the harbor-men fled. I stayed behind to watch, my curiosity overwhelming my good sense. They took what they needed, dragging it back to their boats. When the loading was completed, they rowed into the fog and to the white ship. That was six hours ago."

The Captain listened intently throughout the man's speech. Now, he bid him farewell, thanking him for his time and assuring him the white ship would not return. When we had left the tavern behind, I asked him what it all meant.

"It is as I thought," the Captain answered as we hurried to supervise the men, now purchasing from some of the dock workers and store owners who had returned. "No ship would willingly take on such a passenger, not for the journey he intends or for the pay which he lacks. No, he has bewitched the ship and its men. But men they remain, and supplies they need. Our greatest stroke of luck is his wizardry has cost him his greatest advantage. His ship may be faster than ours, but it is manned by mindless beasts. We may catch him yet. Come, young Weston. The chase is on!"

As the Captain rowed back to the ship, the evil fog began to dissolve before the light of the sun. And for the first time, I believed we might overtake that demon before he reached his appointed place and time with the Devil himself.

* * *

My hopes were short-lived. The men drove themselves like Egyptian slaves, such was their devotion to Captain Gray. Two weeks later, we crossed the Equator. The night was black, but when I looked up to the sky, I found no comfort there. The constellations I remembered, the ones that I had learned with my father during the short summer nights of my youth, were gone, replaced by alien stars and unknown worlds. It only added to my foreboding, my sense that the world as I knew it was in danger of changing forever.

Three weeks in, we spotted a white ship sailing hard against the wind. Captain Gray sprang into action, and I felt the mix of exhilaration and fear that comes with imminent battle. We would have caught them too; I do not doubt that. But no sooner had we closed, so tight I could see the black figure of Thayerson lurking around the aft deck, than a thick fog began to rise from the sea.

It was as dense as any London has ever seen and bitterly cold, despite our latitude and the summer months that held sway in the southern hemisphere. It was as unnatural as it was unmercifully impenetrable, as evil as it was all-obscuring. When it cleared, as quickly as it had risen, the white ship was gone.

That night, Captain Gray called me into his cabin. The map was once again spread out on his table. On one corner sat a book with which I now was very familiar, though the primal fear it inspired in me had not lessened with exposure. I could tell from the haggard look on the Captain's face he had spent many hours delving into the secrets of the *Necronomicon*. He looked up at me and, with much effort, managed a smile.

"Carter, please, come in. Have a seat." He gestured to a chair sitting in front of his desk. "After the events of today, I thought we should have a talk. It is evident to me now, as I am sure it is to you as well, we will not overtake Thayerson, not at sea at least. His powers are limited, but powers they are, and we are incapable of thwarting them. Therefore, I have instructed Drake that, other than a stop at a Royal Navy base near the Horn for supplies, we are to proceed to our final destination, as if there were no ship sailing before us."

"And where is that destination, sir?" I asked the question, even though I knew the answer.

"R'lyeh," he said, rising. "The city of the dead, the greatest city this world has ever seen. It is located here."

He pointed to a spot in the center of a great open space of blue. "This is our destination. It is known as the pole of inaccessibility. It is called that because the nearest land is fifteen hundred miles away at Easter Island. A strange place, and if we did not know the truth, one might wonder why this place of all places is devoid of land. But R'lyeh sits beneath those waves. She did, at least."

I looked from the map to Gray. His eyes were hooded and dark from lack of sleep.

"I have been studying the *Necronomicon*," he said as he sat back down. "The ritual Thayerson performed started the Rising. For that ritual he required both this book and the *Incendium Maleficarum*. He needs only the latter for the next step. The great Citadel of Nazreel has risen, and within it lies ancient Cthulhu in repose. Thayerson will enter the Citadel and perform the final ritual. Then, the Lord of the Seas and Skies will rise. The gate will open, and the Great Old Ones will return. R'yleh will rise from the seas, the sun will melt, and darkness will cover us all."

The Captain fell silent, and with every passing second it seemed as though he had lost hope.

"But we can stop it, right?"

He sighed deeply. "It is possible. The ritual Thayerson must perform is complex and difficult, though I have no doubt the demon within him is well versed in its details. If we can reach the island in time to stop him, there is a spell within the *Necronomicon* that can send the city back into the depths where it belongs."

"And should he complete the ritual?"

The Captain did not respond for a moment. Instead, he reached forward and opened a cabinet in his desk and pulled out a bottle of green liquid. "The French," he began, "believe absinthe either inspires genius or drives one to madness — depending on who you ask. I would take either at this juncture, for when the world has gone mad, only the insane survive."

He poured two glasses and, after turning with a dash of water the orgiastic green into a clouded, milky white, handed me one. We both drank deeply, and I felt pins of licorice dance across my tongue.

"Your questions anticipate my reason for bringing you here. Hopefully, it won't come to that. Our primary objective is to stop Thayerson before he completes the ritual."

"And how do we do that?"

"An interruption should suffice. As I said, the ritual requires precision. Once we stop it, we will use the incantation within the *Necronomicon* to banish the beast within him back to the realm from which he came. It will kill Thayerson, of course, but he has chosen that path himself. Then, it is an easy matter to send the city back to the mossy depths."

"That sounds relatively simple."

Captain Gray frowned. "It does, doesn't it? And it will be . . . if we arrive in time."

"And if we don't?"

"If we don't, if Lord Cthulhu is risen, then it may be too late. In that event, the banishing spell will not work on Thayerson. He will have to be dealt with through other means. There is still one avenue open to us, but a dark one it is. There is one incantation that lies at the heart of the *Incendium Maleficarum*. It is known as the Logos Creed. It has been used only once before," the Captain said, holding up one finger for emphasis. "One time. At the beginning of days, at least days as we reckon them, when the Great Old Ones were cast down and stripped of lordship, when they were banished to the spaces beyond space, to live only in the dreams and subconscious of man, until one day they might return. One time. The words were spoken by God Himself."

I listened as Gray spoke, believing him only because of all that had come to pass.

"'In the beginning was the Word,' Carter," the Captain quoted solemnly. "'And the Word was with God, and the Word was God. The same was in the beginning with God. In Him was life; and the life was the light of men. And the light shineth in darkness; and the darkness comprehended it not.'"

Gray poured another glass of absinthe for us both.

"I have a theory," he said, as he lifted the draught. "That the Word was just that, a word. But what a word it was. God is all powerful, but He did not think the world into being, He did not think light into the darkness. No, all that was made was spoken into being. I believe it took only one word to make it so — His own name."

"The name of God?"

Gray nodded. Then his voice came as a whisper. "And the *Necronomicon* seems to confirm it. If Cthulhu rises, the only way to send him back to the depths is to recite the Logos Creed, the final word of which is the name of God Himself. That name is lost to us, but it can be found at the heart of the Book."

"So it's just a matter of getting the *Incendium Maleficarum* back?"

The Captain chuckled, but there was no joy in that laugh.

"No, it is more than that, though that might be too high a wall to climb as it is. No, my young friend, the saying of the Logos Creed comes with a terrible price, for it is death to utter the true name of the Lord. Whoever does so may save this world, but his life is forfeit."

Gray leaned back in his chair. I knew, then, he did not expect to see his home again. This was to be his final voyage.

"Are you sure?" I asked somewhat desperately. Gray waved one hand dismissively.

"Oh, who can be sure of much when it comes to such things. But, yes, Mr. Weston. I am as sure of this as I have ever been of anything. If we cannot stop Thayerson before he completes the ritual, then I will say the Logos Creed. And, if I cannot, then the lot will fall to you."

As his words washed over me, I rose and took my leave. But when I reached the door, a question dawned upon me.

"Captain," I said. "If God banished the Old Ones before, why would he not do it again?"

Gray smiled. "A question for the ages, my young friend. Perhaps, He will. Perhaps, we are to be His instruments. Or maybe these are the days men have envisioned since God deigned to give them His counsel. Perhaps, these are the last days, and we are to witness the end of the world."

My question answered, I received no succor from the reply. Suddenly, our journey had never been so urgent.

Chapter 38

What seemed like an eternity later, we rounded the Horn of South America and prepared to enter the Cape. The tension in the air, and the way the men went about the work in silence without a word to us or their fellows, confirmed all we had heard about the danger we faced. Even the Captain was tense.

"It is strange, Carter. This is the first time in thirty years I've gone into a crossing like this without the Book. As bizarre as it might seem, I wish I had it with me now."

And I wished it, too. But there would be no help from the Devil on this day. If we were to survive, it would be by God's grace. Or our own luck. I would take either.

It was luck that was with us. The weather was calm that day, the thick gray clouds not offering the storm they might just as easily have. That didn't make the passing easy, by any stretch. The waves were like mountains of ice and our ship was the sled, such was the tossing of the sea. I joined Henry in his illness, though in a strange way, my own occupation with my roiling stomach kept my mind from the danger of our situation.

A day and a half later, we had cleared the Cape.

"Easy passage this time, aye, Captain? Perhaps our luck is turning," Drake said with a laugh. Given I hoped to make the passage again, I prayed this was sarcasm. For all our sakes.

"Steady yourself, my friend," Drake said, reading my thoughts. "The true danger begins now. Ships make the passing of the Horn every day. But no man sails to our destination. Should something go wrong . . ." He held out an upturned hand. There was no need to continue.

So it began, the long voyage into an infinite sea. The birds stayed with us for a few days. But soon, even the gulls were gone, no land close enough to call a home. Then it was just us, with no sound but our own voices and the lapping of the waves against the ship to keep us company. It would have been enough to drive a man mad, were it not for the mission that dominated our minds.

Henry was buried in his books. It seemed as though every time I saw the Captain he was grayer, his eyes heavier. But our efforts were for naught. There was no easy answer, no simple path.

Six days later, we saw the impossible. There, in the place where no foothold should be, Drake reported the unmistakable sign of land.

"What do you see, Mr. Drake?"

"A city, Captain, as best I can tell. A massive city. But we are still at great distance."

We approached cautiously. Though time was of the essence, the Captain feared a trap, and we played our cards as close to the vest as we could. But on the open sea, little can be hidden; Thayerson would be aware of our presence. As we drew closer, Drake's descriptions became clearer.

"It's unlike anything I have ever seen, Captain. Impossible things. Massive structures, great spheres of stone. But it shines, shimmers in the light, glows even, like burnished bronze. The roads run into the sea, and I dare say there are even more wonders that still lie beneath the waves. But in her center, there is a mighty citadel. What we seek is there, I would wager my life on it."

It was then we came upon the ship. It sat at anchor in an inlet where a broad thoroughfare ran down into the ocean.

"She's empty, sir," Drake reported. "Nothing moves on her decks."

"Could it be a trap?" Daniel asked.

Captain Gray stared out at the white ship through his telescope. "It could be," he answered finally, "but I fear we have no time to avoid it. If a trap has been set, then we shall walk into its maw. Mr. Drake, arm the men. We go ashore post-haste."

We left the ship in three longboats, each man armed with a

Winchester rifle, our oars and the splashing of the waves the only sound to be heard. No gulls called, and I doubted birds had made landfall on this island in some millennia. We saw none of Thayerson's men, and as our boats clanked against the stone, I took a moment to hope some ill fate had already befallen them.

We exited our boats carefully, for no man wanted to touch the water, lest some fell beast from the depths snatch him down into oblivion. My eyes wandered over the slime-encrusted monuments that now reached towards the heavens. Many were uncovered completely, while others simply poked their heads above water, mere hints of the grandeur the ocean still contained. And what majesty they did possess. Oh, how to describe their rune-covered faces, their hideous abomination and transcendent beauty, melded together like some Hell-borne offspring of a demonic coupling? It cannot be described, only witnessed. And God help you if you ever see it.

But, in truth, you know the same thing I did, the same dark fact I saw shrouding the eyes of every man on that island. I told myself it was a lie, but there was something undeniably familiar about this place. As if I had been there before, though such a thing could not be. A primordial memory perhaps. Or a dream. A dream of walking these streets, of striding them as the gods of old once did, or of wandering their paths while they yet lie beneath the waves. A city sleeping, waiting to be awoken. Ah, fear and mystery, the aphrodisiacs of a tired mind.

We advanced forward up the boulevard, dividing our group in half, working our way through the ruins in hopes of preventing an ambush. As we climbed, the massive citadel sitting at the acropolis of the city loomed above us, a tower of Babel reaching up to some dark heaven. And then we saw them.

We had crept up into the very shadow of the mausoleum, where some great obelisk or other monolith had collapsed into the midst of the boulevard. Thayerson's men had spread themselves out behind the collapsed stone. Their slack jaws and dead eyes belied the threat they posed, though the rifles in their hands were enough to remind of us of the mortal danger we were in.

Captain Gray looked at me and smiled.

"Ready to make a run for it, Mr. Weston?"

I was not, but if there was ever a time for false bravado, this was it.

"Just tell me what to do."

He nodded and turned to Drake.

"Mr. Drake, I'm going to need you to lead a distraction. Take your men back and around. Join up with Daniel and Jack on the other side. Flank Thayerson's men and attack. Draw them to you and we will move around this left side here. Understand?"

"Aye, Captain."

Captain Gray stuck out his hand. When Drake took it, I knew the two men were saying goodbye, just in case. With a nod, Drake led the men back.

Now, we waited. Minutes seemed to stretch into hours, and with each one that passed we knew whatever foul ritual Thayerson was committing was closer to its completion. Then, the shooting started. Thayerson's men were taken by surprise, and no fewer than five fell before the first volley had ended. Captain Gray and I watched as his plan came to fruition. The men guarding our flank began to move to the right. They lumbered forward, rifles limp in their dead arms. But when they were in range, they snapped to attention, firing precise shots without emotion.

We crept forward, advancing up the last few yards to the gaping jaws of the sepulcher.

"A throne room in life, a charnel house in death," Gray whispered.

Two great stone sentinels, not unlike the base reliefs we had witnessed in the cave beneath Miskatonic, stood guard on either side, kneeling as if approaching a king. These were massive monuments, greater than the wildest dreams of the Pharaoh, an unholy mixture of man and beast.

The mighty doors of the citadel stood open. In this we were lucky. Given their girth and height, we never would have been able to budge them alone. We stepped inside, and despite the high-vaulted ceiling — the top of which I could not see — and lack of windows, the entire corridor was illuminated by some preternatural light that had no source. And at the end of the corridor, standing in front of a sarcophagus in which the denizens of an entire city could be buried, was Thayerson.

He was not a man, not anymore. His skin hung from his body like a loose rag. He was stretched and broken, with crude horns piercing his skull and claws where his hands once were. Those hands were raised above his head; words which I did not know poured from what was left of his mouth.

"It's over, Thayerson!" Captain Gray yelled, raising his rifle. Thayerson froze. Then, he turned. His distorted face appeared to smile.

"No, Captain. But it is finished." His voice seemed to change, seemed to come from somewhere beyond this world as he said, "Ph'lna estraphar morte, Cth-ul-hu!"

The Captain fired a shot, but the explosion of his gun was drowned out by the laughter from that which had been Thayerson. As the Earth began to shake, Thayerson's laughter seemed to surround us, bouncing off the walls and the far ceiling, covering us and pounding on our ears. The Captain didn't hesitate.

"So, that's what it is, then," he yelled above Thayerson's cackle. He removed the *Necronomicon* from the bag he had brought from the ship. "You must get the *Incendium Maleficarum*. It is the only thing that can save us now."

Thayerson faced the great stone box, his arms raised, babbling manically about the return of his master. Captain Gray was now reading from the *Necronomicon*, chanting yet more words I did not understand.

"Thayerson!" I yelled. "Give us the Book!"

He turned to me, and I watched the smile melt from his face as I pulled a large, golden cross from my coat. "The Book!" I commanded, taking a tentative step towards him. His grin returned.

"The age of such icons is over."

He lifted a claw, and with a flick of his wrist, I felt the handle of the cross shatter in my hands, leaving nothing but a jagged rod. The golden cross clattered against the floor, and with that sound I felt my heart sink. But only for a moment. I did the only thing I could imagine — I threw myself at Thayerson.

I felt my body collide with his, felt his cold, clammy-wet skin rub against my face. His balance was off, and we both tumbled to the ground. But it was the Book that concerned me the most. I saw it slam onto the stone floor beside me. With one swift movement, I slid the Book towards Captain Gray, watching as it spun its way to his feet. At that instant, I felt my body lifted into the air, felt a bizarre weightlessness for the split second before I was flung to the ground with as much violence as Thayerson could muster.

"Insect! Foolish beast!" Thayerson spat, lifting himself by some unknown force until his feet seemed to float above the ground. "I would kill you now. But your fate will be different. You shall live to see his glory, and then you will die at his hands."

Thayerson turned his attention from me, and I saw as he stretched out one arm, the palm of his hand upturned. His mouth moved, and though I could not hear his words, I could see the ball of fire that began to grow in the middle of his claw. I looked from it to Captain Gray. The captain was so engrossed in whatever ritual was contained in the depths of the crimson-clad book in his hands he did not notice the swirling death about to envelope him. It was then I felt the lump beneath me.

I pulled myself up on my knees, grasping the broken cross in one hand. I stood, though every fiber of my body screamed against it. Thayerson didn't even notice me, didn't notice as I staggered towards him, didn't notice as I lifted the cross over my head. With every remaining ounce of power I had, I thrust the jagged edge down and into the back of the beast before me. I smelled burning flesh before I heard the scream, a horrible screech followed by the explosion of the swirling fire in Thayerson's hand, an explosion that once again lifted me into the air and slung what had been Thayerson against the far wall.

I fought against the blackness, knowing that succumbing now would be the end of me. I looked at Thayerson's body lying lifeless on the ground, the shining cross still jammed between his shoulder blades. Then my eyes went to the stone coffin. The Earth still shook, and as I watched, the slab that covered the tomb began to move. It slid, slowly but with purpose, across the top of that coffin, until it fell from its perch, slamming against the ground with such force I thought the whole building would collapse upon me. It was then I looked to Captain Gray.

"Run, you fool!" he commanded, his eyes burning with a holy fire. Then he did something I didn't expect. He smiled. He winked. I don't know why, but there was something in that gesture that gave me the strength to pull myself up and run to the door. Yet even as I reached it, I couldn't help but turn around. What I saw then, it haunts me even now, even after a lifetime of seeing things no man should see.

I will describe it as best I can, though I doubt the words of any human tongue can properly give it form. The slab had fallen, and the open coffin sat before us, the air empty above it. But it was not empty for long. A swarm of massive tentacles appeared from within, slapping and vibrating, undulating while searching for something to grasp. Then, two arms, muscular, massive, thick as steel beams and just as strong, with two great claws at the end of each appeared. These claws grasped the sides of the sarcophagus, lifting up the rest of that terrible beast. His head cannot be described, a combination of skull and dragon and Leviathan, with evil red eyes that seemed to possess the power of the basilisk to kill on sight.

It was when the great, leathery wings spread wide to the ceiling that I ran. I ran down out the great doors, past the kneeling statues. I ran down the causeway, with no concern for what I might encounter. I ran, but I still heard the chant of the Captain behind me. Then I heard him pause. After that pause, I heard a word. What was that word? I cannot say, and I know if I could, I would not have lived to see the sunset. But I do know what I heard was as fire, a fire so hot it seemed to burn my ears. And, as one would expect from a fire, there was a burst of light. Had I been facing it, I have no doubt my eyes would have been roasted from my skull.

As bizarre as it may sound, I felt in that fire, in that heat, in that light, and in that pain, an overwhelming sense of joy, of happiness, as if I was standing in the presence of the Lord Himself. But that moment was short-lived — the island began to sink.

I ran faster now, so fast I almost stumbled over the body of one of Thayerson's sailors. Even with the Earth sinking below me, I took the moment to survey a scene as macabre as any I have ever come upon. Thayerson's crew was all dead, each of them lying where they fell. But there were no bodies, not really. Instead there were only masses of flesh. It was as if they had been dead for some months, moldering in the open sun. I didn't look long, as another quake woke me from my amazement.

I could barely stand, as the shaking beneath me grew so violent I didn't know where my foot would land from one step to the next. It seemed an eternity before I reached the sea. My prayers were answered — one boat still waited. The men within — Drake, Henry, Jack, William, and Daniel — were yelling for me to run. This I did, veritably leaping into the boat as I reached it.

"Captain Gray?" Drake yelled. It was all I could do to shake my head. Drake had expected it. He screamed orders to the others, and before I knew it, we were moving away from the island. I looked down at Henry. He was clutching a bloody cloth against his side.

"A flesh wound," he said with a weak smile.

I watched as R'lyeh disappeared again beneath the waves, watched as it sank back to the depths. And I prayed neither I nor any man would ever see the likes of it again.

We did not speak as we rowed away, back to *The Kadath*. We did not speak as we reached the ship. We didn't even speak as Drake pointed to the object that floated with unnatural speed toward us. Nobody said a word as we lifted it into the longboat, placing it into the center of us all. We didn't speak. We didn't have to. It spoke for us . . . though there was only one of us who heard its song.

Chapter 39

Forty-five years it has been. Forty-five years since I heard the Book's song once more, the song that told me I had been chosen yet again. From that moment, somewhere in the unknown seas of the South Pacific, I knew the day would come when the Book would sing no more. I knew when that day came, it would mean the end of me. For I would never relinquish that dark tome, not again. The Book seeks its own. It seeks those through which it can do the most evil. And in me, it expected to find an owner who could return it once more to R'lyeh. It had been so close before.

I have dedicated these past forty-five years to understanding the evil that lies beyond man's imagining, that lurks in the crevices between space, that haunts man's dreams. There have been times when Henry and I have suspected the Rising was upon us, that evil was poised to return. But the stars have never been quite right, not as they were that day, four decades ago. And despite the events of Dunwich and Innsmouth and the insane ravings of a certain Norwegian sailor, the danger has never risen to such a fever pitch again. But then, three days ago, the Book ceased to sing.

I knew it was coming. I felt it. I can't say how, but I did. It was a warm December day, incredibly unusual for Arkham. I was sitting in my office, reading Mather's *Wonders of the Invisible World* for the first time in a long time, when there was a knock on my door.

A young man in an expensive suit entered. He wore a hat and

small, wire-rimmed glasses, a leather briefcase in his hands.

"Dr. Weston," he said in a thick German accent, bowing slightly. "I am Dr. Erich Zann of the University of Berlin. We understand you may be in possession of an artifact of some antiquity. We would like to have access to that object." Then, he smiled. "We are, of course, willing to make a substantial donation to the University in exchange for borrowing it."

I had kept the Book with me every moment of every day for the last four decades. Its song had become so ever-present I barely noticed it. And so, in that moment, when that song finally ceased, the silence was deafening.

"I must say, Dr. Zann," I replied, "I have no idea what you may be speaking of. I assure you our library has many interesting objects, and I am sure you can work out an arrangement to share some of those artifacts with your University."

Zann smiled, but it covered a snarl.

"No, Dr. Weston. I do not believe your library can help me here. I believe you have a tome in your possession. It is bound in crimson leather. It is a spell-book, as ancient as it is valuable. The people I represent," he said, pausing. He had said more than he intended. "They would appreciate having access to this artifact. We would return it post-haste, of course."

"Dr. Zann," I said sharply, "I assure you I have no such artifact. I am afraid you have been misled. If you have no other requests, I am sorry to say that I have work to do, and I will have to ask you to leave."

This time Zann didn't smile. He simply said, "I am staying at the Miskatonic Inn. I will be there for the next seven days. I suggest you re-examine your collection. If you should locate the object I seek, you know where to find me. Seven days, Dr. Weston."

As the door closed behind him, and as silence surrounded me for the first time in decades, I knew I must write this testament. Dark forces are moving in the world again. I will do my best to protect the Book. I shall give my very life to do so. But in the end, I fear the fate of the world will be in others' hands. How many will suffer to save it? How many will die? I cannot say. But if men are not so willing to sacrifice for the truth, then that which should not be, which must not be, which cannot be, *shall be* again. But it is my faith that, in the end, good will defeat evil, light will outshine the darkness, and justice will prevail. God let it be so.

Epilogue

January 31, 1933

Mr. Ashton,

You have our utmost thanks for your discretion in relation to what is apparently the final testament of Dr. Weston. We fear you are correct — Dr. Weston's advancing age had apparently robbed him of his sanity.

In an abundance of caution, we have endeavored to investigate the events described by Dr. Weston. While most of the names and incredible happenings described within the testament appear to have been fabricated, we have discovered a Dr. Zann, though his position as Reich Minister of Cultural History in the newly formed German government casts serious doubt on Dr. Weston's characterization of him as a vicious person.

We have determined your initial assessment is correct. This document is dangerous both to Dr. Weston's legacy and to his heirs. We have, therefore, determined we will destroy the copy of the testament you have provided us. We suggest you do the same. We are convinced Dr. Weston, in his more lucid days, would have been most appreciative.

Sincerely,
Stansbury Charles
Charles & Frankfurt